PRAISE FOR THE NOVELS OF

Maya Banks

"A must-read author . . . her [stories] are always full of emotional situations, lovable characters and kick-butt story lines."

—*Romance Junkies*

"Definitely a recommended read . . . filled with friendship, passion and most of all, a love that grows beyond just being friends."

—*Fallen Angel Reviews*

"Grabbed me from page one and refused to let go until I read the last word . . . When a book still affects me hours after reading it, I can't help but Joyfully Recommend it!" —*Joyfully Reviewed*

"I guarantee I will reread this book many times over, and will derive as much pleasure as I did in the first reading each and every subsequent time." —*Novelspot*

"An excellent read that I simply did not put down . . . a fantastic adventure . . . covers all the emotional range."

—*The Road to Romance*

"Searingly sexy and highly believable." —*Romantic Times*

Berkley Heat titles by Maya Banks

FOR HER PLEASURE

SWEET SURRENDER

BE WITH ME

SWEET PERSUASION

SWEET SEDUCTION

sweet seduction

MAYA BANKS

Heat / New York

THE BERKLEY PUBLISHING GROUP
Published by the Penguin Group
Penguin Group (USA) Inc.
375 Hudson Street, New York, New York 10014, USA
Penguin Group (Canada), 90 Eglinton Avenue East, Suite 700, Toronto, Ontario M4P 2Y3, Canada
(a division of Pearson Penguin Canada Inc.)
Penguin Books Ltd., 80 Strand, London WC2R 0RL, England
Penguin Group Ireland, 25 St. Stephen's Green, Dublin 2, Ireland (a division of Penguin Books Ltd.)
Penguin Group (Australia), 250 Camberwell Road, Camberwell, Victoria 3124, Australia
(a division of Pearson Australia Group Pty. Ltd.)
Penguin Books India Pvt. Ltd., 11 Community Centre, Panchsheel Park, New Delhi—110 017, India
Penguin Group (NZ), 67 Apollo Drive, Rosedale, North Shore 0632, New Zealand
(a division of Pearson New Zealand Ltd.)
Penguin Books (South Africa) (Pty.) Ltd., 24 Sturdee Avenue, Rosebank, Johannesburg 2196,
South Africa

Penguin Books Ltd., Registered Offices: 80 Strand, London WC2R 0RL, England

This is an original publication of The Berkley Publishing Group.

Cover photograph by Andrejs Zavadskis.
Cover photograph manipulation and design by S. Miroque.
Text design by Kristin del Rosario.

PRINTING HISTORY
Heat trade paperback edition / October 2009

Library of Congress Cataloging-in-Publication Data

Banks, Maya.
Sweet seduction / Maya Banks. — Heat trade pbk. ed.
p. cm.
ISBN 978-0-425-23069-5 (trade pbk.)
I. Title.
PS3602.A643S835 2009
813'.6—dc22 2009013514

PRINTED IN THE UNITED STATES OF AMERICA

10 9 8 7 6 5 4 3 2 1

To Jennifer Miller: I'd be so lost without you.
Seriously. Lost. Thank you.

To the ladies on the Writeminded Readers loop:
your support means more to me than you'll ever know.
Much love to you all.

To Karin Tabke, for your unconditional love and support.
Know that you'll always have mine.

Chapter 1

Julie Stanford took a deep breath before shoving aside the curtain to walk into the massage room where Nathan was laid out in all his glorious, naked splendor. Of course, he would be on his belly, with a towel draped across his ass. His very tight, gorgeous ass.

He stiffened slightly as she moved closer, the roll of muscles across his back betraying him. Despite what he might try to portray, he wasn't immune to her. Not by a long shot.

Ah well, it didn't matter. After today, she was so moving on from her fixation with Nathan Tucker. She had fantasies to live, great sex to have and . . . Okay, she'd settle for great sex. No need to get carried away.

Humming to herself, she readied her supplies and then turned to the feast of male flesh before her. Before, she'd always worked with his display of modesty and left the towel over him. She'd never pressed him to turn over so she could do his front, even though she knew damn well the only reason he refused was because he didn't want to get caught with an erection.

But today? She wasn't in an accommodating mood. Nope. This was her last chance to savor him, and she was going to enjoy every minute of it.

First thing she did was whip off the towel and toss it across the room. He jerked and reached blindly back with his hand.

"What the hell?" he muttered as he twisted and maneuvered, all while trying not to turn over.

She grinned and placed her hands over his shoulders to shove him back down to the table. He quieted immediately at her touch even though he went so tense that it would take her the better part of an hour to work out the kinks.

He wanted her. But for whatever reason, he didn't want to want her. And that irritated her. What was so wrong with her? It wasn't like she was a clinging vine, desperate for love and commitment.

The idea that he could be so appalled by his attraction to her stung.

Trying to tamp down her flashing aggravation, she concentrated on the smooth muscles of his shoulders as she worked over his tanned skin. Soon, calm invaded her as she lost herself in the intense pleasure of touching him.

She took her time, determined to make it last. After today she was resigning as his massage chick, and she was off to greener pastures, thanks to Damon Roche.

Okay, so she hadn't exactly talked to him yet. She'd wanted to give him and Serena time to sort out their differences before she hit him up. But he was a nice guy, and she was convinced he'd help her. Faith had been equally sure.

A dreamy smile curled her lips upward as she imagined the possibility of Damon arranging her sexual fantasy at The House.

When Nathan made a sound, she frowned and looked downward. She'd worked her way to his ass, and as soon as she began kneading his tight buns, he'd let out what could only be described as a strangled protest.

She wanted to laugh, and had to swallow hard to prevent it. She needed to snap out of her daydreams and get her head back in the now. Hell, Nathan Tucker was here, naked, under her fingertips, and she was fantasizing about getting it on with two other guys.

Her fingers trailed over the hard globes of his ass before she cupped and rolled the supple flesh under her palms. He made a desperate little sound that had her stifling the laughter again. Yet, he made no effort to stop her.

There was a light smattering of hair at the small of his back that trailed down the cleft, and she followed it with one fingertip. He sucked in a breath and went completely still as she teased the region between his cheeks.

Then, as if she'd never dared to push the boundaries of the massage, she traveled to his thick legs, caressing and molding the bulging muscles of his thighs.

Man, she loved touching him. It was addictive. He was supposed to be gaining the larger enjoyment from the massage, but she wasn't sure that was the case, because she was in heaven.

When she got to his feet, she spent several minutes massaging the arch and instep before finally traveling back up his body. Her mouth watered as she imagined following her hand with her tongue. But no. Not yet. She wouldn't show her hand before it was time. Even if she did have the strongest urge to lean down and bite him right on the ass.

His head was to the side, his cheek resting on the pillow she'd provided. His eyes were closed but there were lines of strain gathered at his temple. She reached down to smooth them away. Her hands slid across the smooth skin of his bald head, then to the base of his skull.

According to Faith Malone, Nathan had always worn his hair longer and shaggy . . . until the day he'd lost a bet with Micah Hudson and was forced to shave it all off. Faith had convinced him he looked hot with a shaved head and goatee and told him all he lacked was an earring to complete the look. She'd brought him to Julie's to pierce his ear, and so began Julie's obsession with Nathan Tucker.

And today would end it.

Impatient and ready to end the buildup, she pulled her hands away from his skin and stepped back. Predictably, he shifted and raised the upper portion of his body as he looked frantically for the robe he'd discarded earlier.

"Turn over," she directed calmly.

His gaze met hers, and she shivered at the intensity in his green eyes.

"No," he said. "Now where the hell is my robe, a towel, *anything?*"

She wouldn't laugh. No, she wouldn't.

"Turn over, Nathan."

There was steel in her voice, and he looked surprised by it.

"What the hell?"

"Afraid I'll see your hard-on?" she asked in an innocent voice. "Really, Nathan, I didn't peg you for a coward. It's not like an erection is uncommon in my male customers. Now turn over so I can finish the massage." She didn't add that it would be his last.

His eyes narrowed, and as if answering the challenge, he turned sharply, rolling his naked body until he was flat on his back.

Her breath left her in one gigantic whoosh. Holy hell in a bucket, but "hard-on" didn't do justice to the magnificent erection jutting from his groin.

Her gaze was absolutely fixed on his cock. She wanted to wrap both hands around it and stroke, touch, caress, and then she wanted to taste. God, she wanted to taste.

She did crude measurements in her head, because damn, he was stacked. Long and thick. She'd had good, but she'd never had *this* nice. Would be a damn shame if he didn't know what to do with it. Not that it mattered to her, because the time for that was over.

"If you're through staring," he grated out.

There was a hint of embarrassment in his voice, and she grinned before allowing her gaze to drift upward until it connected with his.

"Very nice," she murmured. "One has to wonder why you took such pains to hide it from me."

He muttered several curses under his breath. "Can we just finish this?"

"Oh yes," she purred as she moved closer to him again. "I'm going to finish, all right."

He looked at her cautiously, nervousness in his eyes. Smart man.

She climbed onto the table and straddled his thighs just below that nice, straining erection. It was going to kill her to take this nice and slow, but she was determined to have him begging before it was over with.

"What the hell are you doing, Julie?"

Her palms met his abdomen and glided upward over his chest as she leaned over him. She stared down at him unflinchingly.

"You have two choices. You can shut up and not say a damn word until I'm done or I can gag you. In either case, I'm going to have my way."

He cocked one eyebrow as he stared up at her. "Bossy damn woman today. What's got into you?"

"Well, certainly not you," she grumbled.

He started to say something else, but she put her hand over his mouth.

"Not a word, Nathan," she said lightly.

He glared at her but didn't say anything else. She pulled her hand away, very conscious of his cock digging into her belly. She wanted to strip off every piece of her clothing, scanty as it was. But then, this wasn't about her.

Then she caught him staring below her chin and she looked down, following his line of vision. He was focused on her breasts. Her very nice tatas that she'd plumped and stuffed into the too-small bra. The tatas that were about to pop out of the thin halter top she was wearing.

Unabashed by his interest—it wasn't like she hadn't tried for months to get him to look at her—she leaned forward a bit more so he got a really good look.

"I'm pretty sure what I'm about to do violates the code of ethics of my profession," she said huskily. "But you know what? It'll be worth it."

His body tightened underneath her. A quiver worked through his thighs and over his taut belly. She shifted back, sliding her hands over his too-perfect chest, down the thin line of hair leading to his navel.

No longer able to hold back, she bent her head and swirled her tongue around the shallow indentation.

"Shit," he hissed.

She smiled as she pulled away. Her hands closed around his cock as she scooted down to his knees to give herself better access.

Hot steel. He was hard as a rock and pulsing in her hand. With both hands wrapped around his dick, he still had two inches above her grip. Man, oh man, she wanted him inside her, filling her. He was made for a woman's pleasure.

He sucked in his breath when she lowered her head. Her tongue shot out and traced a delicate line around the head. Then she sucked him hard inside her mouth, taking him whole and deep.

His back came off the table like a shot, spasms ricocheting through his body. But he kept silent, according to Julie's dictate.

He tasted wholly male, or like she imagined someone as big and rugged as he was would taste. Strong. He was equal parts satiny, as her tongue glided over the smoothness of his shaft, and rough, as she encountered the pulsing veins and wrinkled flesh of his foreskin.

The crown of his dick was tight. Silky at the top, puckered around the flared edge. She lapped hungrily at it in anticipation of his release. Not that she planned to let that happen for a while yet.

She paused and pulled her head away, keeping her fingers

curled around the base. She glanced up to see him staring down at her, his eyes glittering with lust. Yeah, well, she wasn't going to get any grand ideas that he wanted her. Wrap your lips around a man's cock and shove breasts at him, and he wouldn't give a shit about who you were or worry about deeper attraction.

She winced. Gee, try to not take that personally.

Determined not to look back at him, she lowered her eyes and set about driving him crazy.

Deep. Sucking. Swallowing as she guided him deeper still. His fists were curled into tight balls at his sides as he strained upward to thrust into her mouth.

And then she stopped. She released him slowly, letting her lips glide sensuously over his cock on its way out. He arched helplessly toward her, but she raised her head out of his reach.

"Goddamn, Julie, what do you want?" he asked desperately.

She loosened her hold on his dick and rocked back until her bottom rested on his knees. She stared levelly at him.

"I want you to beg."

He glared at her. "I don't beg. Ever."

She smiled, accepting his challenge. "We'll see about that, Tucker."

She leaned down again, pulling his cock up so that the underside was accessible. With a long swipe, she licked from the base to the head and then rolled her mouth over the crown. She sucked him deep, taking all of him. Her nose met the short, crisp hairs of his groin, and still, she held him deep, swallowing.

His groan split the air. He was close. Really close. But she was determined not to make it easy. What was the point in giving the man the best head of his life if she was going to cut it short? She wanted him to remember. To lay awake at night, his skin alive with want. She wanted him to want her. To realize what he'd never have again.

If that made her vindictive, oh well.

He cursed when she pulled him close to his orgasm and then stopped, allowing him to slide away from sweet release. When he calmed beneath her, she began again, coaxing and unrelenting.

The third time he trembled beneath her, ready to explode in her mouth, she pulled away again.

"Julie, please! God, just finish it. I'm . . . begging."

With a wicked smile she descended, taking him hard. His hips arched convulsively, his ass bumping against the table as she fucked him with her mouth.

"Oh, God," he breathed. "Shit. Julie. I'm going to come."

Her grip tightened around him and she worked her hand up and down in unison with her mouth. His hips shot upward in one continuous bow. His cry ripped over her ears just as his cum shot into her mouth, hot and silky.

She took it all, sucking and swallowing as he shook beneath her. His hips fell as he slammed back onto the table, and she followed him down, her mouth never leaving his cock.

His hand tangled in her hair, the first time he actually touched her. His fingers glanced off her scalp as he almost tenderly stroked through her hair. She closed her eyes, enjoying the moment, the pleasure of his touch.

Then, slowly, she pulled away, refusing to meet his eyes. This wasn't the time to get caught up in the ooey-gooey aftermath when half of what was said was bullshit and the other half was the result of the brain still not functioning after a mind-blowing orgasm.

She slid off the table and straightened her clothes. Across the room his robe, and the towel she'd tossed away, lay carelessly strewn. She hurried for both then turned and tossed them in Nathan's direction.

"That . . . was on the house," she said, proud of the steadiness of her voice. "I won't, however, be available for future appointments. You'll have to find another massage service."

She caught only a brief glimpse of the shocked expression on his face before she turned and walked out of the massage room.

Chapter 2

Nathan roared up into the parking lot of Malone and Sons Security and cut the engine. With an irritated yank of his keys, he got out and slammed his door.

He strode to the door, glowering the entire way. That damn hellcat Julie. After giving him an orgasm that rivaled Mount Vesuvius, she'd had the nerve to blow *him* off.

What the fuck kind of point was she trying to prove? If she wanted his attention, she'd certainly gotten it in a big way. After weeks and weeks of endless sexual frustration, his prayers had been answered. Julie's mouth around his cock, her hands on his body, a vixen bent on seduction.

Yeah, well then she'd turned into a friggin' iceberg. Not only had she fired his ass—could a customer be fired?—but he'd seen neither hide nor hair of her in a week. A week! When before he couldn't damn well turn around without her being there, now she'd disappeared off the face of the earth.

He'd gone into her salon, determined that she, and nobody else, was going to give him a massage. Only this time he was going to have her down on the table under his mouth and hands. Imagine his surprise when a woman he'd never seen before introduced herself as Julie's new massage therapist.

Oh, hell no.

He'd turned around and walked out, ready to strangle Julie. Right after he fucked her brains out.

He swung open the door to Malone and Sons Security and stalked in, making a beeline for Faith's office. He almost ran into Micah Hudson in the hallway. Micah started to say something but took one look at Nathan's face and held his hands up.

Micah backed away, an amused grin on his face. "I'll catch you later, dude. After you've worked the knot out of your panties."

"Fuck you," Nathan muttered as he shoved past him.

Faith looked up as Nathan walked into her office, her eyebrows going up. Usually he was a lot more even tempered, especially with Faith. He loved the girl to death, but today his patience was hanging by a thread.

He put his hands down on Faith's desk and leaned over to stare her in the eye. "Where. Is. She?"

Faith blinked. "Excuse me?"

"Julie," he growled. "Where the hell is she hiding?"

A burst of amusement flared in Faith's eyes, which only served to piss Nathan off more.

"I swear to you, Faith, if you don't tell me where she is, I'm going to strangle that pretty neck of yours."

If he thought that threat was going to get him anywhere, he was sadly mistaken. Faith laughed in his face.

"She finally get to you, Nathan?"

He closed his eyes and was tempted to beat his head on the desk. God save him from impossible women. When he reopened his eyes, he found Faith staring at him, a glint of steel in her expression.

"Come on, Faith," he wheedled. "You're supposed to be my friend."

"What you are is a dumbass."

His mouth fell open. What the hell happened to sweet, generous Faith who made them all coffee and mothered them incessantly?

She stood and placed her own hands on the desk and leaned forward, her lips twisted in a snarl. "You ignore her for weeks, act like she doesn't even exist and then when you decide to take notice, you're pissed because she's not running when you snap your fingers?"

"Not that I don't love watching you get your ass kicked by a girl, but Pop wants you on the phone," Micah called from the door. Amusement was heavy in his voice.

"Get out!" he and Faith said at the same time.

Micah threw up his hands. "Okay, okay. Just don't call me to clean up the mess later." He backed out of the office at high speed.

Nathan turned back to Faith. "What do you mean, I've ignored her for weeks? Do you know how impossible it is to ignore that woman? I'd have to be blind, deaf *and* dumb not to notice."

It was Faith's turn for her mouth to gape open. Then to his utter shock, she reached across and smacked him upside the head.

He yanked back, staring at her in shock. "*What the hell was that for?*"

"Dumbass. Complete and utter moron. If all men were as stupid as you, the world would have a population crisis."

"You can quit with the insults any time."

"Don't stop now. It's just getting interesting," Connor Malone said from the door.

"Out!" Faith screeched at her brother.

Nathan didn't say anything, but he pinned Connor with a glare. Connor's shoulders shook with laughter, but he turned and sauntered back out.

"Office is a damn revolving door today," Nathan muttered.

"It's a revolving door every day," Faith said pointedly. "You just never get the hint. Just like you're too thick to figure out that you could have had Julie at any time. You've lost your chance, and moreover, you don't *deserve* her."

Heat simmered in Nathan's veins. *Lost my chance, my ass.* Just because women had to be so fucking complicated didn't mean that he was the dumbass for not figuring out the mystic woman's code for *I want you.* There wasn't a man in the world who knew how the fuck women thought, and if he said he did, he was a goddamn liar.

"So, you're on her side," Nathan huffed.

She rolled her eyes. "Men are such babies."

"Would you quit with the name-calling? Jesus, Faith, what's crawled up your ass?"

"Why are you here, Nathan?" she asked impatiently.

He gaped at her. His blood pressure was going through the roof. He'd be lucky if he didn't stroke out in her office. He reached for his hair but then remembered he didn't have any.

"Why the hell do you think I'm here?" he roared.

She looked unfazed by the fact he was losing his mind.

"I'm here because that hellcat seduced me and then ran the fuck away. She's avoiding me, and when I went in for my massage, another fucking woman showed up to give me one. And you think *I'm* a chickenshit?"

"No, you're a dumbass," she pointed out in a bored tone.

He threw up his hands and slumped down in the chair behind him. "Okay, Faith, I'm a dumbass. Now tell me *why* I'm such a dumbass, because obviously I'm too much of a dumbass to see!"

She sat down in her chair with a smirk. "Nice sarcasm, Nathan. And I thought that was Micah's job."

"I heard that," Micah called from the hall.

"Not to mention eavesdropping," Nathan growled. "Micah, I'm going to kick your fucking ass if you don't get the hell away from Faith's door."

He got up and stalked over to look down the hall. To his supreme irritation, Micah stood there with Connor and Gray Montgomery and they all wore shit-eating grins that told him they'd overheard every word of his argument with Faith.

"Assholes," Nathan swore. "The lot of you."

"You raise your voice to Faith again and I'll kick your ass," Gray said mildly.

"Oh, like I'd do anything to her even if I'm tempted to strangle her," Nathan said in irritation. "She's being a royal pain in my ass."

"I heard that," Faith called.

Nathan threw up his hands. "Get lost, okay guys? If I wanted the greater Houston area to know what I was talking about, I'd take out an ad."

"That's not a bad idea," Connor said thoughtfully. "We could rent a billboard. *'I'm sorry, Julie. I'm a blind, deaf and dumb moron who doesn't know what to do with his dick,'*" he mimicked.

Nathan sucked in a deep breath, walked back into Faith's office and slammed the door as hard as he could.

"You break my door and you're going to fix it," Faith said.

"Faith, look at me," Nathan said as he walked back to her desk. He leaned over until their faces were a few inches apart. "Cut the crap for a minute and help me, okay?"

Her expression softened. "I can't help you, Nathan. You fucked this up. I'd tell you to fix it but it's really too late. Julie . . . she's hard. Girl holds a grudge forever. She's decided to give up on you and move on. Once she's decided on something, getting her to change her mind is like getting a pit bull to give up a prime steak."

"So her giving me the best blow job of my life during a massage was her kissing me good-bye?" Nathan asked dryly.

Faith's cheeks turned pink, and he felt bad for speaking so bluntly in front of her.

"Sorry," he mumbled.

Faith sighed. "I think that was supposed to be showing you what you're missing out on and what you've given up by not noticing her before."

Nathan's eyes narrowed. "So you knew what she was going to do?"

Faith raised one eyebrow. "I knew she was planning something. Just not what, exactly."

"Vengeful heifer," Nathan muttered.

Faith grinned. "That she is."

"Well screw that," Nathan said as he shoved away from her desk again. "She can't just take those kinds of liberties with my body and walk away."

Faith burst out laughing. She laughed so hard that tears rolled down her cheeks. "You sound like an outraged maiden," she gasped.

He grinned. "Who says I'm not? I was innocent before she corrupted me. If she thinks she can use me and then discard me, she's mistaken."

Faith wiped at her tears and laughed harder. "Innocent, my ass. Dear Lord, I was feeling sorry for you, but now I think my sympathies have shifted to Julie. I'm not entirely sure she realizes what she's gotten herself into."

"No," Nathan said silkily. "She has no clue what she's started. But she will. Very soon."

Chapter 3

Julie hopped out of her sporty two-seater and walked up to Damon Roche's front door. He and Serena were both at home, according to Serena anyway, and supposedly Serena had warmed him up for Julie's request.

Of course Serena might still be mad over Julie and Faith kidnapping her a while back, so Julie couldn't be totally sure that Damon would have a clue why she was here.

She knocked on the door and blinked when a large man wearing shades answered. She squinted for a few seconds as she stared at him.

"Dude, you look straight out of the Mafia," Julie blurted. "I tried to tell Serena that Damon was probably a drug dealer."

To her surprise, Big Dude broke into a grin. "You must be Miss Stanford. Miss James is expecting you."

"And not Mr. Roche?" Damn Serena.

"Mr. Roche is expecting you as well," he returned smoothly. "They're in the living room."

She followed him inside the gorgeously furnished house. No wonder Serena had agreed to move in. Compared to Serena's tiny apartment, this was a freaking palace.

They walked into the living room, where Julie was surprised to see a fire burning in the hearth. Damon sat on the couch and Serena was beside him, her head in his lap as he stroked her hair.

"Miss Stanford is here."

Damon turned, and Serena scrambled up, her long black hair falling over her shoulders in disarray.

"Thank you, Sam," Damon said. "Would you have Carol bring refreshment for our guest? Julie, would you care for some wine?"

She grimaced. "Beer, if you have it."

Damon smiled. "Of course. Sam, have Carol bring Julie a beer. Serena and I will take wine."

Serena got up and hurried over to Julie. Julie found herself in a hug as Serena squeezed fiercely.

"You have to tell me how it went with Nathan," Serena murmured.

Julie grinned. "Just like I planned. And now I'm here for part two of the plan."

Serena rolled her eyes as she backed away.

"You did tell Damon why I wanted to see him, right?" Julie asked anxiously.

"She did," Damon said with amusement. "Sort of. She said she'd leave the actual details for you to explain but that you were interested in using my facilities for a little fantasy fulfillment."

"Yeah," Julie said wistfully. "I'm totally down for some great sex."

Damon laughed, and that's why Julie liked him. He didn't have an uptight, judgmental bone in his body. Plus, he loved Serena to pieces, and what woman wouldn't want that kind of guy for her friend?

"Come sit, Julie. You can fill me in on these fantasies of yours while we wait for your beer."

"Hell, I might need a few beers before I can tell you about them," she muttered.

Serena snorted and took Julie's arm to guide her toward the couch. "Like you've ever been shy. Come sit down and tell Damon what it is you want. As long as it doesn't involve him personally, I'm cool with it."

Julie sent Serena a sly glance as the two settled onto the couch. "You're sounding possessive, girlfriend. Dare I ask whether or not Damon has persuaded you to accept his proposal yet?"

"Julie, shut up," Serena hissed.

"Not yet," Damon said calmly. "But I will." He winked at Julie, and she smiled back.

"I don't know why you don't just put the guy out of his misery," Julie muttered under her breath to Serena. "It's obvious he's over the moon mad about you."

Julie liked to give Serena shit when it came to Damon, but she was hugely relieved that Serena was taking her time deciding, even if Julie did think Damon was pretty terrific. Julie liked him a lot, but she wasn't convinced he was right for Serena long term, or maybe that Serena wasn't right for him long term.

"You're here to talk about you," Serena said sweetly. "Don't make me throw you out of my house before you get to plead your case."

Julie threw back her head and laughed. "Alrighty then." She looked over at Damon. "Faith told me she came to you when she wanted some help in the fantasy fulfillment area."

Damon sat down in the armchair catty-corner to the sofa and propped one long leg over his knee. "Not exactly. Faith wasn't looking for a fantasy. She was looking for something very real." He smiled and looked over at Serena. "Serena was the one looking for a fantasy."

"They both ended up with the real deal. Yeah, I know," Julie said impatiently. "I'm not after reality here. I don't want a permanent fixture. I want hot sex with two gorgeous specimens, and I want it . . . anonymously."

She held her breath while she waited for Damon to react. Serena was quicker. While Damon didn't look overly disturbed by her announcement, Serena turned sharply.

"Have you lost your mind, Julie? Anonymous? And you thought I was the crazy one."

"No, I've got it all figured out," Julie said patiently. "I don't want messy entanglements. Been there, done that, can certainly live without it. I wanted hot sex with Nathan, and clearly that didn't work out. So I'm thinking the best way to go about this is to set up a situation where I have no idea who my hot guys are. We all get great sex out of it and go our merry way afterward."

"How anonymous are you wanting, exactly?" Damon asked.

She looked at him gratefully, relieved that he was at least taking her request seriously. "So anonymous that I don't know who they are or what they look like . . . during any part of it," she said cheerfully.

Serena groaned. "Good God, Julie, what do you want? For them to blindfold you?"

"Yes. Exactly."

"Talk some sense into her, Damon," Serena pleaded.

"Can't do that, love," he said fondly. "What if she'd been able to talk you out of your crazy idea of wanting to be my sex slave?"

"For the love of God," Serena muttered.

Julie grinned. "He's right, you know. You could very well be standing in the way of my future happiness."

"You don't believe that load of horse manure any more than I do," Serena said.

Laughter escaped Julie, and she shoved playfully at Serena. "No, I don't, you heifer, but you could at least give me my own rope to hang myself with. I may have thought you were nuts, but I didn't tie your ass to a chair to prevent you from signing up for slavery."

"Very true," Serena said with a sigh. "But can I at least talk you out of the blindfolds? It seems so . . . scary."

"It's part of the appeal," Damon said evenly. "Think about it, Serena mine. Total darkness. Having to rely on all your other senses. Touch. Taste. Smell. The feel of strange hands on your body, awakening all those senses."

A warm flush stole over Julie. Damn but the man was good.

"I don't want any emotional attachment," Julie said. "I just want two men concentrating on me and my pleasure. No slave shit, please. Unless they want to be mine," she added with a grin. "Minions to do my bidding would be great too."

"You're incorrigible," Serena said as she chuckled.

"No, just desperate and horny."

Damon broke into laughter, and Serena closed her eyes and touched her forehead with her hand.

"Surely there are men at your pleasure palace who wouldn't mind fucking a woman's brains out," she said to Damon.

"Pleasure palace? That sounds so . . . cheesy." He actually looked affronted.

"Sorry," she mumbled. "House of *loooove* then?"

He cracked a grin. "You don't want love, remember?"

"Damn straight. Thanks for that reminder."

"But yes, I'm sure there are any number of men who would be more than willing to take you on," he said as he fought another smile. "We'll do the usual background checks, medical histories, et cetera. Give me a week or so to get everything together and I'll do my best to give you your fantasy."

"If it's not asking too much, I'd like to schedule two nights. Now, ahead of time. I don't want to deal with the awkwardness of doing another after the first night, and if it's already set up, then I don't have to stress about it."

"Of course," Damon agreed. "But if you decide it's not to your liking or if there's anything you want me to change, let me know."

Julie put her hands together in front of her and grinned in delight. "Thanks, Damon. You're the best."

He shrugged. "It's the least I can do to repay you for kidnapping Serena for me."

Serena glowered at both of them, but Julie didn't miss the flash of emotion in Serena's eyes as she looked at Damon.

"I need more details as well," Damon continued. "If you aren't comfortable giving them now, you can e-mail me later, but I need specifics. Boundaries. The do-not-cross lines."

Julie cocked her head and thought for a moment. "I don't have a problem telling you now. I'm not into bondage shit. No way I want to be tied down with strange men, even if I asked for strange men."

Serena laughed and shook her head.

"A blindfold is all I really require because I don't want to know. Don't want to see them, although I'm counting on you not to give me anyone hideous," Julie said.

"Now why the hell should you care if they're hideous if you're blindfolded?" Serena asked in exasperation.

"It's the principle," Julie said. She looked back at Damon. "And no small dicks. If I'm going for the gusto, I want to be treated right."

Damon's shoulders shook as he tried valiantly to keep his composure. "No small dicks. Got it. Anything else?"

"Just give me someone who knows what to do with a big dick," Julie said. "I don't want to have to coach the guy. I want a man who knows what to do with a woman."

"I think I can handle that," he said. "Blindfolds and big dicks. Shouldn't be too difficult."

Then he lost it and started to laugh. Julie grinned before she started chuckling along with him. Serena shook her head but burst into laughter as well.

"I always swore Damon wasn't a pimp, but now I'm not so sure," Serena said ruefully.

"Hey," he said in protest. "Can I help it if desperate women keep throwing themselves at me and begging me to help?"

"He's got you there," Julie said as she dug her elbow into Serena's side. "Between you, me and Faith, the man's got enough experience to run a whorehouse."

"Oh, I'm sure he had plenty of experience before we came along," Serena said dryly.

Julie grinned mischievously. "Maybe we can retire him after he hooks me up."

"Now I sound like a stud horse," Damon muttered. "Serena better damn well not retire me out to pasture."

Serena smiled that silly, goopy smile she got whenever she looked at Damon, the one that made Julie slightly nauseous. Julie cleared her throat before both of them dissolved into slimy little puddles.

"Okay then, if everything's set, I'm gonna skate on out of here and leave you two to do your slave thing."

"For God's sake, Julie," Serena groaned. "Do you ever just shut up?"

Julie blew her a kiss as she got up. "No, but you love me anyway."

"I do but damned if I know why," Serena said wearily as she got up from the couch.

"I'll be in touch, Julie," Damon said as he rose.

"Thanks, Damon. I really appreciate this." She turned to Serena. "I'll see you later this week for your massage, right?"

"You aren't afraid that Nathan will barge in?" Serena asked.

Julie snorted. "I'll just lock up. You and Faith are my only appointments. Besides, he hasn't been around in a few days. Stung pride and all that. He'll get over it and move on. I know I have."

"Just how hung up are you on Julie Stanford?" Micah asked Nathan as they sat down at Cattleman's to eat lunch.

"What the fuck kind of question is that?" Nathan demanded.

It was bad enough that Julie had completely messed with his mind, but now he was fielding comments from the guys about how fucked up he was over the woman.

"It's a simple question," Micah said calmly. "Either you are or you aren't."

"Nothing is simple when you ask it," Nathan grumbled.

"So?"

"So fucking what?" Nathan snarled. "Give it a rest, man. You know what happened. If a gorgeous woman came on to you, sucked you dry and then off, what the fuck would you do?"

"Toss her over my shoulder and lock us in a room for a week?" Micah said with a grin.

"I'm tempted . . . if I could find the wench."

"I just happen to know where she'll be this weekend," Micah said casually.

Nathan pinned him with a stare. "And how would you know that?"

Micah smiled. Smug bastard. "I have my ways."

"Cut the crap, will you?"

Micah gripped his beer bottle and tilted it back, taking a long swig. When he lowered it again, he looked long and hard at Nathan. "There's a reason I'm asking how hung up on her you are."

"And that is?" Nathan asked.

"Because apparently she's serious about leaving you in her dust."

Nathan snorted and downed the last of his beer. "Tell me something I don't know."

"Normally I wouldn't even tell you this, because I usually side with the women, but I think you have a thing for her."

Nathan blew out his breath in irritation. Nice to know he was so fucking transparent. But how transparent could he be if Julie hadn't even figured it out? Hell, she thought he'd spent the last few months ignoring her. As if any breathing man could ever not notice that woman.

"Yeah, maybe," he said grudgingly.

"Well, she's hooked up this weekend for some hot, anonymous sex at Damon's place. And the following weekend as well."

Nathan's jaw dropped about the time the beer bottle fell out of his hand and hit the floor.

"*What?*"

Micah eyed him cautiously, and maybe he did look a little deranged. He couldn't very well act calm, when he felt like a volcano about to erupt.

"Run that by me again," Nathan growled. "Use short words. Don't leave anything out. What the fuck is she doing at Damon fucking Roche's sex club?"

Micah snickered. "I wasn't even sure you had any idea about The House."

"I wouldn't if I hadn't overheard you and Gray talking about the time he hauled Faith out of there. *Faith*, for Christ's sake. If I had any inkling she was wandering in there, I would have snatched her out by her hair. I can't believe Damon allowed her in. I know he's your friend, but that was ridiculous."

"Maybe Faith isn't the innocent you like to make her out to be," Micah said in amusement.

Nathan glared at Micah. "We're talking about Julie, remember? And I sure as hell don't think she's innocent, but I damn well don't want her fucking some stranger with Damon's blessing either. What the hell is he running, some kind of pimp service?"

"Look, I'm not telling you this so you can stop it. Last I checked, you weren't Julie's keeper, and I doubt she'd allow that anyway." His lips twitched as he obviously fought laughter. "But Julie's request was for anonymous sex. She wants to be blindfolded. Do you see an opportunity here?"

Nathan stared at Micah in stupefaction. "Blindfolded? Has she lost her damn mind? What's to stop this joker from hurting her?"

"Jokers," Micah corrected.

"*What?*"

"There's more than one."

Nathan's fingers curled into a fist. "You're shitting me. You're doing this to yank my chain, aren't you?"

Micah licked his lips as he struggled with his composure.

"And would you quit laughing at me already?" Nathan demanded.

Micah dropped his head and laughed. He laughed so hard that tears were streaming from his eyes. Nathan wanted nothing more than to kick his ass.

"I'm not shitting you, man," Micah said as he gasped for breath. "She wants hot sex with more than one guy. She wants to be blindfolded but not tied up. She wants the fantasy of anonymity."

"Fuck me," Nathan swore. "That's going to happen over my dead body."

"Oh? And how do you plan to stop it? Damon's not going to let you within a mile of The House if your plan is to barge in, fists swinging. He runs a very civilized place."

"Civilized, my ass. What's civilized about treating women like pieces of meat?"

Micah raised an eyebrow. "Knowing what you do about me, do you honestly think I would have let Julie walk into that kind of situation if I wasn't sure that Damon would take damn good care of her?"

Nathan leaned forward. "And I'd ask what the hell business of it is yours what Julie does or doesn't do."

"She's friends with Faith and Serena. I'd look out for her just like I do those two," he said evenly. "What business of it is yours? Why do you care, Nathan?"

"Fuck you," Nathan muttered.

"Admit it, you care. It's eating you alive to know that she's going to be fucking some other guy this weekend when you're dying to get into her pants."

"It ain't going to happen," Nathan said belligerently.

"What, you getting into her pants?" Micah asked.

Nathan turned up his middle finger at Micah. "What ain't going to happen is her having anonymous sex with some goddamn stranger."

"And you plan to prevent this how?"

Fuck if he knew. He didn't know this Damon guy as well as Micah did, but Micah could fix that, couldn't he? And hell, if she was that bent on having anonymous sex, he could be as anonymous as the next guy.

A slow grin spread across his face. That was it. He'd exact a little payback for the way she'd played him in the salon with the added benefit of not letting her fuck another man. She wouldn't need another guy when he finished with her.

"I'm not liking the look on your face right now," Micah said warily. "You only get that look when you're plotting. Usually against me."

"I think we should have a beer with your buddy, Damon," Nathan suggested. "Like tonight."

Micah grinned. "I thought you might see it my way."

"Your way? How the hell is this your way? If we did things your way, Julie would be fucking some weirdo at Damon's sex club this weekend."

"Why do you think I told you about it, moron?" Micah said as he motioned for another beer. "And I'm way ahead of you, man. Damon's supposed to meet me here in an hour."

CHAPTER 4

"You did *not* tell me that they were going to be here," Julie huffed as she, Serena and Faith walked into Cattleman's. "In fact, you told me that Damon was at The House tonight. Working on my setup."

Serena shrugged, but her gaze was drawn to where Damon sat between Micah and Nathan.

"Hello? Earth to Serena?"

Faith giggled as they pulled Serena toward the bar. Damon's gaze found Serena's, and he smiled a sexy, toe-curling smile that even had Julie squirming.

"You two are more nauseating than Faith and Gray," Julie grumbled as they plopped onto barstools.

"What did I do?" Faith asked in a perfect rendition of her innocent look.

"So why are they here?" Julie hissed. Nathan was staring at her. She could *feel* him boring holes through her back.

"Why don't you go ask them?" Serena drawled.

"After a few drinks I just might." The last thing she wanted was for Nathan to think she was rattled. Or avoiding him. Even if she damn well was.

"Well you wanted him to suffer," Faith said as the bartender served up their drinks. "Although I'd say he looks more pissed than pained."

"Better to be pissed off than pissed on," Julie muttered.

Serena laughed. "Girlfriend, you pissed all over the guy months ago. Marked him, scented him, howled at the moon . . ."

Julie shoved at her arm and scowled. "Yeah, well, you saw how far that got me. At least now he knows what he's missing."

"Why are you still talking about him?" Faith asked. "Shouldn't you be moving on to greener pastures? Remember? You were going to blow him then blow him off and have Damon hook you up with two prime specimens with big dicks and no brains."

"Why, Faith, you shock me," Serena said in mock horror.

"I'd say she's dead-on," Julie drawled. "She makes a damn good point. Why the hell am I sitting here stewing about Nathan fucking Tucker when I've got a date to be the filling in a stud sandwich?"

Faith and Serena both looked at her with ill-disguised horror.

"The filling in a stud sandwich? Julie, tell me you didn't just say that. For God's sake," Serena said.

"Not one of your better lines," Faith snickered.

"Okay, so it was all I could come up with. Not everyone has your expertise in the area of threesomes."

Serena laughed. "She's got you there, Faith."

"And clearly neither of you are going to let me live it down," Faith said.

"Hell, if I were you, I wouldn't want to live it down. I'd want to relive it. Over and over if possible," Julie said wistfully.

She stole a glance over at Micah Hudson and tried again to imagine him and Gray Montgomery both fucking Faith's brains out. Nope. Couldn't picture it. She shrugged and turned her gaze back to Faith.

"I still think you're putting us on about that whole thing."

Faith rolled her eyes. "You're just a jealous bitch and you know it. I don't know what your problem is. In a few nights, you're going to be indulging in all the hedonistic pleasure you can handle while Serena and I are having a boring evening home with our guys."

"Speak for yourself," Serena murmured.

Julie downed her drink and quickly ordered another one. Liquid courage. Never let her down yet. Last time, Nathan had taken her home and dumped her into bed. Maybe this time she could get Micah to do the dirty deed.

"Going for a quick buzz tonight?" Serena asked with a raised eyebrow.

She didn't respond, just leveled a stare at Serena and then turned her gaze on the guys sitting several tables away.

"Uh-oh. I don't like that look," Faith said.

Serena grinned. "Oh this is going to be good. And you and I get front-row seats, Faith."

"You two are going with me," Julie said sweetly.

"Uh-huh, and exactly what are we doing?" Faith asked.

Julie smiled. "First we're going to have a few more drinks. I assume at this point Damon's not going to leave without you, Serena."

Thirty minutes and a good many drinks later, Julie was feeling no pain, and the demon that had perched so delicately on her shoulder earlier was now hanging from her ear for dear life.

"Shall we, ladies?"

She stood and started toward the table where the men still sat nursing their beers. All three looked up as she approached, and she almost halted at the fire that blazed in Nathan's eyes.

Damn, the man was hot. Her fingers positively itched to run over his bald head and over his gorgeous, muscled body. Broad shoulders, bulging arms. And that chest. Man, did she love his chest. And his ass.

But it wasn't Nathan she focused on. As Damon greeted Serena, and all the guys said their hellos to Julie and Faith, Julie slid onto Micah's lap, and she took his beer from his hand and took a long swallow. She let her lips linger over the mouth of the bottle and flicked her tongue out to rim it.

"Well damn," Micah murmured. "Hello to you too, sugar."

She put the bottle on the table behind her and wrapped her arms loosely around his neck. "Where have you been all my life?"

"Waiting for you to rock mine," he said teasingly.

Nathan sat in stony silence, his eyes glittering. His jaw clenched and ticked, but he said nothing.

"I seem to need a ride home," she whispered. "Gray is meeting Faith here for dinner, and now that Damon is here, Serena isn't going to want to leave."

"Well now," Micah drawled. "Far be it from me to ever leave a woman in distress. However, Nathan here might kick my ass if I make a move toward that door with you."

She let her eyes widen innocently as she turned to Nathan. "Oh, hello, Nathan. I didn't even notice you there."

Damon choked on his beer while Faith and Serena both looked away to keep from laughing. Nathan tipped his bottle in her direction, his face set in stone.

Then she turned back to Micah. "Are you the type to let another man dictate who you take home?"

Micah's expression darkened. "Don't play with fire, sugar, or you'll get burned quick."

She pouted playfully and leaned in closer until her mouth was an inch from his ear.

"Who says I'm playing?" she whispered.

His hands tightened around her hips, and then he tucked his lips to her ear, nuzzling through her hair.

"If Nathan hadn't already staked a claim, I'd have you in my bed so fast you wouldn't know what hit you. And believe me, sugar, I'd be calling all the shots."

She drew away and rolled her eyes. "I've heard all about you, Hudson. And I can't wait for the day a woman knocks you on your smug ass. I just hope I'm around to see it."

Micah smirked. "Ain't going to happen, babe."

"Does that mean you aren't going to volunteer to take me home?" she asked softly.

Nathan bolted from his seat and reached over to snag her wrist. Julie was so surprised by his action that she just sat there on Micah's lap, gaping up at him.

"Cut the bullshit, Julie. I'm taking you home. Now. It's long past time we had a little chat."

Her eyes narrowed, and she moved farther into Micah's embrace, but Nathan didn't let up on his grip.

"We have nothing to talk about, Tucker. And if my options are you driving me home or taking a cab, then I'll go pour myself into a cab."

"Nathan, let it go," Micah said quietly. "Save it for later. I'll drive her home."

Nathan's eyes grew stormy, but he let go of her wrist and then turned and stalked out of the restaurant.

"Asshole," Julie muttered as she rubbed her wrist.

Micah picked her hand up and ran his thumb over her wrist. "You know he wouldn't hurt a hair on your head. And if he had any hair, he'd have already pulled it all out over you and you damn well know it."

She raised an eyebrow. "And what do you know about it?"

He grinned, flashing perfectly white straight teeth. "Women aren't the only ones who gossip, you know."

Her cheeks went warm. "Well, hell."

"Too bad I never started going to you for massages," he teased.

She let her head fall onto his shoulder with a groan. "I'm ready to go home now."

"Come on, Julie, we'll take you home and you know it," Serena said.

"No, I'll take her," Micah said. "I told her I would, and I'd never leave a lady in distress."

"You guys going to hang out here until Gray comes?" Julie asked Serena and Damon.

"Of course," Damon said smoothly.

Faith hesitated, her eyes drooping a little sadly. "For the love of God, people. I'm certainly capable of staying by myself until

Gray gets here. He, uh, he'll probably be late anyway. He's been running behind a lot lately."

"But the point is you don't have to be by yourself," Damon said. "Serena and I are more than happy to wait with you."

Micah lifted Julie to her feet, impressing her with his strength. Then he stood and took her hand, pulling her toward the door.

When they got to his truck, he opened the passenger door for her, and like a perfect gentleman, saw her seated before walking around to his side.

The interior smelled faintly of smoke, and it gave her the first serious jones for a cigarette she'd had in two years.

"I didn't realize you smoked," she said when he started the engine.

He winced and smiled a little guiltily. "I didn't think the smell was that obvious."

"Former smoker," she admitted. "Some people love the smell of coffee. Me, I love the smell of cigarettes."

He reached into the door pocket and pulled out a crumpled packet. "I've got one left. Want to share it?"

She sucked in her breath. Damn. It was only one. Well, half a one. What the hell.

"You trying to quit?" she asked as he lit up.

"Yeah."

"How's that working for you?"

He laughed. "I'm down to a few a day. I keep saying each pack is my last, but at least I'm making them last longer."

He took a deep drag and passed it to her. She slid it between her lips and inhaled, closing her eyes.

"Between this and the booze, you're going to have to pour me into bed," she said as she passed it back. "I'll have a head rush from hell."

"How long's it been for you?"

"Two years."

"Impressive. And here I am luring you back to the dark side. I'm a real bastard."

She laughed. Then she cast him a mournful stare. "Why the hell couldn't I be hung up on you?"

Jesus. Had she just said that? Too much to drink. Or maybe it was the cigarette. Or maybe it was just sheer desperation. She'd all but told him how hung up on Nathan she was now.

Micah smiled and passed her back the cigarette. "You're killing the poor guy. Give him a break, okay? Us men aren't too smart when it comes to women, you know?"

She blew out the smoke and sent him a baleful look. "Okay, so a woman all but throws herself at you for weeks, pushes her cleavage in your face, practically takes out a glowing neon sign saying 'I want you,' and then gives you a massage you'll never forget, and you can't figure out she's attracted to you?"

"Okay, *Nathan* isn't too smart when it comes to women," he said with a chuckle. "Cut him some slack. The poor man doesn't know whether he's coming or going with you."

She scowled. "Well you know what, Micah? I'm damn tired of men not knowing what to do with me. I want a guy who doesn't need an instruction manual, thank you very much. Nathan blew his chance as far as I'm concerned."

"So you're going to torture him endlessly."

"Something like that," she muttered. "Okay, okay, I'll leave him alone. I have bigger fish to fry anyway."

He pulled into her apartment complex and cut the engine. For a moment he sat there just staring over at her with those complex, deep brown eyes.

"You know, Julie, someday a man's going to tame you. I just hope I'm around to see it."

"Ha!" she said as she opened her door. "I'll make a bet that a woman knocks you down a few notches before a man ever *tames* me."

He held out his hand with a smug grin. "Deal."

She took it and stared back just as hard. "What are the stakes?"

"If you win, you get me, any way you want me. If I win, I get you. Any way I want you."

She took her hand back and crossed her arms over her chest. "There's just one problem with your stakes, slick."

"Oh? And what's that?"

"If you're tamed, your girly might have a thing or two to say about me having you any way I want you. If I'm tamed, the guy in question sure as hell won't appreciate having a third in the mix. I'm not saying I'd mind," she added saucily.

"Don't be so sure of that," he said, a glint in his eyes. "As I have no intention of losing the bet, all we have to worry about is this guy who's going to tame you. My guess is, he's not going to mind allowing me my winnings."

Chapter 5

"An instruction manual?" Nathan bit out. "An *instruction* manual?"

Nathan slammed the truck door and stomped around to the front of the truck to meet Micah and to head into the building that housed the Malone and Sons offices.

Micah chuckled. "Yeah, she was pretty clear on wanting a guy who didn't need an instruction manual to satisfy her."

"I'll show her instruction manual," Nathan gritted out.

God, but the woman was making him crazy. Why was he letting her get to him so bad? It wasn't just the blow job—though, damn, the feisty little wench was good with her mouth.

"Have you and Damon talked about this weekend?" Micah asked.

Nathan looked around and frowned. Faith wasn't in her office, but that didn't mean Gray or Connor wasn't skulking around. Or Pop even. He shuddered at the idea of Pop overhearing this conversation.

"Relax, man. Connor and Gray are out with Pop on a job."

"And what are we doing here again?"

"Picking up the paperwork for our job, and then we're going to head south. You're a grumpy son of a bitch when you're not getting laid, let me tell you."

"How the hell would you know whether I'm getting laid or not?" Nathan growled. "Jesus, why are we talking about this?"

Micah laughed as he rummaged around on Faith's desk. "Aha! Here it is. Let's make tracks. We can talk on the way."

"What's turned you into such a chatty bastard?" Nathan asked when they'd gotten back into Micah's truck. He scowled when Micah cracked his window and started digging for a cigarette.

"Damn it. Smoked my last one with Julie."

"What the hell were you doing smoking with Julie? She doesn't smoke. Does she?"

A smug grin creased Micah's face. Then he reached over to open the glove box. Shit fell out between Nathan's knees.

"There is a God," Micah breathed as he pulled out a smashed package of cigarettes.

"Get a damn patch or something."

Micah stuck a cigarette between his lips and fished in his pocket for a lighter. "So you didn't answer my question. Have you talked to Damon about this weekend or are you just going to let Julie go?"

"Fuck you. I'm not letting her go anywhere but to bed with me."

"So you have talked to Damon then. I take it he agreed?"

"Not exactly," Nathan muttered.

Micah turned to blow his smoke out the window. "Will you quit being so damned closemouthed and just spill it?"

"He feels his first obligation is to Julie."

"Imagine that," Micah said dryly.

"Cut the sarcasm," Nathan said with a scowl. "She wants a threesome. An anonymous threesome, with her blindfolded!"

It was all he could do to get the words out. Was she just trying to get herself hurt? He didn't give a damn how tight Damon's security was or that they had video surveillance on the private rooms all the time. It would only take a few seconds to hurt her or kill her, and there wouldn't be a damn thing Damon or his people could do about it.

"Why does that bother you so much?" Micah asked with a sideways look.

Nathan's mouth fell open. Then he snapped it shut. "Damon doesn't have a problem with vetting me to be one of her guys. But I insisted that I'd be the only man in that damn room with her, and he said that he felt obligated to fulfill Julie's wishes."

Micah shrugged. "So? Have a threesome with her. Come on, man. You can't tell me you've never fantasized about fucking a woman while another man is fucking her too. Hell, you watch porn. Half that shit is a bona fide gang bang."

"Would you stand by and let another man touch what you considered yours?" Nathan asked calmly.

Something dark and predatory flashed in Micah's eyes. "As long as she belonged to me? Yeah, it's a huge turn-on."

"You've had threesomes?"

Whoa, this conversation was heading into serious cringe territory. Next they'd be comparing dick sizes.

"You never have?" Micah countered.

"Hell, you act as though it's some natural function, as normal as having sex with a woman. Most men get on their knees and thank God if a woman will sleep with them, much less you and another guy."

Micah laughed. "Women tend to like being the object of so much attention. Two men devoted to making sure she has the most mindless pleasure she's ever experienced?"

"So it's more about the woman?"

Shit, there he went again, sounding like some damn amateur. A blush stole over his cheeks, and he turned to look out the window before Micah could see him and give him hell.

He'd had sex. Lots of sex, damn it. Okay, maybe not *that* much. Still, he'd been around the block more than a few times, but now his experiences seemed pretty dull compared to the crap Micah was talking about.

"Well, yes and no," Micah said seriously. "It's all about pleasuring her, watching her go wild. In turn it's a huge turn-on for a man. I mean what guy doesn't get a serious charge out of rocking a woman's world?"

He had a point there. It wasn't like a guy ever wanted to be a complete failure in bed.

"So she really wants this threesome," Nathan said painfully.

"Don't take it personally. If you've never been to bed with her, it's not as if she's sending you a message or anything."

"Oh, she's sending one, all right."

"So are you going to agree to the threesome or not? Doesn't

sound like Damon's going to give you much of a choice. And hell, dude, have you even given this any thought? Blindfolded or not, she's going to figure out it's you really damn quick with your bald head and goatee. You're going to need a distraction for her."

"Or just tie her damn hands to the bed," Nathan muttered.

Micah laughed. "Well that would be my vote, but I hear that's not what she wants at all. I think it would offend her not-so-meek sensibilities."

"You sound like you know an awful lot about her," Nathan said quietly.

"I like all women, Nathan. Don't get your panties in a wad. It's not like I'm trying to move in on your woman. You want her. I get it. Doesn't mean I don't have eyes or a dick and that they both don't come to attention when she's around."

"Then maybe you'd be a perfect third in this threesome she wants."

Micah tossed his cigarette out the window and cast Nathan a sidelong glance. "Let me get this straight. You want me to be the other guy?"

Nathan shifted uncomfortably in his seat. "Well, if you want the truth, I don't want there to a third person in this equation. I mean, shit, when did sex get so goddamn complicated? But if that's what she wants and if that's the only way I get into the picture, then yeah, I'd prefer it to be you over some stranger. At least I wouldn't have to worry about your intentions."

Micah nodded. "All right. If that's what you want, I'll let Damon know. I'm already a member there, so it'll be just you he has to do all the checking up on."

"This is for the birds," Nathan grumbled. "Seriously. It never used to be this difficult to get into a woman's pants. Now there are security and background checks. Kinky checklists."

Micah chuckled. "The House should be quite an experience for you. I'll suggest to Damon that he give you a tour before this weekend just so you'll know what you're getting into."

"He said she wanted a *private* room. Just her and the two guys."

"Yeah, but you have to get to that private room."

"Great. Just great."

"Don't be such a pussy."

"Hey, fuck you," Nathan growled, but he grinned and shook his head.

This was going to be painful. Hell, it already was. The last thing he wanted to do was get naked in front of one of his best friends and then let that best friend fuck the woman he'd been fantasizing about for months.

But there was something edgy and forbidden about the images flashing in his mind. Watching her come apart between him and Micah? Giving her more pleasure than she could stand?

Yeah, it was a turn-on, but then everything about Julie did it for him. She was an earthy woman, shorter, full figured with hips and an ass that just cried out for a man's hands.

And her breasts. Sweet Jesus, her breasts were mouthwateringly perfect, and he ought to know because he'd seen them often enough in his fantasies. Round with a generous swell. He hadn't seen her nipples, and he was positively dying to get them into his mouth.

He wanted to bury his face right in the valley between the generous mounds. She had to be at least a double D, and Lord but that excited him.

No, he wouldn't be able to feel her ribs, or get poked by her bones. But she'd be soft in all the right places, and he couldn't wait to bury himself inside her pussy over and over.

She was, in a word, stacked. Built like a brick house. Voluptuous. He'd have his hands full with her in more ways than one, and he couldn't goddamn wait.

Chapter 6

"I'm nervous. Why am I nervous?"

Julie looked between Faith and Serena, who stood in her bathroom watching as Julie did her hair.

"And why am I worried so goddamn much about hair?" she muttered. "Like it's not going to get messed up?"

Faith giggled, and Serena just rolled her eyes in the mirror.

"Come on, Julie, it's okay. I'd be terrified," Serena said.

"So says the woman who auctioned herself off—naked—in front of a roomful of horny men," Julie pointed out.

"You want to look good. It's natural," Faith said soothingly. "I wouldn't want to look like a hag in front of men who were seeing me naked."

"Hag?" Julie croaked.

Serena patted her on the arm. "It's just a figure of speech."

Julie set down the comb and the hairspray and sighed. "You know why I'm doing this?"

"Uh, does it have something to do with the naked thing?" Faith asked.

"I saw my ex in the grocery store last night."

"Which ex?" Serena asked.

Julie pinned her with a glare. "Does it matter? He was with his new girlfriend. Okay, he's an old ex. I'm not hung up on him or anything. It was his girlfriend who pissed me off."

"Want me to kick her ass?" Serena asked with a grin.

Julie smooched at Serena's reflection in the mirror. "No, but we can hope she trips and breaks an ankle, can't we?"

Faith laughed. "So what did she do?"

Julie picked up the comb again and pushed at a strand of hair that kept falling over her forehead. "So I'm at the grocery store, I round the corner of the bread aisle, and there he is with Miss Thing on his arm. He smiles and says hello. I smile back and say hello. Miss Thing looks at me once, and she dismisses me like I'm not a threat. Just like that."

"She didn't!" Serena gasped in mock horror.

Julie gave her a mournful look. "I mean, let's face it, most of the time if you're with your guy and you see his ex, you get all prickly. You start sizing her up. Is she prettier than me? Is he looking at her? Was she better in bed? Is he still hung up on her? The claws come out. But no. Miss Thing actually smiled at me. This smug, superior smile that said 'I'm prettier than you, I'm thinner than you, I'll always be better than you.' Then she all but sneered at me when he introduced us and she had this look like, 'he dated *you*? Really?' "

Faith wrapped an arm around her shoulders and squeezed tight. "Her boobs were probably fake, and I bet her roots were showing."

Julie shook against her with laughter. "God, I love you guys, but damn, can't you let me wallow for two seconds?"

"No wallowing," Serena said.

"Why aren't I a threat?" Julie asked mournfully.

"I lock Gray down every time you walk into the room," Faith said.

Julie rolled her eyes. "I wanted to tell her that I could have her man any time I wanted, and that she was probably a cold fish in bed, but then I remembered, she has him, I don't, so that argument wasn't going to cut it."

"Do you want him?" Serena asked archly.

"Hell no, but that isn't the point."

"Did he dump you or did you dump him?" Faith asked.

"I dumped him. Of course."

"Of course," Serena murmured. "Okay then, it's settled. He had to settle for second best, and even now, he's probably drowning his sorrows in a bottle of alcohol while Miss Thing hangs uselessly on his arm."

Julie cracked up laughing. She laughed so hard her mascara smeared. "Damn it, Serena. Now I've got to start all over."

"Don't know why you bother with the stuff," Faith said. "You don't want raccoon eyes during sex."

"Good point," Julie acknowledged. "I'll stick with the basics. Except for lipstick. A woman can never wear too much lipstick."

"Even if they rub it off real quick," Serena snickered.

A few minutes later, Julie took a deep breath and stared back at her friends in the mirror. "Okay, how do I look?"

"Absolutely gorgeous."

"Sensational."

Faith and Serena's voices ran together, and Julie smiled back at them.

"I'm so nervous I could puke. How stupid is that?"

"Not stupid," Serena said. "Just remember, you don't have to go through with it. If you get there and don't feel comfortable, you don't have to do it."

"But if you do, we want all the details later," Faith said with a grin.

Julie hugged them both then shooed them out of her bathroom. "I'm going to be late if I don't get out of here."

Everything was done and arranged. All she had to do was walk inside, and her night of fantasy would begin. But here she sat in her car with sweaty palms like a virgin behind the bleachers with the quarterback.

She and Damon had agreed that Cole would handle her arrival, because having Damon do it? Weird much? She knew Damon's security monitored the rooms with video surveillance, but she'd rather not have a personal relationship with anyone seeing her naked, doing two guys at the same time.

Then again, if she didn't get a move on, she wouldn't be doing anyone.

Excitement skirted up her spine as she got out of the car. Nervous had no place in tonight's activities. She was a confident, sexual woman. She could handle whatever was thrown her way.

Before she could knock, the door opened, and an extremely good-looking man smiled back at her.

"Julie?"

She nodded. "You must be Cole."

White teeth flashed as his smile broadened. "Come in, I've been expecting you."

"I hope you aren't the only one."

He laughed as he put his hand to her back to usher her down the hallway. "Indeed not."

She knew from Damon's tour which room would be hers, but it didn't make her any less excited as they went up the stairs. At the end of the upstairs hallway was the common room where anything went. Publicly. There were several private rooms, however, and Cole guided her to the one on the opposite end of the hallway from the common room.

"I'll leave you to undress. I'll be back in a few minutes to blindfold you and see if there's anything else you need before your men arrive."

She couldn't help the grin. *Her men.* It sounded positively decadent.

Cole retreated from the room, and she made her way to the bed to run her hand across the sumptuous linens. Not wanting an awkward moment, she hurriedly shed her clothing and stuffed it into the closet.

The room had been prepared as Damon had promised. The blindfold was on the bed, a beautiful scarlet red sash. Symbolic. She liked it.

On the vanity next to the bed was an array of sexual paraphernalia that she probably wouldn't have even thought of. Condoms, of course, but there was also lubricant and an array of sex toys, some of which she wasn't even sure of their purpose. It would be fun as hell to find out though.

A sound at the door had her guiltily whirling around. Cole came back in, and she instinctively covered her nakedness, as if her hands were going to cover that much flesh.

"Are you ready?"

She blew out her breath in a sharp staccato. "Yeah."

He smiled and patted the bed. "Hop up and I'll get the blindfold in place. Then all you need to do is lie back and relax."

She crawled onto the bed and turned her back to Cole. A second later, the silky material of the sash slid over her eyes, shutting out the light. He tied it securely, tightening it so it wouldn't slip.

Then he took her hand and guided her backward until she lay on her back on the soft bed.

"Welcome to your fantasies," he murmured.

She heard him leave, and silence fell over the room. She hadn't expected to feel so vulnerable with the blindfold. If she'd realized before, she would've never requested it, but the nervous anticipation was exciting in a way. She liked the tightening sensation in all her nerve endings. She was already aroused and there was no sign of her studs yet.

She smiled dreamily as she let her imagination go. There was something to this not seeing. This way, she could imagine whoever she wanted. They could look exactly as she wanted, and how was she to know any different?

The soft sound of the door opening made her inhale sharply. They were here.

CHAPTER 7

Nathan stood in the doorway, staring at Julie lying on the bed, and all his breath left his chest. God almighty, the woman was gorgeous. He heard Micah's quick intake of breath behind him and knew he wasn't any less affected. Damn it, but his first instinct was to rush in and cover her with a blanket so Micah wouldn't see her. This had to be the dumbest idea he'd ever hatched. Why the fuck had he asked his best friend to have sex with the woman *he* was lusting over?

Because the alternative was fucking her with a stranger?

Leave it to Julie to come up with a sexual fantasy that gave him hives. How could the woman think he wasn't interested in her?

Maybe because he tried too hard to play it cool.

Micah nudged him, and he continued to move farther inside the lavish room. She heard them enter and turned her head in their direction. She licked her lips nervously, and his dick immediately stood up and paid attention.

He hoped this worked. Micah was scarily thorough when it came to making sure she wouldn't find out it was him. Nathan felt like a first-class moron changing his soap and deodorant for the occasion, not to mention wearing light cologne. He *never* wore cologne.

Keep her touches to a minimum, because Lord knew she'd spent enough time touching him. A woman as tactile as she was would probably have his physique memorized.

And silent. Stay silent. That one was obvious enough, but not as easy as it seemed when he wanted nothing more than to tell her in excruciating detail precisely what he planned to do to her.

Micah seemed to be waiting for him to make the first move, a fact he appreciated. Micah wasn't the type to ever let anyone else call the shots, but in this he seemed willing to sit back and let Nathan dictate the pace. Which was kind of stupid, given that Nathan had zero experience in this whole threesome arena, while Micah seemed to practice them regularly.

Why couldn't he have normal friends?

Drawn by the erotic sight of Julie, naked with only a bloodred sash tied around her eyes, he moved in close. He wanted to touch her. To run his hands over her skin and feel all the curves and soft swells.

She jumped when he put his palm down over her belly. Then she moaned softly when he let his fingers wander upward, brushing the undersides of her breasts. He cupped the mounds and ran his thumb over the puckered crest of her nipple. Such a wonderful contrast of silky smooth skin and velvety ripples.

He drew the nipple between his thumb and fingers, stroking and pulling just enough to get it to elongate. She raised her hands, blindly seeking him, but he stepped back. It was agony, because he wanted her hands on him, but he couldn't take that chance.

No longer caring that there was another man in the room with them, Nathan started pulling off his clothing. The sooner he could get skin to skin with her, the sooner he'd be in heaven.

Julie trembled in anticipation. When would he touch her again? Those hands. Wonderful hands. Slightly rough, which told her he worked them enough that they were calloused. They were gentle, yet firm enough to give her a decadent thrill as they traveled her body.

She could hear the soft rustle of clothing. Where was the other man? She jumped again when another hand curled around her ankle. Ah, there he was. His touch was different, more assertive. Less coaxing.

His fingers brushed along her leg, working the sensitive spots on the inside of her thigh, under her knee, then higher still until he was precariously close to her pussy.

Restless, she stirred, opening to him, but he backed off, and she moaned in frustration. His soft chuckle echoed in the quiet room.

Her first lover was back. She felt his presence before he ever touched her. The bed dipped as he crawled up beside her. There was a pause. Was he watching her? Looking at her? Did he like what he saw?

She arched her body invitingly, and then she gasped when his lips touched her belly. His hot tongue dipped into her navel, rimming it then grazing her skin with his teeth. She reached down, wanting to touch him, but the other man grasped her wrists, and to her surprise, pulled her arms up over her head, holding her captive there while his partner continued to lick a path up to her breasts.

The bristle of a beard scraped against her skin. God, she loved that. Nathan immediately came to mind. Him and that sexy goatee. Oh yeah, this blindfold idea was great. Now she could fantasize that it was Nathan running his tongue over her body.

His lips found her nipple, and he nuzzled gently, coaxing the bud into erection. Her mind went fuzzy as pleasure exploded through her body. His tongue laved over the point, and then he used his teeth to graze the delicate skin. She could no longer contain her cry when he sucked it strongly into his mouth.

He went taut against her at her exclamation, as if the audible sound of her approval pleased him very much. If that's what it took, she'd be more than happy to reward him every time he pleased *her.*

To her complete shock, his hands and mouth left her breasts, and he framed her face with his palms then crashed his lips down over hers. It was as though he hungered for her far more than she hungered for him. He tasted her, devoured her, *absorbed* her.

Not content to lie there passively even though her arms were still trapped above her head, she kissed him back just as urgently. She opened her mouth to let him in, but she also thrust her tongue over his, wanting entry just as she allowed him access.

His beard scraped roughly at her chin, abrading the tender area. He tasted and smelled positively divine. Wholly male. Strong and powerful.

She studied the feel of his body pressed so close to hers. His chest wasn't too hairy, but neither was his skin smooth. The dips and lines of his muscles, the fact that there was no give in his body, told her how solidly he was put together.

It was killing her not to touch him. She was a tactile person. Touching others was her living, her joy.

"I want to touch you," she whispered.

He chuckled softly and the hands tightened around her wrists. No they weren't going to allow her to touch. Why not? This was her fantasy, damn it.

But she forgot all about protesting when he moved down her body, his hands cupping her hips as he kissed a line straight to her pussy.

The man holding her wrists bent over her. She could smell him as he sucked her nipple into his mouth. God, the combination of these two men was the most powerful aphrodisiac she'd ever encountered.

A single finger slid through her folds, parting her and pressing into her heat. His mouth found her center, his tongue plunging deep.

The lips at her breast became more insistent, going from one to the other, sucking and nipping sharply. He was more demanding than the first. Not as gentle and sensual. The differences were compelling. Between her legs, her gentle lover made love to her with all the care and finesse of a man who instinctively knew how to please a woman. The man at her breasts was harder, with an edge to his movements that excited her even while she soaked up the attentions of the other.

Nathan picked his head up and saw Micah sucking hungrily at Julie's breasts. A bolt sizzled through him. Shock. Jealousy. And then, strangely, lust. It should piss him off that another man was taking what he considered his, but in a barbaric way, it aroused the hell out of him.

And God, but she was beautiful, stretched between them,

arching, begging for more, her skin glowing with a sheen of sweat. Her scent was driving him insane. He couldn't get enough of her taste.

He ran his tongue over her quivering entrance, circled it with the tip and then traveled up until he sucked her clit gently into his mouth.

He was rewarded by a sharp cry and she bucked so hard against him, he had to hold her hips with both hands. She was wild and so damn responsive. It was all he could do not to rear up and drive deep into her body. Only the knowledge that he wanted to make this truly spectacular for her kept him from doing just that.

Micah raised his head, and Nathan saw the glittering need in his friend's eyes. There was something harsh and almost primal. He moved to the side and motioned Nathan away for a moment.

Curious as to what Micah was doing, Nathan eased away, though he kept his hands on her, wanting, needing to touch her at all times.

Micah coaxed her to her knees, helping position her just so. For all Micah's demanding, hard edges, he was exceedingly careful. Or maybe he knew how difficult this was for Nathan to swallow.

He might be new to the whole multiple partners aspect, but he didn't need Julie's damn instruction manual to figure out what to do next. As Micah positioned himself at Julie's mouth, Nathan reached for a condom, his hands shaking as he rolled it on.

He watched in fascination as Micah eased his cock into Julie's mouth. He held her jaw with one hand, his thumb stroking across her cheek while he guided himself past her lips with his other hand. Both their expressions were a study in carnality. Desire. Lust. Extreme satisfaction.

Nathan leaned down and kissed the small of Julie's back, letting his lips linger as his hands drifted over her hips, over the swell of her buttocks. He ran a finger down the cleft of her ass and lower, until he delved into her wetness once again. He wanted to make damn certain she was ready for him. The last thing he wanted to do was hurt her.

She squirmed and moved her ass back as if seeking him. The tip of his cock butted against her skin, and he moaned. She took her mouth off Micah's cock long enough to look over her shoulder.

"Don't make me beg," she whispered.

It was all he could stand. No, he wouldn't make this proud woman beg for anything. Not when he was all too willing to give her exactly what she wanted.

He positioned himself and slowly, carefully sheathed himself in her heat.

They both groaned, and Micah even let out a sound of agony as she made moans of contentment around a mouth full of his dick.

Nathan stayed inside her, his hips flush against her ass. Reaching underneath to cup her full breasts, he toyed with her nipples, stroking them to stiff peaks.

When she wiggled against him again, he withdrew slowly, dragging his cock through the velvet clasp of her pussy. She moaned and threw her head back, taking more of Micah's cock. It sent Nathan beyond his measured control.

He slammed into her, rocking her onto Micah's dick. She took them both deep, her body trembling uncontrollably underneath Nathan's hands. He stroked and caressed, unable to keep his fingers from touching her as he plunged into her welcoming body.

Uninhibited. He loved it. This was a woman who gloried in

her sexuality, who wasn't afraid to ask—no, *demand*—what she wanted, and she was so goddamn beautiful doing it.

He reached out, wanting to tangle his fingers in her silky hair. Micah relinquished his grip on her head as Nathan pulled slightly, wrapping the tresses around his palms, letting them slide sensuously over his fingers.

She let out pretty little sighs each time he stroked inward. She convulsed wetly around him, her body holding him, reluctant to let him leave each time. He pushed deeper, seeking her sweet spot, wanting to give her the ultimate pleasure.

Good, so good. He closed his eyes, enjoying the electric, razor-sharp currents gathering in his balls, tightening and drawing them together. Man, he wanted this to last, and if he didn't slow down, he was going to explode.

He met Micah's gaze over her body, and Micah lifted an eyebrow in question. As much as Nathan didn't like the idea of another man sliding into her sweet pussy, he wanted to feel her mouth around his bare cock, and he also wanted Julie to have her fantasy.

He gave a short nod and carefully withdrew, pulling at the condom. Micah reached for one as he walked around the bed and hurriedly jerked it on. Practice. Yeah, Micah had clearly had a lot of practice at this. It was enough to make Nathan feel like a rank amateur in comparison. The only reason he wasn't ready to crawl under the bed was because Julie seemed to genuinely enjoy his lovemaking. And for that reason, he could continue to ignore Micah's participation in this whole thing.

Julie quaked in anticipation as her first lover's fingers lovingly brushed over her face. He pushed back her hair, tucking it tenderly behind her ears, and then he let his hands trail down her neck and forward under her chin until he cupped it.

She wanted to taste him. Wanted to please him like he'd taken such great pains to do for her. She parted her lips and ran her tongue over her swollen mouth. The tip of his cock butted against her bottom lip, and his thumb stroked her cheek, asking her permission.

No longer bracing herself on the mattress with both hands, she reached eagerly up to grasp his cock in her fingers. Guiding it to her mouth, she sucked him deep, her body catching fire as he hissed his satisfaction.

Behind her, firm hands gripped her ass. This lover reached underneath the globes with his thumbs, pushing upward and parting her just before he stabbed deep.

The differences in their sizes, their shapes, fascinated her. They tasted different. They made love to her differently. Her second lover stroked deep, not waiting for her to adjust to his size. He was slightly longer, but not as big around. He certainly reached deeper into her body, but she didn't clasp him as tight, and she missed the delicious friction.

Then he picked up his pace, and she forgot all about her analysis. His hands gripped her insistently as he pumped into her, fast, hard, demanding.

By contrast, her first lover was making love to her mouth with all the gentleness and care he'd shown when he was inside her pussy. Deep, but careful. Sensual, almost like a massage. That was it. His slow, measured movements reminded her so much of how she massaged. Lovingly, caressing, as though he enjoyed the act of touching her, of feeling her, as she did.

The dual pace set off a spark inside her that was like a fuse being lit. It burned fast, racing up to the inevitable explosion. She gripped his cock tighter around the base, wanting him to come with her. She sucked harder, exerting firmer pressure as she moved both hand and mouth in rhythm.

His hands tangled in her hair, pulling her closer, burying himself deeper inside her mouth. Breathless. He swelled within her, taking as much as she would give. Her second lover was fucking her with savage intensity, reaching inside her to her most sensitive depths.

Then his fingers stuttered across her clit, plucking and rolling just the right way. Oh God.

Warm fluid spurted onto her tongue and the hands in her hair tightened around her head, holding her, giving her no choice but to swallow him whole.

They exploded together, him in her mouth as she gave a muffled cry. The tension in her pussy wound tighter until she simply burst under the strain, the pleasure so magnificent, so sharp. It was too much and not enough all at the same time.

The sticky fluid filled her mouth, and she swallowed quickly as she sucked every inch of him deep. His fingers trembled against her scalp and his hips spasmed as he thrust rapidly. Then he stilled and she lovingly lapped her tongue around his softening erection as she washed away every drop of semen.

When she finally let him slide from her mouth, he gathered her face in his hands and kissed her forehead, then her cheekbones. His lips slid higher to kiss each temple as he stroked her hair. The gentle kisses melted her heart. He took such care with her.

Carefully the man at her ass withdrew and she found herself being turned onto her back, her legs parted and warm lips nuzzling between her thighs. The other man laced his fingers with hers and held them to the mattress at her sides. They seemed so determined not to let her touch them.

Her clit spasmed and jumped almost painfully as he licked at the still-quivering nub. When she would have protested the sharp, post-orgasm sensations, the man at her head bent and kissed her softly on the lips.

She forgot everything but the two mouths on her, drinking and sipping as they coaxed her down from the bomb burst of just seconds ago.

Her second lover's tongue lapped lightly at her pussy, going lower, delving into her opening, covering every inch of sensitive skin.

She moaned into her first lover's mouth, allowing him to drink up her sounds as he licked over her lips. He nibbled lower, biting gently at her neck, grazing his teeth in little short arcs.

Chill bumps rose and danced across her skin, racing from breasts to pussy. Before he ever got to her nipples, they were taut. Upright and straining like little beads awaiting his kiss.

His mouth closed around one so carefully and reverently she nearly died on the spot. Amazingly, as soon as his lips made contact with the puckered crest, she felt the stirrings of another orgasm, curling deep and rising like a thin smoke plume.

"Yes," she sighed. "Oh yes."

She felt him smile against her breast and an indescribable thrill ran through her at the thought of him being pleased with her.

The licks at her pussy became firmer, drawing her higher and closer to her orgasm. He seemed to know a woman's body so well, taking care around her most sensitive parts and being harder in the places she wanted him to be more assertive. He didn't ravage her clit, and seemed to realize just how supersensitive she was after that first orgasm. He took such care, sucking ever so gently, holding it in his mouth as he flicked little licks over the center.

She wanted to box both men up and take them home with her. She'd never leave her bedroom again.

"Harder," she whispered to the man at her breast. "Just a little harder."

He readily complied, sucking more urgently at her nipple. He went to the other, giving it equal treatment. Then he pressed her hands more firmly into the mattress and tapped her wrists in warning. His message was clear.

Then he released her and palmed both her breasts, kissing one and then the other. While he caressed one, he suckled the other, driving her mad. She wanted more, needed more.

The mouth at her pussy became more demanding, licking and sucking with just enough pressure to make her insane with wanting. She reached for the orgasm lurking precious inches away.

Bucking and bowing her body up in mindless need, her hands started to fly up, but she let them fall back in quiet acceptance of her lover's request. It should have irked her to no end, but he hadn't demanded. And he'd been so good to her, so gentle. She wouldn't deny him the one thing he'd asked of her so far.

And then, shockingly, the man between her legs picked up his head just as the other man slid down her body, his chest pressed to her belly as his mouth covered her pussy in a hot rush. She exploded instantaneously, coming hard in a hot liquid rush.

He drank her greedily as she came on his tongue. He sucked and lapped like a man starving, and it gave her such an erotic thrill that yet another mini orgasm rushed on the heels of the second, a sharp, painful burst that left her screaming her release.

She lay weakly against the bed, her legs limp. Exhausted, she rested there as he kissed and licked between her legs.

She wanted to say something, but the words lodged in her throat. She didn't want to come across as needy. This was sex. Good sex, but sex nonetheless. No way in hell she was going to get all girly and emotional.

Her first lover moved off her and she wondered if he would leave now, but no, he carefully arranged her body like he wanted her on the bed and then tucked her against his hard form. His heart beat fast and furious against her back as he spooned against her.

Softly and soothingly, his hand ran over her body, petting and caressing her as he kissed the curve of her neck.

And then he pulled her even closer, twining his legs with hers as he wrapped an arm securely around her waist. Did he intend for her to stay? She reached for her blindfold, but he took her wrist and lowered it back to her side.

He sighed. In regret? He kissed her neck again, letting his lips linger for a long moment. Then he rolled away, and she bit her lip to keep from calling out, to apologize for breaking her own rules. She had her reasons for wanting things to be anonymous, and evidently so did he. It wasn't fair for her to change the rules now.

His footsteps mingled with those of the second man, and then the door shut softly, and she was left alone. She lay there for a long moment before finally reaching for the sash covering her eyes.

The lights had been turned low, and she blinked to bring the room into focus. Empty, but then she'd known they'd left. It was what she'd asked for, but had she not reached for the blindfold, would he still be here, holding her? And why did she want him to?

She snorted in disgust and rolled from the bed, putting shaky legs over the side. She hurriedly dressed, not wanting Cole to come back while she was naked, although he'd seen her already. Before she'd been expectant. Cocky almost. Now she was shaken and disheveled and she definitely needed some recovery time to think about what the hell had gone on here. She damn sure didn't want to do it in the buff with a gorgeous man looking on.

A knock at the door startled her, and she bolted around as it opened a crack and Cole stuck his head in.

"Everything okay?" he asked gently.

She nodded.

"Damon arranged for a car to bring you home. One of his men will drive your car. He thought it better if you didn't drive yourself."

She smiled. Had Damon known how the evening would affect her? That her mind was mush and she had the muscle tone of an overcooked noodle? She would have to remember to thank him for his consideration and needle Serena some more about making the poor man wait for her to accept his marriage proposal. If her girlfriend didn't want to marry him, Julie might reconsider her strict no-relationship vow and marry the man herself.

Cole reached for her hand and squeezed when she placed her fingers over his palm. He didn't say anything else as he led her from the room, and for that she was grateful.

Even when he handed her into the waiting car, he merely nodded before backing off. As she rolled away from the stately mansion, she wondered about her two mystery lovers. Leaning her head back against the seat, she closed her eyes and relived those erotic moments when their mouths and hands worked over her body. She'd had good sex before, but this? This went beyond a quick, sweaty fuck, or even the more sensual lovemaking she'd indulged in. And she couldn't figure out why.

Sure, it was a new experience, and damn, but she knew what sweet little Faith saw in the kink. But her first lover . . . he was something special. It hadn't just been sex to him, and it galled her to be so damn girly right now and say mushy shit like that, but the man hadn't fucked her. She'd been around enough to know the difference. Lover number two had fucked her and fucked her hard. Lover number one had made sweet, bone-melting love to her, and damn, but she wanted to know why.

Chapter 8

"So are we ignoring what happened?" Micah asked.

Nathan cast him a disgruntled look as the two headed into Malone and Sons.

"Work ain't where I want to talk about it," he muttered.

And yeah, ignoring it worked for him just fine. He was still reeling from the experience, but that didn't mean he wanted to gush on about it like a damn girl.

"Look, I don't want to recap. You just seem kind of weird about it. If it's going to mess things up, then I'd rather call it quits now. Just remember, it was your idea."

Nathan was prevented from replying as they entered Faith's office. The smells of fresh coffee and doughnuts made his mouth water. Damn, but the woman took good care of them all.

"Morning, sweet thang," Micah said as he kissed Faith smack on the lips.

Nathan shook his head. It amazed him that Micah hadn't gotten his ass kicked by a jealous man yet. He went through life loving women, and didn't much give a shit who else loved them.

"Morning, you two," Faith said. "Why's Nathan so grumpy?"

Nathan frowned and slouched in a chair with his cup of coffee.

"PMS," Micah offered.

"Morning," Connor drawled as he walked through the door.

He stopped long enough to ruffle Faith's hair, which started an immediate argument between them. For two people who had absolutely no blood relation, they'd gotten the sibling squabbling down pat. Even though Pop had adopted Faith, Nathan swore she looked enough like Connor to be his real sister.

"Where's your man this morning?" Connor asked Faith.

She scowled. "Just because I'm wearing his ring doesn't mean I have to keep up with him every minute of every day."

"Quit giving her a hard time," Micah said mildly. "I don't want her to threaten to cut off our coffee again."

"Dude, you are one pussy-whipped son of a bitch," Connor said with a laugh.

Micah arched one eyebrow. "You say that as if it's a bad thing, my friend."

Connor slung one leg onto Faith's desk and slid over until he was sitting on the edge, coffee in hand. He reached for the doughnut box and rifled through it until he picked up one with sprinkles.

Nathan cracked up. "Speaking of pussy. You're eating a doughnut with sprinkles, man."

Connor looked down and frowned, then shrugged and stuffed

half the doughnut in his mouth. "More sugar," he said in a muffled voice.

He pinned Nathan with a stare. Uh-oh, here it came.

"So, you catch up with Julie yet?"

Heat crept up Nathan's neck, and he shifted uncomfortably in his seat.

"Yeah, Nathan, you catch up with Julie?" Faith asked, her eyes gleaming with unholy glee.

"Leave the guy alone," Micah said. "He'll work things out with Julie in his own time."

Connor chuckled and wiped sugar from his chin. "He has to catch her first."

Gray strode through the doorway of Faith's office, his blue eyes stormy. Ignoring the others, he stalked to Faith's desk, slapped his palms down on the surface and leaned over until his eyes were level with Faith's.

Nathan exchanged surprised looks with Micah and Connor. This had to be worth the price of admission.

"Why the hell did you cancel our wedding?" Gray demanded.

Connor eased from his end of the desk and took a step back. Micah's eyebrows shot up and Nathan studied Gray's tense body language, but none of the men made any move to give the couple their privacy.

Faith's cheeks lit up in a blush. "Not here, Gray."

Gray didn't even look around. His gaze never left hers. "Why?"

"Because it's not private!"

He shook his head. "That's not what I meant, and you damn well know it."

Nathan's brow crinkled. Faith and Gray having problems? Gray was head over ass in love with the girl. It was killing him that they hadn't tied the knot yet, and now she had canceled the wedding?

Or maybe all the women of his acquaintance were just nuts. Serena was balking over Damon's wedding proposal, although Nathan didn't entirely fault her for that. Serena seemed to be an intelligent woman, and maybe she had reservations about all the female flesh Damon dealt in.

A scowl crossed his face just thinking about the idea that Damon might have seen Julie naked.

Hell.

"You don't trust me."

Nathan looked up to see a look of hurt cross Faith's face as she launched her accusation. Uh-oh. If she teared up, he was out of here. He was positively useless when it came to a woman crying. Micah didn't look any more comfortable. Connor was scowling, though, and had taken a belligerent stance, legs apart, arms crossed over his chest.

It seemed the entire world had gone mad. Maybe Jupiter was out of alignment, or Mars or Venus, or whatever the fuck the planets did when people lost their minds.

"Trust? Trust? This has nothing to do with trust and everything to do with you pulling the rug out from under me. Damn it, Faith, what's going on here?"

And if Faith was hurt, Gray looked terrified. It was a fascinating thing to see this big man, an ex-cop, brought to his knees by a sweet, shy woman like Faith. Nathan remembered just how devastated Gray had been when Faith had been kidnapped. He'd never forget the terror in the other man's eyes. Love did some freaky shit to a man, no doubt.

Lust might make a man stupid, but love made him vulnerable.

"I won't have this conversation here," she said fiercely. "If you want to talk, then you can bring your carcass home on time and talk to me then."

Oh hell. The men exchanged quick looks and Nathan let out a silent groan. Gray was busted in a big way.

Gray's eyes softened. "Is this what this is about? My being late?"

"Gray, read my lips. I will not have this conversation in front of my brother and your friends."

"Hey, baby doll, don't be that way," Micah reproached. "You were here way before Gray. Just because he's a guy doesn't mean he automatically gets our loyalty."

Faith frowned unhappily. "I'm sorry, Micah. I didn't mean it that way. Look, why don't I just leave? Pop will be in any second, and he wanted to talk to you all. I'm just the coffee and doughnut provider and you all know it. I'm not having a personal discussion in front of God and everyone, I don't care how much I love you all."

"Goddamn it, Faith," Gray swore when she rounded the corner of her desk and headed for the door.

She nearly collided with Pop, who put his hands out to steady her.

"Whoa there, girl. Where you going in such a hurry?"

Pop's grizzled face softened in love for his only daughter. He was an ornery coot, but he loved Faith to pieces. Hell, they all did. Nathan wondered what in the world had gotten her so worked up. Gray didn't look like he had any more of a clue than the rest of them.

"I'm going to head home, if that's all right with you," Faith said softly. "I'm not feeling so great this morning."

Pop looked up, his eyes hard as he searched out the others for an explanation. Then he looked back at Faith and patted her on the shoulder. "Of course I don't mind. Go home and get some rest. I'll send over some lunch for you later."

She smiled wanly. "Thanks, Pop." She reached up to kiss him on the cheek, then disappeared out the door.

"Well hell," Gray muttered.

Pop strode in, a scowl bunching the wrinkles around his eyes.

"One of you want to tell me why my girl just left here so upset?"

"Ask him," Connor said, thumbing in Gray's direction. "Apparently Faith called off the wedding."

Even Pop looked shocked at that announcement. His glance at Gray was almost sympathetic.

"She got bridal jitters?" he asked Gray.

"Hell if I know. I didn't even know she'd called the thing off until I called to confirm our reservations only to discover she'd canceled them."

"That would explain you coming in here hell on wheels," Micah said dryly.

"Well yeah, knocked my feet out from under me." Gray stared around at the others and then at Connor. "Does anyone know something they're not telling me?"

They all shook their heads as fast as the question spilled out. As if any of them wanted to get involved in Faith's and Gray's personal lives.

Connor looked thoughtfully at Gray, some of his animosity fading. "She talked about you being late. Could it be she misunderstood? I mean, this surprise you're planning . . . Faith's a levelheaded girl, but once a woman gets an idea planted in her head, a man is well and truly screwed at that point."

"Are you saying she might think I'm cheating on her?" Gray asked in a strangled voice. "All because I'm late?"

"Ai yi yi, you two are giving me a headache," Micah complained. "There are plenty of other reasons a woman might get upset over a man being late home from work all the time."

"Oh yeah? Name one," Nathan said.

Micah shrugged. "Well, if he's coming home tired, she might feel neglected or like he's lost interest, or maybe she feels he's keeping secrets from her. Women are freakishly tuned in to when a man is holding out on them, I swear."

"How the hell do you know so much about the female mind?" Connor demanded.

"I've had relationships. It's all common sense. You just have to put yourself in the mind-set of a woman."

Four sets of eyeballs skittered over Micah like he'd lost his damn mind.

"Now who the hell tries to do that?" Pop demanded. "No man in his right mind ever *wants* to try and figure out what goes on in a woman's head. I tell you, it's an exercise in frustration. Good way to give yourself a stroke about thirty years too early. Hell, son, I've been through two wives and three live-ins. God help me, but I prefer life as a bachelor."

Connor chuckled and shook his head. Even Micah grinned.

"He's probably right," Gray said wearily. "I've been spending all my time out at the new house. I wanted everything to be perfect so that when we came back from our honeymoon, I could surprise her with the house. Honestly, by the time I get home, all I'm thinking about is food and bed."

"Ouch," Nathan said. As dim-witted as he was when it came to women, and his current predicament sure didn't show him to be a fount of knowledge on the female species, even he could figure this one out.

"Yeah, ouch," Connor said in sympathy. "Sounds like my sister has got her feelings hurt. She's always been sensitive that way. You know that, Gray."

"Now don't go bad-mouthing your sister," Pop said gruffly. "She hasn't had the best time of it in life. She's bound to be a little insecure, especially in a new relationship. Gray just has to work harder at making sure she knows where she stands."

Gray winced and rubbed his hands over his face. "God. I can't believe I'm standing here being lectured by an old fart and three guys whose idea of a steady relationship is knowing the name of the woman they're sleeping with."

Pop punched him in the gut. "Who you calling an old fart? I'll take your scrawny ass any day of the week."

"And Nathan knows her name, he's just not sleeping with her," Connor drawled.

"Yeah, yeah, you just couldn't resist a potshot. Sure, kick a man when he's down," Nathan muttered.

He avoided Micah's gaze. There was no way in hell he was spilling the beans about what had gone on the night before. If it meant getting teased by the others because he couldn't pin the little witch down, then so be it. Better that than getting his balls handed to him if it got back to Julie what he'd done.

"Have you tried *talking* to her, son?" Pop asked Nathan in exasperation.

"Don't we have projects to discuss?" Nathan demanded. "I'm fairly certain my private life isn't one of them."

He was roundly ignored by the others.

"He can't get close enough to her to talk," Connor snickered.

"It seems to me that you have offended her female sensibilities by being a typical, thickheaded male," Pop said sagely.

"No kidding."

"So, go talk to her. Ask her out. Seems to me that's what you should have done months ago instead of going to her for massages. A man's got to speak up for what he wants, or risk losing it."

Everyone groaned. Pop was on a roll, and when he got on a roll, well, there was no shutting him up.

Gray sighed. "He's got a point. It's only when men try to do romantic bullshit that they get into trouble. I should have just taken Faith to buy the damn house and let her do all the decorating instead of busting my ass for the last several weeks to get it ready. Now I've got a woman who apparently thinks I don't want her. As goddamn if."

"Well, you know where she is," Micah said with a grin. "I'm sure we can handle your projects for the day. I never do like to see an unhappy woman. I'd just as soon see Faith back to her old self by tomorrow."

Nathan felt yet another damn blush work its way up his cheeks when every single one of them turned and stared expectantly at him.

"What?"

"Seems to me you've got a woman who needs to hear precisely where she stands too," Pop said. "Go on. Take the day. Get out of my hair. But I'd prefer it if you boys got your heads on straight tomorrow so we can get some work done around here."

"I'm just glad I'm still single," Connor said. "Too much drama for my tastes."

"You'll get yours," Pop said as he dug around on Faith's desk for the paperwork she'd left. "The smug ones always fall that much harder."

Chapter 9

"I sorta called off my wedding."

"Say wha?" Julie sputtered, her hands stilling on Faith's back.

Of all the things she thought Faith might say, that wasn't one of them. Something was definitely up with her. When she'd called to schedule a massage at the last minute this morning, Julie had canceled two hair appointments and another massage, knowing the real reason Faith was coming in was to talk.

But canceling her wedding? The mind boggled.

Faith remained quiet for a long time, and then Julie realized she was crying. Oh hell.

"Don't cry, honey," Julie said as she handed her a tissue. "I hate it when someone cries. It's horribly catching, you know? I'll be blubbering like an idiot right along with you and I won't even know why."

Faith picked up her head and laughed softly but her face looked positively mournful.

"Want me to continue with the massage or do you just want a shoulder to cry on?"

Faith sat up and wrapped a robe around her. "I'm being an idiot. I know I am. I should be talking to him, but I'm just so afraid of what he might say."

Julie leaned against the opposite table and stared over at Faith, who looked for the world like she'd lost her best friend. Hell, maybe she had. "You've lost me here. First, why don't you tell me why you called off the wedding and then we can get to why you aren't talking to him."

Faith sniffed, a delicate, feminine sound that annoyed Julie. When Julie cried, she let out big honking noises that sounded like a sick goose. Faith got to be all pretty and dainty. But then Faith was miserable, and Julie had just had the best night of sex in her life, so she supposed looking dainty and feminine wasn't all it was cracked up to be.

"I think he might be cheating, or that's what I'm afraid of." Her shoulders slumped and she looked like a deflated balloon. "That came out wrong. I don't think he's cheating, but I think he's no longer interested in me."

"Okay, but you said you think he might be cheating," Julie said gently.

"It's a fear, but honestly, I don't see him as the type. He's just too blunt. I don't think he'd stay with me if he was seeing another woman."

"But you think he'd stay if he wasn't interested in you?"

Faith flushed. "Yeah, it sounds pretty stupid, I know."

"Why on earth would you think any of it? Faith, have you ever seen the way he looks at you? I'm not defending him, okay? I just wonder why you've arrived at these conclusions. Is it your own insecurities, or has he given you a solid reason for believing them?"

"Why do you have to be so damn levelheaded?" Faith grumbled.

Julie reached out and impulsively hugged her. "I'm sorry. You're right, you know. My job is to say what a bastard he is and to offer you my unconditional support. We're supposed to go get loaded on ice cream followed by copious amounts of alcohol."

Faith offered a tremulous smile. "No, your job is to keep me real and make sure I don't screw up the best thing in my life with my ridiculous anxieties."

Julie squeezed her hand. "Now for the obnoxious questions. What makes you think he's lost interest in you, and why aren't you talking to him about this? How did he take you calling off the wedding?"

"I'm a total coward. I'm afraid I used up my allotment of courage when I decided to own my sexuality and go after what I wanted," she said with a sigh. "I didn't exactly tell him I was calling things off. He found out this morning and stomped into my office. In front of all the others."

Julie cringed in sympathy. "Ouch."

Faith's brow wrinkled in confusion. "He seemed so . . . hurt."

"Why don't you lie back down and let me give you your massage. You can tell me all about it and you'll feel the magic of my fingers."

She held up her hands and waggled her fingers enticingly. Faith looked down at the table.

"I'd rather not. My boobs aren't taking it well. Maybe I'm just PMSing or something."

Julie frowned. "What do you mean, are they sore or what?"

"I'm just off," Faith said tiredly. "I'm not myself, and I shouldn't be making major life decisions when I'm missing a few brain cells, you know?"

Julie slid onto the table beside Faith and let her legs dangle as she glanced sideways at her friend. She took Faith's hand in hers and squeezed. "This is more than getting your period, Faith. I've seen you PMSing, and please. It's like Miss Sunshine stubs a toe or something. You're disgustingly cheerful even then. So tell me what's going on."

"I'm just tired and yucky feeling. My boobs hurt, and I can't stand my office in the mornings. The smell of coffee makes me want to puke."

"Oh shit."

Faith turned sharply. "What?"

"Uhm, Faith, honey, you know I love you but even you can't be this dense."

"Stop insulting me and tell me what the hell you're talking about."

"When was your last period?"

Faith's brows scrunched up in concentration. "Well, crap, I don't know."

"I think you ought to be at the drugstore buying an EPT instead of canceling your marriage plans."

"But I'm on birth control. I mean, I've been on it for a long time."

The panic in her voice made Julie wrap an arm around her and squeeze. "Is it the end of the world if you are?"

Tears welled in Faith's eyes. "It is if Gray's already tired of me."

"Is the only reason you think this because he's been late getting home from work?"

Faith shook her head. "It's been every night. And Julie, the other guys live in the same apartment complex. They're all getting home on time, and I talk to Pop several times a week. He's not working late. And when Gray gets home . . . he's just so tired. He hasn't been interested . . ."

"In sex?" Julie prompted.

"Yeah," Faith said in a quiet voice. "Me, sex. He comes home, he eats, he takes a shower, we go to bed. All of this *before* we're even married. I hate to think how it will be once we've tied the knot and become an old married couple."

"Hmm, yeah, I understand your point. I don't blame you for being worried, but you've got a lot to consider here. One, you might be pregnant and it's been my experience—not personal, mind you—that pregnancy hormones turn normal women into raving bitches. Two, these hormones might be making you a tad oversensitive. Three, there might be a perfectly reasonable explanation for Gray's behavior. You won't know until you talk to him. Preferably after you've taken that EPT test."

Faith gave her a watery smile then threw her arms around her, hugging her tight. "You're right, you know. You always are, Julie. I swear I don't know what I'd do without you to keep me grounded."

"You mean I'm a total bitch and you appreciate me for it," Julie said dryly.

Faith pressed her lips to Julie's cheek and smacked noisily. "You're the best bitch I know."

"But you can't go in there!"

Both women jerked their heads toward the door just as it thrust open and Nathan strode in, Julie's new massage therapist running behind him, her hair flapping like a flag.

Nathan skidded to a halt as he spied Faith, and his mouth

snapped shut. A dull flush reddened his cheeks, and he hastily backed up a step.

"Ah hell. I didn't know you were here. I mean, I thought you were home."

Julie raised a brow and followed the direction of his gaze to where Faith's robe had gaped open at her breasts. She reached over and pulled it shut, which caused Nathan to look upward at the ceiling and Faith to grab both lapels with clenched fists.

"You wanted something?" Julie drawled.

Nathan redirected his gaze to Julie, his green eyes glittering with determination. "Hell, yeah, I want something. I want you to stop avoiding me."

He turned back to Faith, who was now decent. His eyes softened when he saw the evidence of her upset. Faith did have that kicked-puppy look going on. A guy would have to be made of stone not to go all gooey around her. But what surprised Julie was that his gaze kept going back to *her*, and when it did, he positively sizzled.

Very interesting, indeed.

"Faith, are you okay, honey?"

Faith smiled and kept a tight grip on her robe.

"I didn't mean to barge in. Okay, I did, but I had no idea you were here. I thought you'd gone home. Hell, that's where Gray went . . ."

Both women arched an eyebrow at that.

"Gives you time to get to the drugstore," Julie murmured. "You can come back here and pee on your stick in my bathroom."

"Yeah, uhm, I think I'll do that," Faith said as she hopped down from the table. "Give you two time to do whatever it is you're going to do."

As she moved past Nathan, he reached out to cup her elbow. "Faith, are you okay?"

She smiled and reached up on tiptoe to kiss his cheek. "I will be. Don't blow it this time, okay?"

He grimaced and looked beyond her to Julie as Faith left the room. With determination etched into every one of his features, he advanced toward her.

Julie swallowed, suddenly feeling like a very big fish in a very small bowl.

"Now that we're finally alone, you're going to listen to what I have to say," he said softly.

Chapter 10

Nathan leaned forward, placing his hands on either side of Julie's hips, trapping her where she sat on the massage table. Damn but the man smelled good. She actually found herself leaning more into him, her nose precariously close to the part of his shirt that was unbuttoned at the neck.

"So, uhm, what was it you wanted to say?" she asked casually.

"Date."

She raised an eyebrow in question.

"You. Me. Date. Go to dinner. Have a normal conversation. Preferably one where you'll sit through the entire meal, and I don't have to chase you down."

Her lips twitched as she battled a smile.

"A date, huh."

He nodded. "As of now, you've never given me a massage. Whatever happened in the past stays there and that includes any misunderstandings that went on in your head."

"Does that caveman approach work on all the girls?" she asked.

He blinked in confusion then stood back, running a hand over his head. "Damn it, Julie, what do you want from me? For some reason known only to you, you've decided to drive me around the bend."

"And you haven't driven me nuts over the past few months?" she asked incredulously. "I mean, come on, Nathan. What's a woman have to do?"

He closed his eyes and blew out his breath. She could swear his lips were moving in an effort to count to ten. She almost laughed out loud. Maybe she wasn't the only frustrated one here.

He moved back in, crowding her, stepping between her legs so that his heat and delicious scent enveloped her. He cupped her face in his hands and stared down at her, sincerity burning in his eyes.

"Look, can we just start over? Please? My name is Nathan Tucker and I'd love to take you out sometime. Preferably tonight. If you're available, that is."

Her eyes widened in surprise and then she smiled. "Okay, Nathan Tucker. I'd love to go out. Tonight is fine."

He looked suspiciously at her. "Really? Just like that?"

She nodded, pressing her lips together to keep from laughing. "Amazing what happens when you just ask, isn't it?"

"I could say the same for you," he said darkly.

Before she could respond, he leaned down and took her mouth. There was no other term for it. It wasn't a gentle kiss from someone who was unsure of his reception. It was a kiss from a man starved.

"Mmmm."

It was all she could muster as he devoured her lips. Warm and soft, his tongue delved into her mouth, sliding over her tongue, over and under and over again. He tasted every bit as good as he smelled.

He crowded in closer until she was at an angle, her face turned up to his. She put her hands down on the table to brace herself as he towered over her. Damn but the man could kiss.

When he pulled away, his breathing was ragged, and his eyes were glazed with passion. He looked totally and utterly flustered, and he didn't try to hide it behind a Mr. Cool veneer.

He fished in his pocket and pulled out a crumpled piece of paper and thrust it toward her. "Give me your number. I'll pick you up at seven, if that's okay."

She took the piece of paper then slid off the table, bumping against him when her feet hit the floor. He didn't back away, and for a moment she stood there, her breasts brushing against his chest. Part of her wanted to kiss him again. Hell, she wanted to throw him down on the table and have her wicked way with him, but he was going to have to work for it this time.

She sidestepped him and walked over to where a pen lay on the counter. With a hasty scribble, she wrote down her number, then walked back over to hand it to him.

"No changing your mind," he said.

It was probably meant to be a threat or an order, but it came out more as a request, a fact she found endearing. It was interesting to see this man at a disadvantage, unsure of himself.

"You be there at seven, and I'll be ready," she said.

He looked as if he wanted to kiss her again. He even swayed

slightly in her direction. Then as if deciding against it, he turned and stalked out the way he'd come in. At the door he paused and turned around.

"I'll see you tonight."

She smiled and nodded.

As soon as he disappeared, she balled up her fist, raised her arm and pumped her elbow down in a victory exclamation.

Score one for her. Finally.

This whole owning her sexuality, going for what she wanted thing wasn't a bad idea after all. If she hadn't gone after Nathan, no matter how disastrous it had been, she wouldn't have gotten fed up and gone to Damon, which had resulted in a mind-blowing sexual fantasy come true. Now she had fantastic sex on one hand and Nathan Tucker finally coming to heel on the other.

Not bad for a day's work. Not bad at all.

Faith skulked down the aisles of the drugstore like a teenage girl after a pregnancy scare. Chastising herself for remotely caring if anyone saw her buying a damn pregnancy test, she snagged the first one she saw and turned it over to read the back.

Then she realized she'd picked up an ovulation predictor kit. With a sigh, she bent down and focused on the boxes. Her head wasn't screwed on right today. She kept remembering how Gray had looked when he'd stalked into her office.

Surely a guy who'd lost interest wouldn't look so . . . hurt. Angry. Yes, he'd been angry too, but those blue eyes she loved so much had also yielded worry and pain.

What a mess she'd made. Calling off the wedding had been an impulsive action brought on by the desire to react. A reaction to her panic and stupid hysteria. She'd love to blame it on pregnancy hormones but that would mean she was pregnant, and she didn't really need that right now.

No, she was just stupid and now she'd probably ruined everything with Gray.

She snagged the box that promised the earliest results and headed for the cashier. Thank goodness she was only minutes away from Julie's. She could use Julie's bathroom and then cry on her shoulder if necessary.

When she entered Julie's salon, Julie met her at the door and herded her back to the massage room.

"Got it?" Julie asked.

Faith held up the bag and sighed. "I'm being ridiculous, but I appreciate you letting me."

Julie smiled. "What are friends for? If they won't let you be irrational twits, who will?"

For a moment, Faith sat there, the bag crumpled in her sweaty hand. Then she looked up at Julie and shook her head. "I'm being a coward. I might as well get this over with."

"Take your time, honey. I've got no appointments."

Suddenly remembering that when she'd left Nathan had been here and now he was gone, Faith yanked her gaze back up to Julie.

"What happened with Nathan anyway? Did you toss him out?"

Julie grinned. "No, he asked me to dinner and I accepted."

"Come on, is that all?" Faith sputtered. "Details. I know I'm missing some details."

"Okay, so he kissed me senseless then asked me to dinner."

"And you said . . . ?"

"Yes, of course."

Faith sighed in relief. She loved Nathan to pieces, and as clueless as he was, he still deserved a chance.

She almost swallowed her tongue as she realized that she was hoping for Nathan what she was unwilling to grant Gray—a chance to explain himself.

Hysterical ninny. Stupid, stupid, stupid.

"I need to get out of here," she mumbled as she stood. "I should be home, talking to Gray."

"I agree."

Faith whirled around to see Gray standing in the doorway staring at her and Julie, those blue eyes burning. She clutched the brown bag to her chest and stood there trembling, all her courage deserting her in a wimpy rush.

Gray took a step forward, then another, until he stood just a foot away, so close she could almost feel him touching her.

"What's going on, baby?" he asked in a soft, worried voice.

Her grip was so tight on the bag that her fingers were bloodless, pale tips. He reached out and carefully tugged it away from her. Oh no . . .

He unrolled the top and peered into it, going completely still. She couldn't even see him breathe. Then he looked back up at her. Only the betraying shake of the bag told her its affect on him.

"Don't you think we should go home and do this together?"

Her chin trembled, and she fought back tears. He was precisely right. This was something they should be doing together, facing it together.

Silently, he reached for her hand, palm up, just waiting for her to take it. Closing her eyes, she extended her arm, allowing her palm to slide over his.

As he pulled her forward, she turned to Julie. "Thanks, Julie. I'll see you later, okay?"

Julie smiled. "Take care, hon. And let me know, okay?"

Faith nodded and allowed Gray to lead her outside to his truck.

"My car," she protested when he opened the passenger door.

"We can get it later. Right now I want you with me."

He paused briefly to run his fingers down the side of her cheek, pushing aside the hair gathered there.

"Get in, Faith. There's something I want to show you before we go home."

Chapter 11

Realizing there wasn't much time for her to get home and get ready for her date, Julie left on the heels of Faith and Gray. It had certainly been an interesting day. The only thing that would make it more interesting would be if Serena showed up because she was dumping Damon or had finally accepted his proposal.

Relationships were quite simply a giant pain in the ass. Too much drama. They were laden with misunderstanding. No one ever communicated worth a shit as evidenced by Faith's departure from the common sense she usually possessed.

Good sex should be the ultimate goal. Anything else was just icing and, well, too much sugar was never a good thing.

Julie drove to her apartment, tapping her nails on her steering wheel the entire way. This was the time where she was probably supposed to be bemoaning the fact that all her friends were in relationships and happy as clams and here she was, still single. She was supposed to be envious and lacking, right?

Only, at the moment she felt fortunate to be financially secure, to not be an emotional wreck and, God forbid, have a pregnancy scare. Not that she didn't think Faith would be a terrific mother and adjust to the situation in record time, but the idea still sent a shudder down Julie's spine.

Maybe one day, but not anytime soon. No, she had no desire to settle down and breed a bunch of peeing, puking, burping, crying little munchkins.

It was six by the time she parked in her spot. Not that it took her eons to get ready, but she wanted to look damn good tonight. After all the entire point was to let Nathan Tucker know what he was missing.

What demon possessed her, she wasn't sure. As she let herself into her apartment and headed for the bathroom, she reflected on the idea that she was probably being more than a little vindictive.

Was it hurt pride? No, she didn't think that was it. Nathan was hardly the first man to ever be oblivious to her signals. She'd always adopted a fuck-it attitude when it came to men. So why was she so uptight over Nathan Tucker?

Because you want him more than you've wanted other men.

And there it was. The truth hurt but it was still there in black and white. For whatever reason, she wanted Nathan more than she'd ever wanted another man, and the fact that he hadn't wanted her in the beginning did sting.

A cool shower helped to clear her head and sooth her savaged nerves. It really did irritate her that Nathan affected her so much. She was normally cool and confident, but he'd managed to turn her into a raving, desperate lunatic.

Most women her size probably wouldn't wear tight, formfitting jeans, but she didn't have any compunction about displaying her body. To be honest, she'd tried skinnier and leaner, and it just didn't look good on her.

Once, after breaking up with a dickhead who snidely told her she could stand to lose a few pounds, she'd gotten serious about losing weight. She'd dropped thirty pounds, but it just hadn't worked for her. She *liked* herself the way she was, and she was pissed as hell that she'd let a man change the way she looked at herself, even if it had been a temporary thing.

After that, she'd forgotten all about ideal sizes, had rounded out and added back her ample curves, and quite frankly she liked herself a lot better, and she had her self-respect back.

Her mother wasn't perfect by a long shot, but what she had given Julie from the time she was a child was a strong sense of self. Not a day went by that she hadn't told Julie how beautiful she was, how smart. She'd imbued her daughter with the belief she could do anything, be anything. She'd grown up believing that. She still did.

She needed to call her mom and check in. Make sure she didn't need anything. Lord knows her brother wasn't going to step up. As much as it galled her to have any contact with the moron her mother had married, she couldn't very well turn her back on her mom.

Besides, there was always the outside chance that her mother might actually surprise her and leave the jerk.

Chuckling over the absurdity of that notion, she finished dressing, applied light makeup and brushed out her hair until it fell softly over her shoulders.

The only area she paid special attention to was her lips. She applied rich red lipstick because she wanted Nathan to look at those lips and remember them around his cock.

She cracked a grin and then checked to make sure she didn't have lipstick on her teeth. Satisfied with her appearance, she went in search of her shoes. With ten minutes to spare, she went back into the living room to wait for Nathan to arrive.

Oddly she wasn't nervous. Excitement hummed through her veins. Finally she was going to be on a real date with him. After months of cat and mouse, of hinting and endless flirtation, the man had gained a clue. It didn't speak well of a lengthy relationship if she had to beat him over the head with a baseball bat every time she wanted his attention.

When her doorbell rang five minutes early, she had to stop herself from bolting to the door. Chiding herself for being way too damn eager, she took her time going to let him in.

She opened the door to see him filling up the entrance, his hands shoved nervously in his pockets.

"You shouldn't just answer the door without checking to see who's outside," he said with a frown. "What if I had been some rapist or serial killer?"

She let her hand rest on the edge of the door and cocked her hip to the side as she studied just how damn good he looked in his Carhartt jeans. They molded to all the right spots, cupping him as lovingly as she would have, given the opportunity. And the simple T-shirt he wore shouldn't have been anything special, but it spread tightly across his chest, outlining in perfect detail every ripple and bulge of his muscles.

Damn it, why couldn't he be mediocre? Or passably handsome? Why couldn't he be one of these guys who had only his personality going for him? Why did he have to be the total package for her?

"Are you listening to me, Julie?"

She blinked. "Huh?"

"I said you shouldn't be answering the door without knowing for sure who's on the other side. It's dangerous."

"Oh, well, I knew it was you. Who else would it be?" she asked lightly.

"That's not the point. From now on, check before you open the door, okay? They should have peepholes on these doors."

"You're off the clock, Nathan," she said as she gestured him inside.

He flashed a quick grin as he stepped inside the small foyer. He filled up the entire entryway, and suddenly she felt pretty small beside him.

"Just let me get my purse and we can head out," she said.

He nodded and stood waiting while she ducked back into the living room. Seconds later she returned.

"You ready?"

"Sure, let's do it."

He motioned her ahead of him and they walked out the door. She turned back to lock it, and he waited on the sidewalk until she rejoined him. Then he walked her to his truck and opened the passenger door for her.

It was a long damn way up and she eyed the seat skeptically. Even the "oh shit" handle was out of reach.

To her surprise, Nathan put his hands around her waist and lifted her up as easily as if she was one of those small, dainty females. She landed in the seat with his hand still resting firmly on her thigh. For a long moment, he stood there, looking at her with heat radiating from his eyes.

Slowly he pulled his hand away as if reluctant to stop touching her. He backed up and shut the door then strode around to his side. He slid in with no problem whatsoever, but then he was a good foot taller than she was.

"A person could get a nosebleed in this thing," she said.

He laughed. "Not everyone is as short as you."

"Why do men like big tires and jacked-up trucks anyway?"

He slid her a sideways glance and grinned. "Guys like big toys. Besides, it's fun to go off-roading in it. I'll have to take you mudding some time."

She rolled her eyes. "The only mud I'm interested in is the kind a gorgeous guy wraps me in during a day at the spa."

"I could wrap you in some mud."

She laughed. "Oh I bet you could."

He turned back to stare out the windshield as he navigated through traffic. "Have you heard from Faith?"

Though he asked the question in a casual voice, she could hear his concern. It was pretty sweet and obvious he cared about her.

"Actually no. After you left she came back. She, uhm, had to go get something but then Gray showed up."

Nathan winced. "Yeah, I sorta told him where she was, but he was so worried. I couldn't let the poor guy sweat like that. Besides, they need to work their shit out."

Julie nodded. "True, and I think they will. She had already come to the conclusion that she needed to go home and talk to him rather than park herself at my place and cry on my shoulder.

Not that I minded. But Gray showed up and she went home with him. I haven't heard from her, but then I don't expect to until tomorrow."

"I hope it works out. She seemed pretty upset this morning at the office."

"You're really worried about her, aren't you?"

He gave her another quick look as if to gauge whether she was joking. "Of course I am. Faith's like my little sister or something. I don't want to see her hurt."

"I wasn't implying you weren't sincere. I just think it's sweet the way you look out for her."

"My mama did teach me how to treat women," he said with a saucy grin.

She raised an eyebrow. "Did she? Guess I'll have to be the judge of that."

He reached over and touched her cheek, brushing aside her hair so he could slide his knuckles along her jaw. "I plan to treat you very nice."

Shivers danced over her skin until her shoulders twitched in response.

"I didn't ask you what you preferred to eat, but Serena said that Riganti's is really nice, and she's friends with the head chef, so I pulled a few strings and got us their best table for the night."

"Wow. Pulling out all the stops."

"Maybe I think you're worth it," he said in a quiet voice.

She swallowed. What the hell was she supposed to say to that? In two seconds flat they'd gone from playful teasing to . . . what exactly? Bone-melting declarations? Clearly he had no intention of playing fair.

"Are we dressed for Riganti's?" she asked skeptically as she glanced over their jeans. Not that he didn't look positively spectacular in his.

His smile flashed. "Let's just say we have a private setting. No one's really going to notice what we're wearing because they won't be able to see us. You struck me as the casual dress type, and this is about as dressy as I get, so I took a chance on not offending you with my choice of wardrobe for the evening."

"What can I say, I'm a girl who likes my comfort."

"A girl after my own heart."

He was so going to have to stop with the leading statements because she got a disgusting thrill every time he made them.

When they pulled into the parking lot of the restaurant, Nathan cut the engine and opened his door. "Hang tight. I'll be around to help you out. I'd hate for you to break a leg getting down."

Though he was totally teasing her, she actually might break an ankle, so she waited until he opened the door and reached for her waist with his big hands.

It was ridiculously thrilling to be with a man strong enough to toss her around like she was one of those women who weighed a hundred pounds soaking wet.

And he took his time letting her slide down his body until her feet hit the ground. For a moment he stared down at her, molding her against the juncture of his thighs.

Finally he reached for her hand, tucking her fingers against his palm. He pulled her away from the truck and shut the door behind her.

"I don't know about you, but I'm starving. I hope they serve meat in here. Serena wouldn't have sent me to a granola restaurant, would she?"

Julie laughed. "Serena is probably more of a carnivore than you are. The girl loves her red meat."

"And you?"

Either he was incredibly naïve or he was a huge flirt. She was placing her bets on the latter.

Ignoring his blatant innuendo, she leaned farther into his side as they walked toward the entrance. He let go of her hand and wrapped his arm around her waist, encouraging her farther into the crook of his arm.

A man just shouldn't feel this good. It caused a woman to do and think crazy things. She nearly laughed out loud at the absurdity of that thought. Attacking the man during a massage was as crazy as it got. There was nowhere left for her to go but up from there.

Chapter 12

Faith and Gray rode in silence. Uncomfortable silence. There was a lot she wanted to say, but she wasn't about to have such an important conversation when he couldn't even look at her because he was driving.

Every once in a while he glanced over, and she could see the worry, the confusion in his eyes. But she also saw resolve, as if he wasn't about to let her go without a fight. She took comfort in that. They could work this out and chalk it up to one of the many misunderstandings they'd no doubt have over the course of their marriage.

"Where are we going?" she asked, finally breaking the silence.

He reached for her hand, curling his finger around hers. "You'll see. We're almost there."

She recognized the area as an affluent neighborhood just north of Houston. They drove deeper into the residential area where the houses grew larger and more beautiful, the landscaping speaking of professional hands.

Then he turned into the circular driveway of a large stone house. The yard looked as though it hadn't been tended to in a while, or at least only a cursory hand had been applied.

"Come on," he said as he got out.

She met him around the front and he took her hand to lead her to the front door. To her surprise, he pulled out a key and inserted it into the lock.

"Gray?"

He drew her inside, and the smell of fresh paint quivered over her nose. The house was empty. No furniture, nothing on the walls except the gleam of new paint.

"This is where I've been spending so many evenings," he said gruffly.

She stared around at the foyer, the stairs and the open living room beyond.

"But Gray, we can't afford this house, I mean, we already picked out our house."

He smiled and pulled her through the living room. "I got a good deal on this one, and I knew you really wanted something larger, something we could grow into. When I saw it I just knew I had to have it for you. It was a foreclosure. Needed a lot of work. I've done what I could myself. Painting, new carpet, stuff like that."

She looked around, trying to absorb all he was saying. So many of her dream items were featured prominently in the house. The big fireplace, the big picture windows and a patio leading off from the living room through glass doors.

"Oh my God," she whispered. "This is really our house?"

He nodded. Then he hesitated. "That is, if there's still going to be a wedding."

Shame coursed through her. She squeezed her eyes shut, not wanting to look at him. A tear trickled down her cheek to her mortification. Boy, when she screwed up, she went big.

He gathered her close, ignoring the stiffening of her body. He wrapped his arms around her and cupped the back of her head with one hand. His fingers wandered through the strands of her hair as he simply held on to her.

"Don't ever do that to me, Faith," he whispered. "You scared the shit out of me this morning. When I realized you'd canceled the arrangements, I went a little nuts."

She inhaled, holding and savoring his scent as she laid her head against his chest. "I'm sorry, Gray. I wish I could give you a reason. It was irrational of me, and I'm so sorry. It was stupid and childish, and I wouldn't blame you if you didn't want to marry *me* after all this."

He leaned back and tilted her chin until she stared into his eyes.

"I only have one question, Faith. Do you love me?"

Her heart shifted and melted under his intense gaze.

"So much it scares me."

"That's all I need. You loving me. Nothing else matters."

"I do. So much," she said with an ache in her voice.

"I vote we leave the tour of the house for another time and go home so we can address more important matters."

His hand slid down to lay flat against her belly, his fingers splayed out. God, there might be a baby in there. A mixture of panic and awe coursed through her at the thought.

"Yeah, let's go home," she said around the knot in her throat.

* * *

Nathan sat across the table from Julie watching her eat. He watched her smile, how her eyes lit up in response every time she spoke. How she laughed with no reserve. Was it any wonder he was always so damn tongue-tied around her? Or that it had taken him months to work up the courage to ask her out?

He'd had sex with her. Twice, technically, and even then the idea of asking her on a date had left him with a raging case of gut rot.

He wanted to ask her why. Why had she given him a blow job and then fired him as her client? Why not just say she was interested?

Why hadn't *he* said he was interested?

"Tell me about you," she said as she leaned forward.

The motion pinned her breasts to the table, plumping them up toward her neckline until they mounded like two ripe melons. All he could see was her lying on the bed at The House, and all he could remember was the feel of so much willing sweet flesh in his arms as he slid into her over and over.

How the hell was he ever supposed to have a normal conversation with her again? Preferably one where his dick wasn't fighting for equal airtime?

"What do you want to know?"

"Well, all I know is what Faith's told me or what I've learned from listening to general conversation. She said you used to be in the army and went to work for Pop as soon as you got out."

He nodded. "Yeah, I joined up out of high school. There was no way Ma could have paid for me to go to college. At the time I only planned to stay the minimum and let them pay my way through college, but I enjoyed it so I re-upped. I'd probably still be in if an injury hadn't taken me out."

Her forehead wrinkled and her eyes lighted with sympathy. They were such a warm brown. Like chocolate.

"It wasn't anything serious," he said hastily. "I mean, I could have stayed in the army but I couldn't remain with my specialty. Just didn't seem like much point after that."

"Oh. Still, that had to suck."

He grinned. "I thought it did at first but I came home, licked my wounds. Pop gave me a job and here I am. It's great. I like the people I work with, I make good money and I'm close to my mom and my sisters."

"Sisters?"

"Yeah, I'm the only boy. Was hell growing up with all those women, let me tell you."

"You're so full of shit. You loved it and you know it. Your eyes are all warm and gooey just talking about them."

He grinned self-consciously. "Yeah, busted. It wasn't fun when they all had PMS, but they're a great bunch of women."

"How many sisters?"

"Three. Two are married but the baby is in college."

He could see the question she wanted to ask but was too polite.

"I send Ma money so Tracy can get her degree."

"That's awfully sweet of you," she said in a quiet voice.

He shifted uncomfortably, heat creeping up his neck. "She's a smart kid. I consider it an investment. She'll probably own the world in a few years and then she can support her big brother."

Julie smiled and put down her fork. "I just love a guy who blushes. It's incredibly sweet."

Fuck if his face didn't light on fire, and the heifer knew it. And why the hell was she talking to him like he was her big brother or something? Her mouth around his dick had certainly removed any possibility that they were going to be *just* friends.

Sweet? He frowned in disgust. Yeah, it was just one beat off her telling all her friends that he was just *adorable*. Next thing he knew, he'd be the guy all her friends considered their big brother. The one they all went to when they had guy trouble. Always the confidant and never the main event.

He had the sudden urge to beat his head on the table. Maybe he should be talking about dodging bullets or rescuing hostages from some hellhole in South America. Women went for that kind of shit, didn't they? Anything but sweet. Have mercy.

"You look like you just swallowed a bug," she said as she peered at him.

"You called me sweet," he said in disgust.

Her eyebrows went up. "You'd rather me call you an asshole?"

"At least asshole wouldn't make me sound like a pussy," he grumbled.

She looked incredulously at him. Swept over him with her gaze, up and down then back up again.

"You're the last man I'd ever worry about coming off as a pussy," she said, her eyes gleaming.

"Oh?" Now it sounded like he was fishing for compliments, but this woman's head was harder to get into than Fort Knox. How the fuck was he supposed to know what she was thinking at any given time? She was as erratic and helter-skelter as a drunk butterfly. Who knew what the hell she'd ever do or say next?

"Strong. Rugged. Sexy, even. A bit dense, but otherwise, very nice," she purred.

Now even his ears were red, he was sure. "I've been told I'm a man and it's my lot in life to be dense."

"Well, you have me there," she said out of the side of her mouth.

"So what about you?" he asked as he sat back to study her. "What's your story?"

She looked mildly discomfited by the question, and for the first time looked at a disadvantage. And to think he couldn't imagine this woman ever not on top of things. She exuded confidence. She was sure of her place in the world, and that, to him, was about the sexiest quality a woman could possess.

She raised her wineglass to her lips and took a long sip. Her perfectly manicured nails tapped a moment on the crystal as she seemed to collect her thoughts.

Then she grinned and set it back down again. "I would love to lie to you and tell you that I've traveled the world collecting men for my harem, or that I've rubbed elbows with the rich and famous, but the simple truth is, I'm a small-town girl who's never been out of the great state of Texas. Sad, isn't it?"

His brows drew together. "You could have fooled me. You seem so . . . I dunno, knowledgeable, and I don't mean book learning as much as you just seem to have lived a lot of life."

"Well thank you, I think. That almost sounds like a compliment."

"It was intended to be one. You seem to have your head on straight. You're confident and beautiful. I imagine you could go anywhere you wanted and fit in."

She looked completely caught off guard by his assessment. For a long moment she just stared at him as if trying to figure out his angle. This was a cynical woman, and he could see the wheels turning in her head. She thought he was plotting his way into her pants. Flattery, pretty words, all the usual stuff.

The problem was, he sucked when it came to wooing a woman. And while he'd love nothing more than to go home and strip every piece of clothing off her with his teeth, he could wait. If she expected a full-on assault, then he was going to give her just the opposite if it killed him.

"You make me feel like a fraud," she finally said with a rueful smile.

"That wasn't my intention."

She shook her head. "Oh, I know. I'm beginning to think you're actually a sincere guy."

"You say that as if it surprises you."

Her eyes glinted with amusement. "It does."

"Okay, so tell me more. You've never been out of the state of Texas. Any plans to change that?"

She leaned back with a thoughtful look. "You know, I hadn't really given it any thought. I'm so busy with my salon. Don't get me wrong, I spend plenty of time dreaming, but I never really thought about making it a reality."

"What do you dream about?"

She blushed. Actually blushed. He had to snap his jaws shut to keep from gaping, because anything that made this woman blush had to be good.

"My dreams aren't up for discussion until at least the fourth date," she said with a cheeky grin.

He smiled and reached for his glass. "I'll keep that in mind."

He sipped at the wine and tried not to grimace. Anything more refined than beer was wasted on him. This entire restaurant gave him hives, but he figured this was a place that Julie would slide right into.

"You want to ditch this place and go get a beer?"

He blinked and stared at her over the glass that was frozen in midair on its way down to the table. Had she read his freaking mind? Surely he hadn't voiced his thoughts aloud.

"Not that I don't like where you chose for dinner," she said in a rush. "But this is way more Serena and Damon's speed. I'd just as soon head over to Cattleman's and have a beer and some greasy French fries."

Yes. Dear God, *yes*. He had to control the urge to scramble out of his seat and haul her out behind him.

"You sure?" he asked calmly. It sounded so much better than *hell yeah!*

She shrugged. "It's up to you."

He held up his hand to motion for the check before the words were completely out of his mouth. Beer and French fries sounded damn good to him. Even better, tasting beer and French fries on her lips later.

Chapter 13

Faith sat on the counter in the bathroom, her legs dangling over the edge. Gray stood between her knees holding the paper bag with the EPT test.

"Before we do this, I think we need to make a few things clear," he said in a husky voice. "Or at least talk about the possibilities."

She nodded as a flutter of panic scuttled higher in her stomach.

"How do you feel about the possibility of you being pregnant?" he asked gently.

She closed her eyes. Why couldn't he say how he felt first? Ah well, honesty and all that stuff. If her not embracing the idea upset him, then maybe . . . No, she wouldn't think about things like leaving the wedding called off. She and Gray were on the same page. She had to believe that.

"Terrified?"

His eyes softened, and he leaned in to press his lips to her forehead.

"You know I want children. Eventually. But Gray, I have to be honest. I'm praying so hard for this to be one huge false alarm."

"Me too," he admitted.

Her shoulders sagged in relief.

"Tell me, baby, is this why you called off the wedding? Did you get scared or think I might be upset if you were pregnant?"

"I wish I could say yes," she said glumly. "But the fact is, I didn't even think about the possibility of pregnancy until Julie mentioned it. My boobs have been tender, and I've been so hormonal. I was convinced you weren't interested in me anymore," she added in an embarrassed voice.

He stilled and then pulled away, his eyes narrow. He looked . . . angry.

"Okay, maybe we should talk about a few more things before you take this test. What on earth gave you that idea? Are you not happy with the dynamics of our relationship any longer? You need to tell me if it's not working, Faith. We talked about all this before, but you're entitled to change your mind, you know."

Ugh. This was getting way more complicated than she wanted.

She reached up to touch him, needing that brief moment of contact before she went on. "I love our relationship, Gray. I haven't regretted ceding the power, the decision making, putting myself into your hands completely and wholly. I wanted to be taken care of, and until recently thought you did such a wonderful job of making me feel, well, taken care of."

When he opened his mouth, she placed a finger over his lips.

"I was an idiot, Gray. I swear I'm not usually so irrational. I just got scared. I'm not even sure what the hell happened. You've been wonderful, and I feel so unappreciative. I acted like a child sulking because she wasn't the center of attention. If I could take it all back I would. I just snapped."

"Snapped?"

He looked so perplexed she almost laughed.

"Yeah, uh I sort of had seduction in mind last night and when you didn't show up yet again after work, I got pissed, then I got overly emotional, and then I convinced myself in a fit of self-pity that you weren't attracted to me any longer and were avoiding me like the plague."

His mouth dropped open, and his eyes gleamed with silent laughter.

"Don't you dare laugh," she muttered. "It all sounds perfectly ridiculous now, but at the time I was convinced I was about to be single again."

At that his amusement vanished. He touched the tip of his finger to her chin, his eyes boring holes through her.

"You aren't the only one who screwed up, Faith. Yeah, my intentions were good, but how were you supposed to know that? I shouldn't have tried to keep the house a secret, and I damn sure shouldn't have spent so many nights over there with no explanation. In hindsight I'm lucky you didn't think I was cheating on you. All I can say is that it ain't ever going to happen. You're it for me, baby. And I sure hope to hell I'm it for you."

She sighed and nuzzled her cheek against his hand. "You are it for me, Gray. I guess we can be stupid screwups together."

He found her lips, kissing lightly, then deeper. "I love you."

She smiled against his mouth. "I love you too. Forgive me?"

"Of course. Now, we need to talk about this other matter between us."

He raised the paper bag so that they both stared at it. You'd think a snake was hiding in it with the way they eyed it so cautiously.

"If . . . if you're pregnant, we can do this," he said. "No, it's not how we planned it, but it won't be the end of the world. We'll adjust, and we'll be damn good parents."

Her lips trembled and she stared into his eyes, drowning all over again in love.

"I can't believe I almost did this without you."

"Don't make a habit of it," he growled affectionately.

"You going to watch me pee on the stick?"

"How 'bout I stand over here and study the ceiling while you do the deed. Then we'll embark on the longest five minutes of our lives."

She chuckled, and he lowered her down to the floor then moved away from the toilet. He leaned back against the counter while she tore away the packaging and concentrated on the instructions.

"Think we'll look back on this day and laugh ten years down the road?" Gray asked.

She pursed her lips as she turned the plastic tube the right way and then looked back up at him. "What if I am pregnant? I wouldn't want our child to ever know we sat here and prayed he or she didn't exist."

"First of all, who says we'll say anything? Second, I'm sure if you are pregnant, then we'll spend parts of the next eighteen years and beyond wishing he or she didn't exist."

She laughed, feeling some of the tension escape with each

burst. "Okay, don't talk to me for a minute. I don't pee well under pressure."

He chuckled but fell silent as she wiggled and maneuvered until her underwear was where it was supposed to go and the plastic was where it was supposed to go.

"How do you keep from peeing on your hand?" Gray asked.

She froze and looked up to see a bemused expression on his face. Then she burst out laughing.

"Wouldn't it be easier to pee in something else first? That just seems to be an awfully small target," he said doubtfully.

Her shoulders shook so bad that she couldn't keep the test in place.

"Leave it to a man to make perfect sense of a female issue," she muttered. "But then a man probably invented the damn thing to begin with."

"Want a cup?" he asked with a grin.

"Please?"

Laughing he left the bathroom and a moment later returned with a foam cup.

"Not that this is likely to keep any more pee off my hand," she said as she eyed it.

Gray dutifully remained silent while she administered the test. When she was finished, she laid it gently on the counter and the two of them stared at it like it would go off after the allotted time.

She blew out her breath, puffing her cheeks as the air whooshed out. "Okay, so now we wait."

"Come here," he said, holding out his arms.

She slid easily into his embrace, pressing against his muscled chest. Her fingers idly brushed over where she knew the scar lay under his shirt. A reminder of how close she came to losing him. She closed her eyes, willing those memories away.

"You know we'll handle this, no matter what," he said.

She nodded. And she did know. It wasn't as if either of them had anything against children. She just wanted . . . time. Time with Gray. Time to enjoy it being just the two of them. Later when they were comfortable in their relationship, comfortable with each other and some of the new and shiny had worn off, then they could think about children.

"Here's what I suggest," he said as he pulled her away from his chest. "I think we should go out and celebrate. Dinner, some good conversation and then come home and make love until we pass out. The only unknown is what we'll be celebrating, right?"

She leaned forward and linked her arms around his neck. "That sounds absolutely wonderful. Especially the part about making love until we drop. I've missed you, Gray. As much as I love surprises, I don't like them at the expense of you being away so much."

He kissed her nose and then her cheeks and finally her lips. By the time he nuzzled a path down her neck, she'd forgotten what it was they'd been talking about.

"I have plans for you tonight," he murmured.

A delicious thrill ran up her spine and exploded at her nape. She *loved* it when he got all mysterious and brooding and sexy.

Then she frowned. If she was pregnant, they'd have to curb some of their sexual activities, wouldn't they? Not that Gray would ever hurt her, but the lash of a crop, a belt, sometimes a flogger . . . A dreamy sigh escaped her lips as she imagined him stroking her skin, raising red-hot heat across her body.

No, she couldn't think that way. If she was pregnant, it would only be a temporary restraint on their part. But then she began to imagine sleepless nights, never being alone. No more kneeling in the living room as he fucked her mouth. No more lying over the arm of the couch while he fucked her long and hard.

With a groan, she buried her face in his neck, quivering with nervousness.

"Baby."

The single endearment stroked over her ears, soothing and quieting her worries. She was being selfish. Children meant change, and if she was pregnant, she certainly couldn't escape the inevitable.

She raised her head, disgusted by the sheen of tears hanging in her vision.

"I think it's been five minutes."

She started to look over but he caught her chin, forcing her gaze back to him.

"I love you."

"I love you too," she whispered. "Think we should look now?"

He reached over without looking and snagged the test. His hand covered the result window as he pulled it between them.

"You look," she said.

Slowly, he opened his hand, staring down at the test lying on his palm. When he frowned, her heart dropped.

"What does it say?"

"You're not pregnant," he said softly.

Her eyes widened. Simultaneously relief and, oddly enough, disappointment swamped her. Why was she disappointed?

"That's a good thing, right?" she asked cautiously, still unsure of his reaction. He didn't seem happy.

He stared back down at the test. "Yeah, it's a good thing. We're not ready. You're not ready, honey, and I don't want you to have a baby until we're both sure it's what we want."

"I hear a *but* in there," she said gently.

He pressed his lips together in a rueful expression. "Would you believe that just for a teeny, tiny moment I was imagining what our baby would look like? Whether it would be a girl who was as gorgeous as her mama, or a boy who was as ornery as his father?"

Her heart ached just a bit too, so she knew exactly what he meant. For a little bit she'd actually allowed herself to indulge in the fantasy of what a child would mean. And even though she knew without a doubt they'd escaped a kink in their relationship they didn't need, a part of her was disappointed.

"What it means is that you and I will make wonderful parents when the time comes," she said with a smile.

He cupped her chin and kissed her again. "We'll make a great mom and dad. In five years or so."

She laughed. "Exactly! Now, you and I have a date to go celebrate not being pregnant."

"You know," he said thoughtfully. "I have an even better idea."

"Oh?"

"Let's get married. Tonight."

She gaped at him. "But we can't get married tonight!"

He gave her a sly grin. "We can in Vegas."

A sharp tingle of excitement ran circles around her belly and then climbed up her throat.

"We could call Damon, who has already offered us the use of his jet. We go to Vegas, get married, spend a few days having really great sex and then we come home and move into our dream house."

"Oh, Gray," she breathed. "You really know how to present an argument, don't you?"

"I sure as hell hope so. Is it working?"

She gripped his hands in hers, the test still trapped against his palm.

"I should ask you if you still want to marry me."

"Of course I do. Oh gosh, do you really think we could do such a crazy thing? What about our jobs? I'm not sure Pop could spare us both. And what if Damon can't loan us the jet on such short notice?"

"Then we go book a commercial flight. If all else fails, we get in the truck and we drive. Come on, Faith. Let's get crazy and do it. I'm tired of waiting. I want you as my wife."

"Let me call Pop," she said breathlessly. "If he can spare us then yeah, let's do it."

"Tell you what. You call Damon. I'll call Pop. I'll need to smooth his feathers for upsetting his daughter anyway."

She kissed him exuberantly, letting all her excitement and passion bleed into that one kiss.

"Last one packed is a rotten egg!"

"Hi, Julie. I know you're out with Nathan and didn't want to bug you on your cell, so I thought I'd leave a message here. I'm not pregnant. God, am I relieved. Gray and I are both relieved. I mean, the test said I wasn't."

There was a long pause, and Julie could positively see Faith grappling with the sudden realization that tests weren't completely infallible. She grinned and shook her head.

"These tests are reliable, aren't they? Oh shit. Okay, well, I won't think about that right now. Anyway, I wanted to call to tell you that Gray and I are getting married. Tonight, I mean. We're flying to Vegas to tie the knot and won't be back for several days. Try not to kill Nathan while I'm gone. Give the man a break. He's obviously crazy about you. You and Serena try not to have too much fun without me. We'll catch up when I get back. And hey, thanks for the shoulder today. You're the best."

She made noisy smooching noises and then hung up.

Julie erased the voice mail and put the phone back on the kitchen table. The girl was certifiable. She'd called the wedding off, had a pregnancy scare and had eloped to Vegas all in twenty-four hours. And she had the nerve to call herself boring?

Clearly Julie needed to be taking lessons from her.

It was late, and Julie was tired, but she knew without a doubt she wouldn't go to sleep very easily. Too much occupied her mind, Nathan Tucker being the main distraction.

He'd surprised her tonight. He'd seemed alternately comfortable and ill at ease with her, almost as if she made him nervous. Was that why he'd never made a move before? His shyness was actually pretty endearing.

She had no idea where things were going with Nathan. He'd dropped her off without so much as a kiss good-bye. The tension between them had been palpable, but he must have the restraint of a saint because all he'd done is look at her with those gorgeous green eyes fringed with those too-long lashes. She'd melted into a puddle, and he'd simply told her good night.

She'd been plotting to jump him and drag him into her apartment while he could have been talking about the weather as calmly as he'd handled their farewell.

Maybe he just wasn't interested in her that way. But why go to the trouble of asking her out? Would she ever figure this guy out? He hadn't asked her out again. He hadn't given her the *I'll call you* line. He hadn't even said *See you*. Had the date gone *that* bad?

With an indelicate flop, she landed on the couch. Reclining, she put her head on the back and closed her eyes. Sexual frustration sucked. Men sucked.

Chapter 14

Micah leaned back in the chair in front of Faith's desk and turned his head as if to make sure they were still alone. "We still on for round two?"

"I wish to hell you wouldn't put it like that," Nathan grumbled. "And yeah, it would seem so. I mean, she asked for two nights. I guess I ought to be grateful she didn't ask for a week or something."

Not that he'd mind a month. Hell, he'd like a lot longer, but he wanted the blindfolds off and he wanted her to see him, to know it was him, to want him as much as he wanted her.

Micah eyed him with what could only be deemed amusement. "So how did the date go?"

Nathan grunted as he poured a cup of shit coffee that Micah had brewed and sipped cautiously. "It went."

"That good, huh?"

"It went exactly how I wanted," Nathan defended.

"So, what happened? You're acting like a bear with a sore paw this morning."

"It's called frustration," he growled.

Micah chuckled. "You not have a good time? Or is she still holding out and running circles around you? I knew I loved this girl."

"We had a great time," Nathan said tightly. "She was great. Perfect, actually. I was determined to play it straight. She seemed convinced I was going to jump her, and I was determined to prove to her that I wasn't just after sex."

Micah leaned forward. "You aren't? Do tell. This gets more interesting by the minute."

Nathan sighed and ran a hand over his smoothly shaven head. "You ever look at a woman and just like what you see? I'm not talking about sex. I'm talking about liking her. The entire package."

"This reminds me of being in the third grade and having Emily Robbins tell me that she liked me but she didn't *like* me like me, because she liked, liked, *liked* Bobby Ray Coleman."

Nathan aimed a pencil at Micah's head and let fly. Micah ducked and the pencil bounced off the water cooler by the door.

"Okay, so you like her. The whole package. I get the feeling you're about to get all deep on me, man. We should probably be having this conversation over drinks, and one of us should be drunk. Preferably me."

"I wonder if anyone would miss you if you just disappeared one day," Nathan said.

Something peculiar flashed in Micah's eyes before they

became bland again. "Nah, just Pop, and he could replace me quick enough."

"Don't tempt me then."

"All right, all right," Micah said, waving his hand impatiently. "So you like her. You don't want sex with her except if she doesn't know about it. Weird, man. I gotta say, you're one kinky bastard."

"Micah," Nathan growled.

He chuckled. "Okay, continue on."

"She expects me to want sex. I don't think she trusts men very much. I think she likes us as a species just fine, but I get the idea they've done a number on her, or maybe she just hasn't been very impressed by what she's experienced so far."

"So you want to prove her wrong. By having anonymous sex with her?"

Nathan glared at Micah who was contorting his face to keep from laughing.

"If I had my way, she'd be at my place, in my bed and we damn well wouldn't have any company. But since I don't have a choice in the matter unless I want her off fucking God knows who at a place where she could easily get hurt by some guy who wouldn't give a fuck about her or her pleasure, I have to go with what I've been given."

He turned away in irritation. He felt like a slimeball deceiving Julie like this, and okay, maybe he did think the threesome thing was pretty damn hot, but he still objected to having more than one dick in the room when he was having sex.

"Look, man, I know it isn't ideal, but you have a couple of choices. You come clean about your participation and go from there, you pretend you don't know a thing and ask her out for the same night and see what happens or you keep quiet and give her the best sex of her life."

"With you present," Nathan said darkly.

"If it bugs you that much, I can always slip out. If you're good enough, she won't even notice I'm gone," he said with a grin.

Nathan sighed. "That wouldn't be fair to her. Hell, none of it is, but I'm just enough of a selfish, conniving bastard that I can't stand the idea of another man touching her."

"So I take it you're going with option C."

"Fuck me," Nathan bit out. "She's making me crazy, Micah. It's not just lust. She *does* it for me. I'm telling you this is my dream woman, and she acts like . . . well, she called me *sweet* for God's sake."

"Ouch. Next thing you know, you'll be dickless and wearing pink."

"Thanks for that," Nathan muttered.

"Sorry I'm late," Pop said as he ambled through the door. Connor was on his heels.

"Where's Faith?" Nathan asked. He was still concerned after yesterday's showdown between her and Gray.

"Not like her to miss work," Micah said with a frown.

Pop smiled, and it was one of those shit-eating grins. "We're going to have to manage without Faith—and Gray, for that matter—for a few days."

Nathan exchanged looks with Micah and then they both turned to Connor. Connor shrugged and jerked a thumb in Pop's direction.

"Ask him. He has all the deets. I'm just the older brother. No one tells me anything."

"Faith and Gray flew to Las Vegas last night to get married. I imagine by now they've tied the knot and are tucked away in the honeymoon suite somewhere," Pop announced.

Micah chuckled. "Gray's a smart bastard. Hustled her off to Vegas before she could change her mind again."

Nathan frowned. "Is that what she wanted? He didn't coerce her, did he?"

Pop smiled. "It's nice of you to worry about her, son. Connor wasn't too happy with the way things went down either, but I talked to both her and Gray last night. Faith sounded over the moon. Whatever their issues, they seem to have worked them out."

"When I saw her yesterday, she seemed awfully upset," Nathan said doubtfully.

"She loves him," Micah said reassuringly. "I'm guessing there was a misunderstanding over the time he was spending out at the house. And we all know Gray is shit-faced when it comes to her."

Nathan had to concede that point. He'd seen Gray after he'd left the hospital after being shot because Faith was missing. He'd refused treatment, rest or anything else until she'd been found. It wasn't a sight he'd ever forget.

"Okay, so let's quit the gossip and get to work," Pop said. "Not that you make it worth a shit, but get us some more coffee going, Micah."

Micah sent Nathan a questioning look as he got up. Nathan knew what he was asking. Was he going through with Julie's threesome a second time? With a resigned sigh, he nodded. But this was going to be the last time, damn it. Sometime between now and the next time she decided she wanted an anonymous interlude, he was going to convince her that he was the only man she needed in her bed. Preferably for a hell of a long time.

He hadn't called. She'd honest to goodness expected him to call after their date and all she'd gotten was a big wall of silence.

Julie locked up her salon and walked toward her car, the frown she'd worn all day wearing a hole in her brain. She slid into the passenger seat and drew in a deep breath, appreciating as always the smell of expensive leather.

Her cell phone had remained silent. She'd checked messages on her home phone for the past two days and had come up with a big fat zero.

With her second night at The House looming, she was in a huge quandary. Go with it or call it off?

As she backed out of her parking space, she shook her head. Why the fuck was she waiting around on a man? Again. This was the kind of stupid shit she had done when she was younger and a hell of a lot dumber.

She hadn't panted after a man in a long time, and damn if she was going to start. Okay, so she'd been panting an awful lot. Drooling, more like it, but that didn't mean she was going to stay at home, twiddling her thumbs while she waited for Nathan to make up his mind.

No kiss, no come-on, no promise to call her, no asking her out on another date. The evening had ended in silence and the silence remained. Hello? Slow to get the message much?

"You're a dumbass, Julie. You've let another guy twist you around and make a total ninny out of yourself."

Just saying it made her feel better. The first step in becoming smarter was to admit what a dumbass you were.

She wished she could just be angry, but the truth was, she was hurt by Nathan's indifference. He seemed interested enough when they were together. He'd said some really sweet things and he'd seemed sincere.

"Don't they all," she muttered.

She swung into her favorite take-out place and waited for her order. Dinner alone at her apartment wasn't on her list of favorite ways to spend the evening, but with Faith out of town getting hitched and Serena having plans with Damon, it left her options slim. It wasn't as if Nathan was knocking down her door.

She had walked into her apartment, juggling purse, keys and food when her phone rang. Thoroughly disgusted with the way she leapt at the thing, she forced herself to let it ring more than twice before she answered.

"Hey, Julie, it's Serena."

"Oh, hey."

She had to force a light, cheerful tone because her disappointment was damn near crushing. *You moron.*

"Damon wanted me to check with you to see if things were still a go for tomorrow night?"

She frowned. "Why wouldn't they be?"

Serena paused. "Well, you know, you and Nathan went out . . ."

Julie snorted in disgust. "He's not interested, Serena. And I'm not waiting around for him. I get the feeling I'm his backup plan or something. Fuck that."

"Ah, damn. I was hoping he'd call you."

"You and me both," she muttered, too low for Serena to hear. "Well, look, it's not the end of the world. The threesome . . . it was dreamy and it has the added benefit of not making me crazy. Honestly, I was nuts for getting involved with Nathan to begin with. He's obviously not that into me."

Serena sighed. "Okay well, I'd hoped it would work out. But he's a moron if he passed up an opportunity to have you."

Julie grinned. "I love it when you get all loyal on me."

"I'll kick his ass next time I see him."

"Nah, he's not worth it. Besides, you'd just hurt yourself. Don't worry about me, Serena. I plan to have fun and forget all about Nathan Tucker."

As she hung up the phone, she shook her head in disgust. Her vow of forgetting about Nathan Tucker seemed to be a common one. So when was she actually going to heed it?

Chapter 15

"I want you to come to The House tonight," Damon said as he forked a small bite of steak onto Serena's tongue.

The two were enjoying dinner in front of the fireplace, which Damon kept burning year-round, no matter the outside temperature.

She cuddled into his side, forgoing the next bite that he offered.

"You're asking," she said in a puzzled tone.

It wasn't as if he had actually phrased it as such, but normally he wouldn't say anything at all. If he wanted to take her to The House, he did so. Their relationship was a study in submission. Hers. It was something she still questioned at times, but she'd never backed away. No, she wanted it, craved it, too much. Much as she craved him. His love, his protection.

"Julie will be there tonight," he said after a hesitation. "And as you know, so will Micah and Nathan. Even though they won't be in the common room, I wanted you to know that they would be there before I took you."

She cocked her head sideways, studying his features. His warm brown eyes that softened with such love every time he looked at her.

"Does the idea that they could see me excite you?"

Damon was nothing if not honest. Even to his detriment. She could see the arousal in his eyes and knew the answer to her question already, but she wanted to hear what he was thinking. She thought she knew some of his thought process, but to hear him? Already a low thrum of desire swelled in her belly.

"What excites me is for them to see that you're my woman. My love. The woman who has trusted herself into my care. Not just them. Anyone. In my eyes, there is no woman more beautiful than you when you dance under the lash of my crop. For others to see and recognize that beauty gives me immense satisfaction."

She had no words, no response. She sat there, staring at him with wide eyes, her heart fluttering wildly.

"Does my barbarity shock you?" he asked.

For a moment concern sparked in his gaze, but he regarded her calmly, as if he trusted her to accept him.

She touched his face, allowing him to slide his lips over her fingertips in a gentle kiss. "Has my reluctance made you insecure? It's not what I ever intended, Damon. I've tried to be so careful to be fair to you in my caution."

He smiled. "You've done nothing wrong, Serena mine. I won't lie to you. Do I expect the people you know to even know you're there? No. But the *idea* of them being there, of the possibility that they could walk into the room and see you naked, under my hands, so submissive. Mine. *Mine.*"

"And if I said it bothered me, that people I'm close to would see me this way?"

"Then I would never make you go."

But an essential part of their relationship would be gone. Irreparably damaged. Trust.

"And if I told you that I would stand naked in front of the world while you marked me as yours?"

"Your trust humbles me," he said in a nearly silent, aching voice. "Sometimes late at night I lie in bed with you next to me, your wrist bound to mine, and I simply marvel at the idea that you're mine. That after spending so many years searching, I've finally found you. I know you worry that I'm in love with an idea, a façade that you can only hold up for so long, but you're wrong, Serena. I love *you*, not an idea."

Love. It bathed her in its warm, heady glow, comforting. Constant.

"Take me where you go, Damon. It's all I want. I'm in your hands. Always."

He silenced her with a kiss. His lips touched hers with a reverence that shook her to the core. There was so much feeling. Too much for her to bear. He shattered her every time he showed her his love.

When she didn't stop to analyze, when she merely accepted, she was completely and utterly bowled over by the intense connection between them. Searching back, it was too soon, too young, too fresh to be so strong, so stable, so . . . permanent. Wasn't it?

There were rules for relationships, surely, that didn't include falling in love in such a short period of time. They were supposed to date, bicker, break up, fight, get back together, ponder getting married, children, baby names and then be engaged for at least a year before settling into marriage like an old couple. Right?

Damon had taken everything she'd ever considered about love and turned it on its head. Ever since they'd embarked down the path of her fantasies, their relationship had a surreal quality that she still struggled with.

But if it wasn't real, what was it? No one could fake this kind of emotion. Who was she to say that what she felt, what *Damon* professed to feel, what he showed her with each glance, every touch, was an illusion?

The realization of just how wrong she was staggered her. Every day she expected to be the last, as if one of them would wake up and realize they were deluding themselves or each other.

While Damon had been giving their relationship his all, she'd been giving it a time limit.

A low sob welled in her throat, catching and stealing her breath. She swallowed and swallowed again, but it tore out as painful as her lack of faith.

Damon went still, and then he pulled away, concern deep in his eyes. "Serena, what's wrong?"

He put his hands to her face, touching lightly, seeking, running them down her neck and over her shoulders then back up again.

"Nothing is wrong," she choked out. "Everything is very, very right."

He gazed at her with the look of a man completely befuddled by a woman. How was she to make him understand anyway? There was no way for her to make it right with mere words. No, not unless they were the right words. Just the perfect ones.

"What shall I wear?" she whispered. "And when should I be ready?"

He fingered the band around her arm, the beautiful piece of jewelry he'd gifted her with. The symbol of his ownership. She'd never once taken it off, and she knew if she were to remove it that the impression would be branded onto her skin.

"Your stockings," he said after a moment's consideration. "The black ones. And your heels, the ones I just bought for you."

"What else?"

"Just your silk robe. The short one that hangs just below the band of your stockings. Nothing else."

"When should I get ready?"

He kissed her again. "Now. I find I'm unable to wait any longer. We'll leave as soon as you're dressed."

Chapter 16

Tonight she stood at the side of the bed, her back to Cole as he slipped the blindfold snugly around her eyes. Julie sucked in her breath as the room went dark. Immediately her hands went out, seeking the edge of the bed in reassurance. Cole caught her by the waist and held her there for a moment until he was sure she had her bearings.

For one brief second, she wondered . . . But no, he couldn't be one of her men. The hands were all wrong. His were smooth. Too smooth. Not rough like her guys.

"I'll leave you now," Cole said next to her ear. "Get comfortable. They'll be in shortly."

She crawled onto the bed and instead of lying down, she rested on her knees, letting her hands curl into fists on the tops of her thighs.

She didn't have long to wait. The door quietly opened, and the brief disturbance in the air told her they had come. Footsteps, barely audible, whispered along the floor. She sat there, fists clenched tight as she heard them discard their clothing.

Why was she so nervous? She was trembling, her mouth dry as she waited. She hadn't been this antsy the first time, but then she knew what waited for her this time.

A sudden thought hit her. Would they even be the same men? She swallowed back her panic. No, Damon wouldn't do that to her, would he? She hadn't specified that they'd be the same men, and she had no guarantee her original lovers would even want her again.

A hand slid over her right shoulder, and she breathed a sigh of relief. The light rasp of those work-roughened hands soothed her nerves. It was him. Her gentle lover.

He let his fingers wander downward to cup her full breast. He weighed it in his palm for a long second before brushing his thumb over the peak, coaxing it to full arousal.

She emitted a soft gasp when his lips touched her shoulder. Just a soft brush that sent chills racing up her neck, tightening all the tiny hairs at her nape. A warm, silken glide. The hairs of his beard scraped delicately over the curve of her neck, his soft breath spilling over her skin.

Her back arched as she bowed upward, seeking more of his touch, his tongue, those wonderful lips. His other hand slipped down her back, to the hollow above her behind and then caressing lightly over her buttocks.

Another gasp stuttered out when the other man's lips closed over her nipple, sucking hard. He nipped at the bud, grazing the puckered skin with his teeth.

Then a second mouth closed over her other breast and she moaned, throwing back her head to give them better access.

The dual sensations, so different and yet thrilling, captivated her. She knew without seeing which was which. Her gentle lover plucked softly at her nipple, toying, loving, while the other man suckled hard.

Carefully they laid her back and to her surprise turned her over onto her stomach. Hands, lips, the soft glide of tongues slid over her shoulders, her spine, her ass. She floated, lulled by the decadent wash seeping over her.

Firm thighs straddled hers. Fingers curled beneath her ass to grip her legs, spreading them slightly. She sucked in her breath when a cock nudged between her cheeks, sliding downward, seeking her pussy.

He arched over her, raising his hips and then sinking, lodging himself firmly into her wetness. Trapped between him and the bed, all she could do was process the sensation of being pinned, penetrated, as he held himself deeply within her body.

Back and forth. Slowly he glided, rasping over her swollen, damp tissues. The dragging sensation spurred electric currents, each one racing through her belly to her breasts, drawing her nipples into hard knots.

Fingers dragged through her hair, and at first she thought he was merely petting her, but then he touched her cheek, tapping the hollow just enough so she parted her lips. She started to raise her head, but he held her down, letting her know she was fine and to relax.

So she lay there, her cheek pressed to the mattress as he positioned his cock at her mouth and then slid inward. He laid his palm over her face in a gentle cup as he thrust in and out.

Her belly was flattened as her other lover rode her, his big body leaned over her as his hips flexed and strained. She could feel every one of his muscles tighten when his flesh met hers. It was heady, delicious, and she never wanted it to end.

His fists met the bed on either side of her hips with a thump as he dug in and began thrusting with more vigor. Long, deep, he buried himself completely, wedging himself as tightly as he could go.

They were careful not to overwhelm her, and she didn't know if she was grateful or frustrated. The one fucking her mouth was exceedingly gentle, and yet this *wasn't* her gentle lover. No, he was the one deep inside her pussy. Why was her more insistent man being so careful with her mouth?

A single finger trailed down the cleft of her ass, stirring a remembrance of how she'd done the same to Nathan. Man, did he have a nice ass. She shivered and wiggled a bit when he stopped and toyed with the puckered ring of her anus.

His thrusts had stilled now, and he concentrated more on playing with her ass, rimming the entrance with a light touch and then pressing inward as if trying to insert the blunt tip of his finger inside her.

She held her breath, unsure of whether she liked this or not, but as he continued the gentle toying, she found herself responding, arching upward to meet his seeking hand.

He stilled and rubbed his palm over her ass cheek, coming to a stop. He was still buried in her pussy, and he didn't seem hurried. He brushed his thumb across her anal opening and then went still again.

Then she realized, he was silently asking her permission. God, did he want to fuck her ass? She'd tried it before, albeit with a less skilled lover. Quite frankly it had sucked before, but would it be different with these two men?

She relaxed her mouth when she realized it had gone tight around the cock sliding in and out. Then deciding she could always call a fast halt, she arched her hips, seeking his hand, telling him just as silently as he'd asked that it was okay.

But no, his hand went still again, and he squeezed firmly. Okay so despite his utter silence, he wanted a verbal response from her. Damn the man.

She lifted her head just enough that the cock could slide over her lips and fall away. She turned in her other lover's direction, though she couldn't see him, she knew his gaze was locked on her, waiting.

"I trust you," she said steadily.

His hands tightened on her ass and he thrust forward. She could hear his breath, harsh in the stillness, and then he leaned down and his hand touched her cheek, his thumb brushing across her lips as if to tell her that sooner or later, he'd be there too. Everywhere. In that moment she understood. It wasn't just about anal sex. He wanted to take her in every conceivable fashion, almost as if he were laying claim to her body and soul.

It was a fanciful thought, but the night was one big fantasy so she couldn't be hard on herself for succumbing to the magic.

The man at her head made no move to slide back into her mouth. She felt him move away, and a moment later, warm, slick oil dribbled into the crack of her ass.

Still embedded in her pussy, her lover carefully worked the oil over her tight ring. His finger delved inward, just barely, before retreating again. He was patient and careful and seemed devoted to making the experience as enjoyable for her as possible.

More oil rained down in a warm rush, sliding around his

fingers as he played. She gave a little gasp when one tip finally slid inward, breaking the taut resistance of her opening. He didn't move. He simply left it there, allowing her to become accustomed to the sensation of his finger.

Finally he inched forward, burying the finger to the knuckle. A sound that was an odd mixture of a sigh and a moan whispered past her lips when he carefully pulled back, retreating until just the tip was inside the opening, stretching it. Just when she felt it begin to close back, he eased forward again, reopening her.

More oil slicked his way, and he added a second finger, gradually stretching her as he applied the lubricant.

It was maddening. She squirmed, her skin itchy and unsettled. She wanted more, wanted him to just do it, and yet the care in which he introduced her to the act touched her.

She went completely still when he slid his index finger in, pad down against the thin layer of skin separating the walls of her vagina and her ass. He seemed fascinated by the feel of his own cock through the skin as he ran his finger up and down along the hard bulge.

And then he moved his hips, sliding his cock up and down against his finger. He was going to drive her insane. She wanted that cock in her ass. Deep, unrelenting, spreading her wide and filling her over and over.

She twitched and squirmed, bucking upward until he held her down with his free hand.

Goddamn it, he was going to make her beg.

Sinking her teeth into her lip, she raised her head and pushed herself upward with her arms. Finally he got the message and slid out of her pussy.

Oh God. More oil. It dribbled down, sliding into her opening, stretched by his fingers. It filled and then overflowed, and he massaged the extra into her skin with slow, methodical movements.

His hand left her for a moment and she heard a slight sucking noise. Oil over latex. He was lubricating his cock.

The bed shifted as he rose on his knees. His thighs pressed solidly against her hips as he leaned forward, guiding the crown of his dick to her opening.

He didn't immediately press for entry. Instead he tucked the head against the opening and rested there, allowing her to get used to it. Then carefully, he started to press forward, stretching the resistant ring around the broad tip.

Her fingers curled desperately into the covers. She wanted to scream, she wanted to cry out, she wanted to tell him to fuck her and fuck her hard. Her body was going in six different directions, and she didn't have the first clue which direction she wanted to follow.

With an almost delicate give, her body ceased resistance, and he slipped past, into her body. Oh God, oh God. Her chant was silent, her nerve endings too fried to say anything. He was big. Bigger than big. He felt huge inside her ass, and he'd stopped as soon as he'd gained entry. She wasn't taking all of him or even half. And yet she felt split wide open, as if she couldn't possibly take another inch.

And then he moved forward, proving her wrong as he worked a little deeper.

She wiggled. She squirmed. She was on the verge of coming completely and utterly undone. Her breathing was too fast, she knew, but there was little she could do to slow it down.

Part of her wanted to scream for him to quit while the other part of her wanted to yell at him to just do it. Take her. Fuck her until she had no inkling that they were separate beings.

An almost primitive rage built within her. She wanted to turn around and snarl at him, take him and take him hard. Claim his mouth, his body, jump on him and fuck him as hard as she wanted to be fucked.

No longer willing to wait, to be patient or to enjoy his gentle initiation, she pushed back, taking more of him, as much as she was able before he halted her with his hands. They shook against her, betraying his seeming control. This was as hard for him as it was for her.

Now he was lodged halfway into her ass, and she panted, trying to suck more air into her tortured lungs. His hands came to rest over her hips, his touch light, inquiring.

"You're not hurting me," she said with a moan. "More. I need more."

Her words seem to shake loose his gentle regard. He tilted his hips and sank deep, his hips coming to rest against the fleshy globes of her ass. The crisp hairs surrounding the base of his dick tickled her skin as she squirmed harder.

"Goddamn it, move!"

A low chuckle reverberated over her skin. Even his damn laugh was sexy. Low and husky. Where the hell was the other guy?

He leaned down and pressed a kiss between her shoulders, right along the ridge of her spine. Damn, that was a sensitive spot, and he felt good. So good. How could something so simple as a well-placed kiss turn her to butter?

Not content with that one little kiss, and not seeming

inclined to accommodate her demand to move, he trailed his mouth lower, taking a line down the middle of her back, dragging that beard and his full lips over her skin.

His hands splayed out over her hips, his fingers wide and sprawling. Finally he moved, dragging his cock back, nearly withdrawing completely before sliding forward in one long, delicious thrust.

He stroked and petted her skin, soothing her, reassuring her that he wouldn't take things too far. It was as if he spoke, because she knew, she *knew* he was holding a tight line of restraint.

And she had no choice but to play it his way in her current position.

He retreated again and then fed his cock into her ass inch by agonizing inch until once again he pressed firmly against her cheeks.

Full, so full. Stretched around his dick, pinned to the bed underneath his muscled body.

Then to her utter shock, he leaned down, slid his arms underneath her belly and lifted her up. He pulled her back, leaning as she sat on his cock, her back pressed solidly against his chest.

Her bottom rested on the tops of his thighs, and he scooted awkwardly toward the edge of the bed. He rolled slightly to his side, his cock still buried tight in her ass, each movement sending it deeper. She gasped, part in pleasure, part in pain, as the fullness overwhelmed her.

When he attempted to move his legs, he slipped out. Before she could move back toward him, her other lover grasped her firmly around the waist and lifted her. Dear God, this man had to be strong. He'd lifted her as easily as a sack of potatoes, and she was no dainty lightweight.

He lowered her down, and the other man reached for her,

curling his hands around her waist as they both lowered her onto his straining cock again.

When he missed, he hastily reached down to grab his erection and guide it into her ass.

Her upright position pressed all her weight downward so that no part of his cock wasn't inside her. His arms came around her, holding her reassuringly. His hands palmed her breasts, rolling the tips between his fingers.

Gradually he roved downward, letting his palms glide over her belly and then lower, between her legs to her pussy. He fingered her gently, petting and stroking the sensitive folds, parting them and then delving into her wetness.

The other man grasped her legs just above her knees, and he spread her thighs, opening her further. Her first lover started to recline, holding her tightly against him as he lay back.

Holy hell. They were going to . . . Shit. Her brain and body went into overload. She trembled uncontrollably, her legs shaking, her mouth dry and her senses screaming for mercy.

Mercy, hell, she didn't want any such thing.

He stepped between her parted legs, between the other guy's parted legs. She'd sell her soul to be able to see them right now, but her imagination was going to have to suffice, and she'd never been accused of not having one.

Placing one hand on her belly just below where the other man's hands cupped her breasts, he tucked his cock against her pussy and pushed.

Her body resisted the dual invasion, but he persisted, exerting steady pressure.

Tight. She was so incredibly tight with one cock buried in her ass. It made her pussy nearly inaccessible.

He pulled back after she flinched, and she heard the soft squeegee sound of the oil being squirted. A second later, he pressed against her pussy again, this time his passage eased by the slick liquid.

In one hard thrust, he was in to the hilt.

Fire burst and exploded around her. Thank God they both stopped, not moving even a centimeter as she fought the wicked thrill of having two cocks stuffed into her body.

Their hands glided over her body, so light and caring. It baffled her, this extreme care they took with her. To them she should have just been an easy lay, some chick who wanted a quick fuck, but they didn't treat her like a piece of meat. Because of that, the experience . . . ah, the experience. It was grander, more exciting, more mind-blowing than she'd ever imagined.

She'd envisioned thirty minutes of sweaty sex, them humping her like dogs in heat then rolling off to be on their way. And she'd been okay with that. Originally. But damn if they hadn't wooed her with their hands, their mouths, their tenderness.

Now she wanted everything they had to offer, all they wanted to give her. Whatever they wanted, she would give. She was theirs for as long as they wanted their sweet seduction to last.

The man over her leaned forward, his mouth roving over the breasts being held and plumped by the man under her. He held each breast up, offering them to the other man's mouth like an appetizer. God, she wanted to *see*. How must she look? Like an enchanting seductress? Beautiful? Desirable?

As he suckled at her breasts, he pumped against her in steady rhythm. His thrusts moved her up and down on the cock in her ass. One hand slid between them, finding her clit as his pace increased.

She moaned helplessly as her orgasm built and swelled like an incoming tidal wave. Exquisite pleasure, the sweetest of agonies, bombarded her. Rained down like hail. Never had she experienced such cutting ecstasy. It hurt, it was beautiful, it was sweet, it was pain.

Her hands flew out, landing against the chest in front of her. Her fingers curled around his shoulders, holding on as she tried to breathe.

Higher. Longer. Harder. Tighter. The ripples began in her pelvis and fanned out, rushing faster and faster until she spun like a tornado.

They rammed into her, both sliding so deep. So, so deep. With a hoarse cry, she splintered and came apart.

The cock in her pussy jerked away. The bed dipped and impatient hands turned her face, a thumb prying at her mouth to open. The first jet of his release landed on her tongue just as she parted her lips. Then he slid inward, holding himself deep while he twitched and spasmed.

The man under her went still, waiting, his hands tenderly holding her hips as his cock snuggled deep in her ass.

The hands at her face went soft, stroking her cheeks as he executed short, quick strokes over her tongue. Finally he slipped away, and she swallowed then licked the stickiness from her lips.

To her surprise, he cupped her cheek and kissed her tenderly on her other cheek. It wasn't a passionate kiss. Oddly it was one of reverence. A sweet kiss.

Then she found herself being pulled away. The cock slipped from her ass as the man under her stood and cradled her in his arms. He laid her on the bed, and for a moment she was left alone. Surely they weren't done. No, someone was sitting at her head now.

Her cheeks bloomed with heat when a warm, damp cloth soothed over her skin. Ah, they'd stopped to clean up as well. As soon as they were done, a body pressed down over hers, and a cock settled against her pussy.

He shifted and moved his hips but didn't seem to be in a hurry to gain entrance. Finally the tip slipped inside, and with a sigh he sank deep.

His forearms were pressed to the bed, and she could easily imagine him just over her, staring down as his hips flexed and rolled against her. She spread her legs, arching upward to give him a better angle.

This was as vanilla as sex could be and yet it was sexier than anything she'd done with them yet. One on one contact, his body pressed so tight to hers, his warmth filling her.

She could sense him staring at her, intently, as if he found her the most desirable woman in the world. She raised her hands, wanting to touch him, but she got no further than his muscled arms.

Fingers curled gently around her wrists, pulling her hands away. The other man kissed her exposed palm as if to apologize but he kept her away from the man fucking her.

With a growl of frustration, she broke the silence.

"Why can't I touch you?"

He stilled above her, growing tense. His hands wandered down her body as he raised up to his knees, his cock still angled to reach her deepest parts.

She sighed knowing she wasn't going to get an answer. "I'm sorry. I'm not complaining. Honestly."

He leaned down again, framing her face in his hands, and he kissed her. Before she could kiss him back, he drew away. His way of telling her it was okay? She smiled. There was something to be said about wordless communication. It was certainly effective.

She stretched like a lazy cat, the aftermath of her orgasm making her lethargic. The gentle rhythm of the cock sliding through her post-release screaming nerves stirred the beginnings of her arousal all over again.

The first night had been more hurried, as if they, like her, were so taken in by the experience that it was over before it even began. Tonight was different.

They'd taken pains to take their time and even now there was no rush to release. Would they make love to her all night? Her pussy clenched in anticipation. They'd opened her imagination up to all sorts of possibilities, and now she was anxious to explore.

CHAPTER 17

Beautiful. She was absolutely magnificent. His only regret was that he couldn't see her eyes, that she couldn't see *him* and know that it was him making love to her and not some nameless schmuck chosen for his dick size.

Nathan clenched his jaw as sweat beaded his forehead. He was ready to come, and it was taking every ounce of his restraint not to spend himself in her softness right now. He wanted her to orgasm again, though. This time with him. Just with him.

He lowered his head to kiss her neck, the delectable curve to her shoulder. He loved how she shivered and squirmed as if his touch was the most pleasurable thing she'd ever felt.

With every thrust, she swallowed him, welcomed him into her body, and God, did she feel good. Swollen, so feminine and hot. Like a velvet clasp, holding him and stroking him as he stroked her.

She turned him inside out.

Raising back up, he looked down to where their bodies were joined and he withdrew, watching as her sheath sucked wetly at him. Her feminine curls were trimmed short in a neat triangle, but her lips were bare and soft, a sweet surprise hidden by the nest of dark hair.

Drawn to the softly swollen flesh, he ran a finger down the lips that hugged his cock. Back and forth, he moved, exerting just enough pressure to send himself deep before retreating.

He touched the hooded nub above where his cock dove inward. She jumped and then let out another breathy sigh that damn near had him coming. He stopped to collect himself, to try and hold on to his tenuous control.

Idly he toyed with her clit, enjoying how it swelled and strained, how she arched and writhed underneath him. Gently he pulled at it, careful not to hurt her, taking it between his thumb and forefinger as he stroked it.

When finally he felt her melt around his cock, going wet and wild in anticipation of her orgasm, he grasped her hips and bent to suck one pink-tipped breast into his mouth. Wanting to go with her, to take her with him, he thrust hard and harder still.

Her legs came up to wrap around his waist. His hands slid around to cup her ass, squeezing and holding her to him as he pounded into her again and again.

He nibbled and then licked at the sweet nipple just as he felt himself losing all sense of time or place. Frantically he grabbed at her, pulling her, pushing her, wanting her closer, straining to be inside her.

Faster, harder, the sweet friction against his cock drove him mad. The room around him blurred but not her. She remained as sharp and as focused in his vision. Constant. Beautiful. His.

Yes, she was his. She just didn't know it yet.

His balls drew up painfully. Fire gathered at the base and pushed upward, burning a path up his cock, holding, wavering. God. Then he erupted with a muffled gasp, jerking, heaving uncontrollably.

He couldn't get enough of her, couldn't get inside her deep enough. Her cry seared a path to his soul. His woman. His pleasure.

Gathering her fully into his arms, he held her while she went liquid around him, her legs weak and shaking as they slid down the length of his limbs. He held her, supported her, didn't want to let her go.

He inhaled her scent, holding it and savoring her natural sweetness with the musky scent of their passion. Addiction.

Her hands trailed down his back, tentative, as if she expected to be reprimanded. He closed his eyes, luxuriating in her touch, the silky feel of those wonderful hands. Hands that he'd spent so many hours enjoying, fantasizing about when he wasn't with her. Hands that knew him intimately, that had touched every inch of his body.

Just for a moment, he let her, because the alternative was pulling away.

"Beautiful," he whispered against her skin softly, so she wouldn't hear.

Beautiful. He'd called her beautiful. At first she thought she'd imagined it, so faint was his whisper, but the word had spilled over her skin and carried to her ears.

It aroused her in a way no physical motions ever would.

They lay there, him blanketing her, her infused with his warmth, their bodies still joined. Finally he stirred, withdrawing from her with careful ease.

Coolness rolled over her skin, and she hugged her arms to her chest in a protective measure against the loss of his heat. To her surprise—and dismay—she heard the rustle of clothing and then the sound of the door opening. And closing.

Disappointment rendered her motionless. She lay there on the bed, arms folded over her middle as the chill settled more firmly over her.

They were gone. Just like that.

The door opened again, and her heart leapt. Gentle hands—different hands—soothed over her shoulders and then to the sash around her eyes.

She blinked at the sudden light, and Cole's face came into focus as he stared down at her.

"They wanted to give you a break," he said. "I'm having a tray brought up with something to eat and drink. If you're willing, they'll be back in half an hour."

She struggled to sit up, and he reached for her hand to help her. Yes, he'd seen her naked, but it was still discomfiting to sit around in the buff while they discussed her sexual debauchery.

"Thank you," she said huskily. "And yes . . . I'm willing."

Cole smiled, and his blue eyes twinkled. "They are lucky men to have such a willing woman."

She glared for a moment before realizing he was yanking her chain. "Damon's told you about me, I take it."

"Not in so many words. There are some things about a woman

that a man doesn't need to be told. Take you, for instance. Strong willed. Beautiful. Defiant. Not a woman a man could ever easily rein in."

Beautiful. As odd flutter scuttled in her stomach. The word seemed to come so naturally to the men here, as if they appreciated the female form in all its varieties and not just those generally accepted in society.

She cocked her eyebrow as his other words settled in. "Why the hell would you want to rein a woman in?"

He chuckled. "Why indeed? I think, Julie, that you are a woman who is all the more breathtaking for that fact."

A flush of pleasure spread over her cheeks.

"You think I'm flattering you."

She shook her head slowly. "No, Cole. I think for whatever reason, the men here are different."

He eyed her questioningly.

"It would seem that Damon has the good sense to surround himself with men who appreciate and celebrate the differences in women. Not the sameness."

Cole flashed her a gentle smile. "I'd say you have the good sense not to listen to the men who don't appreciate your differences."

"Damn straight," she said with a grin.

"I'm very tempted to dismiss the two men who wait so anxiously to make love to you again," he murmured.

Her eyes widened. "Now why would you do that?"

"So I could have you all to myself. And trust me, Julie. You wouldn't miss having the extra guy around."

Well damn. A hot buzz sizzled up her spine. At least now she knew what Faith and Serena saw in this place. She didn't have to be submissive to appreciate the reverence with which women were treated here.

A knock at the door sounded, causing Julie to jump and then cover herself with her hands, which was pretty laughable given her bountiful attributes and the amount of skin not covered by her graceless pose.

Calmly, Cole went to the closet and drew out a robe. He settled it around her shoulders then waited as she put her arms through the holes. When she was done, he tied it snugly at her waist and then called for the person at the door to come in.

Another handsome man entered carrying a tray—were there no ugly men on the premises? While it was nice from a feminine perspective, it seemed a bit unrealistic. But then this place was all about fantasy.

Cole took the tray and dismissed the young man with a simple gesture. As he carried it to the bed, he met her gaze with a questioning glint in his eyes.

"Want company or would you prefer to eat alone?"

She looked down. "Well, now that I'm not naked, I'd prefer company unless you have other debaucheries to attend."

He laughed and settled onto the bed beside her. "I like you a lot, Julie. You're different. So many woman—and men—come here, most curious, a few rubberneckers, most having no idea of themselves. You, on the other hand . . ."

"Oh, don't stop now," she said as she slathered creamy cheese spread on a cracker. "I've always wanted to be psychoanalyzed in a den of iniquity."

"You present a man the best kind of challenge."

She rolled her eyes. "Please don't give me the line about wanting to chase down and subdue me."

"Nope. A different sort of challenge. The challenge is to meet your needs and expectations."

Her eyebrows went up. "Ah now, that challenge I can live with. What woman wouldn't like the thought of a man busting ass to please her?"

"I have a feeling many have tried and failed."

"Hmm. I'm not so sure about the trying part but yeah, plenty have failed all right."

She licked her fingers and then reached for the bottled water on the tray. She drank thirstily, closing her eyes in pleasure. When she opened them, Cole was staring at her with quiet intensity.

"You're coming on to me, aren't you?"

His expression didn't change but a hungry gleam entered his eyes. "If I am?"

She cocked her head to the side. "Doesn't it strike you as odd to be having this sort of conversation after I've just fucked two strange men and plan to fuck them again after intermission? That would bother most guys."

"I'm not most guys. All you have to do is say the word and it'll be you and me. Only I'd prefer to take you away from the den of iniquity, as you put it."

She stared back at him, considering all he'd said. He was truly a gorgeous man. And she just knew he'd be a generous lover. But. But what? What the hell could possibly be holding her back?

With a disgusted sigh, she recapped her water and shoved it away.

"The truth is, I don't know what I want right now," she said quietly. "Furthermore, I don't want to have to make decisions. I wanted to chase a few fantasies, dust myself off after making an ass of myself over a man. That's why I'm here. So far I'm not complaining."

"Fair enough," Cole said with a nod. "But when you're done with your chasing, you know where to find me. I can be a patient man, particularly when the outcome is worth waiting for. And honey, just so you know, you should never have to make a fool of yourself over any man. There are plenty of us only too willing to be the fool for you."

Wow. Just wow. What the hell was she supposed to say to that?

"You make it damn hard to not be all self-centered," she said.

White teeth flashed as he grinned. "I want you to be self-centered. Indulge while you can, because if you ever come knocking on my door, I'm not likely to let you out of my bed. Ever."

"I do love a selfish man," she said mournfully.

He checked his watch as she slid the last piece of fruit between her lips.

"Your guys are waiting, I'm sure. As I would be if I were in their place."

She pushed the tray away and stretched sensuously.

He stood by the edge of the bed and ran his finger lightly over her cheekbone. "At least let me help you undress again. It's the least you can do for rejecting my advances."

She laughed. "You seem so sure my rejection will stand."

"I think your interest is held elsewhere. If I didn't think it, I would be a hell of a lot more persistent."

Crap. Now she was a walking transparency. Nice. Damn

Nathan Tucker. He was ruining her love life and he wasn't even around.

She held up her arms in supplication, too disgruntled to argue with Cole. The fact was her interests *were* held elsewhere. No matter how hard she tried, Nathan Tucker still occupied her mind. She was even pretending it was him making love to her. Thanks to the blindfold.

Cole's gentle smile of understanding just further served to show her what an idiot she was being. He tugged away the sleeves, and his appreciative stare warmed her naked skin as the robe fell away.

"I'll replace the blindfold," he said as he reached for the sash. "But first I want to taste. Just one taste."

He hesitated long enough for her to protest if that was her wish before he lowered her to the bed until her back pressed against the rumpled covers. There was a hungry, almost primal look to his eyes that puckered her nipples long before he lowered his mouth to take one.

Warm and light, his lips circled the straining knot. He sucked lightly at first and then harder. His tongue lapped over the tip but he never broke suction.

Her belly knotted and desire ran crazy circles in her belly and slithered lower into her pelvis. Her clit puckered, her pussy clenching and straining.

"You don't play fair," she groaned.

His eyes gleamed. "Never forget it."

He kissed her lips, not waiting for her to respond in kind before lifting away from her again.

He secured the sash around her eyes, and the room went dark once more. He touched her gently on the cheek and then retreated, his footsteps sounding farther away until the door opened and he left the room.

She only spared a brief moment of regret, interrupted when the door opened again. Her breath caught as a quiver of excitement slipped down her spine.

They were back.

Chapter 18

Nathan strode in the bedroom after glaring holes through a departing Cole. Having to stand outside while Cole put the moves on Julie, *his* Julie, and pretend that nothing was going on had him busting a nut.

Micah nudged him and shook his head. In other words, calm the fuck down.

He held his hands out in front of him and stared as if he could will himself to stop shaking. He didn't want to touch Julie while so much anger rushed through him.

Possessive. Who knew he had such a possessive streak? If asked, he'd have never thought he was the jealous type. Too much mental energy involved. And what woman was worth that kind of aggravation?

He sucked in several breaths and focused his attention on the bed where Julie lay. Instantly his anger was replaced by a red-hot haze of lust. All he had to do was look at the woman and he was a walking hard-on.

He snuck a look at Micah who, while not unmoved by the sight of Julie, didn't exhibit the insanity that Nathan felt. No, Micah was Micah. Cool as a cucumber. Which was fine with him, because he'd rather Micah not feel the same rioting emotions toward Julie.

It was for that reason that he'd been able to watch Micah touch her.

Micah glanced back as if seeking permission, and when Nathan didn't press forward, Micah reached for Julie's hand.

Curious as to what Micah had in mind, he stood back as Micah pulled Julie to her feet to stand beside the bed. He could see her trembling from his vantage point, and he wanted to soothe her, to let her know he wasn't going to allow anything to happen that she didn't want. But then he realized it was excitement, not fear, when her nipples beaded and formed hard points.

She clutched Micah's hand trustingly as he guided her toward the middle of the room. He stopped her and lowered her hand to her side. He touched her cheek and held a finger over her lips in a signal that they'd be just a moment.

Then he stepped back and looked over at Nathan as he reached for the fly of his jeans.

Still curious and feeling more than a bit naïve, Nathan shucked his clothes, but still he waited for what Micah would do.

When Micah tossed the last of his clothing away, he reached out to touch Julie's shoulder. With a firm grip, he pushed downward until she got the message and bent her knees, sliding gracefully to the floor.

Nathan frowned, then hurried over to the bed to get a pillow. He came back and motioned for Micah to lift her back up. Confusion riddled Julie's features until he tucked the pillow under her knees and then she smiled her thanks.

Now that her mouth was directly in line with his cock, he knew exactly what Micah had in mind. So did his dick. It surged upward, straining outward just an inch from her lips.

Nathan touched her hair, running his fingers through the strands that hadn't been tied down by the sash. With a shaking hand, he cupped her chin and angled her so that his cock was aimed at her lips.

A delicate, feminine sound escaped her mouth as she parted her lips. Was there ever a sweeter torture for a man?

When she sucked lightly as he slid into her mouth, he had his answer. It just didn't get any sweeter.

He rose up on tiptoe in order to get as deep into her throat as he could. His ass tightened, his balls tightened, he was one big muscle spasm from head to toe as she flicked her tongue over the head of his dick.

Wanting to make it as easy for her and as pleasurable for him, he cupped her face between his hands and held her gently in place while he fucked back and forth.

Like quicksilver, his release gathered, fiery and sharp. He pulled away abruptly and pinched the head of his dick between his fingers. Christ, he'd been in her mouth all of a minute and he was ready to blow his top.

Micah moved in, nudging her chin over. She turned, blindly seeking him even as she reached a hand to steady herself on Nathan's leg. Her touch reassured him, steadied him as Micah found her mouth and sank in deep.

It did odd things to him, watching his friend fuck his woman's mouth. It appalled and aroused him in equal parts until, quite frankly, he wasn't sure what the hell he thought about the whole thing.

And then it hit him. It was her. If it had been any other woman, he'd be turned on as hell. He'd fuck her brains out alongside Micah and have a hell of a time doing it. But this was Julie. Julie, who he considered his. Julie, who he had some fucked-up feelings for.

He nearly groaned aloud. This was all wrong. And he was helpless to stop it.

After the first time Micah turned her to him, she readily caught on and halted Micah's session on her own, turning back in Nathan's direction.

He cupped the back of her head tenderly, his fingers caressing her scalp. While the first time he'd done most of the moving, this time she moved her head back and forth, sucking him deep, licking and rolling her tongue around the flared ridge of the head.

As much as he wanted to come all over her mouth, he wanted to make her squirm in absolute pleasure. He didn't want her on her knees in front of him; he wanted her under him, beside him, next to him, on top of him. Flush against him. Skin on skin. He wanted to feel her body ripple against him as she came undone.

He pulled away and before she could turn to Micah again, he reached down and lifted her up, hoisting her upward so that her legs fit over his hips. She gave an alarmed gasp, but he ignored it as her slick heat settled over his cock.

He parted her folds with careful fingers, settling at her entrance. His dick was straining upward, wanting her, reaching for her moist haven.

Cupping her ass, he lifted slightly and then slid into her pussy. They both moaned.

Then he panicked as he realized he was going to be so busted if her hands went any higher than his shoulders.

Micah moved in behind Julie, fitting his cock to her ass. With both men to hold her up between them, they easily drove into her body. Micah gripped her upper arms, preventing her from moving them higher. He pulled downward, grinding her onto his cock. The motion sent Nathan deeper into her as well.

Making sure that pleasure and not pain reflected in her features, Nathan wrapped his arms tighter around her, pulling her closer to him so that Micah's angle of entry was better.

"God, you're big," she whispered.

Nathan's gaze flew to Micah. Were they hurting her? A sheen of sweat beaded Micah's forehead. It was creased with intense concentration. Pleasure. Almost pain. But no pain carved lines into Julie's face. No, her head was thrown back, her lips parted as tiny little gasps spilled out every time they slapped against her ass and thighs.

Taking his cues from Julie and her obvious enjoyment, Nathan thrust harder, driving deep and holding before retreating again.

Her body shook with the force of the two men slamming into her. How much could she take? She was a good deal smaller than him and Micah, and even if she was plump and curvy, it didn't mean she could take the continual bombardment they were meting out.

And before he'd made sure that he was the one to introduce Julie to anal sex. Not that he knew if he was her first. It didn't matter. He was determined not to hurt her, to make it good for her. Now Micah was fucking her ass, and Nathan had no way of ensuring he was as gentle as Nathan had been.

He closed his eyes. This had to stop. He was making a complete cluster fuck of this entire situation. His dick was starting to shrivel under the weight of his brain overloading.

Carefully he pulled her away from Micah and started toward the bed. He wasn't going to make Micah go home with a case of blue balls, but neither did he want them to work Julie over in the middle of the room.

Still buried in her pussy, he gently laid her on the bed. Reaching back for her legs, he hoisted them high on his hips as he settled more firmly between her thighs.

She probably wanted a kinkfest, complete with another double penetration. But all he wanted was to make love to her. He wanted to slide so deep inside her that her body acknowledged who she belonged to, even if she didn't know it was him loving and pleasuring her.

He looked down as he withdrew and let out a curse. He'd been so overtaken with the urge to possess her that he wasn't even wearing a condom. What the hell must she be thinking? This wasn't the time to lose his head and leave her unprotected. He didn't have any diseases, that was for sure, but the last thing he wanted to do was knock her up.

Oh hell. He pulled out of her in a hurry before the idea of her pregnant with his baby could make him lose what little sanity he had left. Yeah, she was probably on birth control, but there was no need to take any chances.

He turned blindly in search of a condom, and Micah tossed a packet into the air. With clumsy fingers, he tore the wrapper off and hastily rolled the latex on.

Now that he'd felt her sleek heat, he loathed the idea of a barrier.

He stared down at her luscious body, and he knew in that moment he wanted nothing more than her on top of him, her sweet, rounded ass cradled on his thighs. His hands cupped around that sweet ass.

He lay down beside her then reached for her. Micah was there to help her as he turned her and urged her to straddle Nathan's hips.

For a moment Nathan merely stared up at her, his hands roaming over the curve of her hips to her plump breasts. He loved the feel of all that silky, satiny skin over his palms. She was soft where he was rough. She made him feel strong. An able protector.

To his surprise, she didn't wait for him. She reached down and curled her hand around his cock. She didn't hurry, though. She toyed with the band of the condom, touching the bared portion of his cock below before gliding her hand over the latex-sheathed portion. Then she dropped her hand again and cupped his balls in her soft palm.

A groan escaped, billowing up from the deepest portion of his chest.

She fondled them carefully, and with each touch, he grew harder until he was one giant, painful erection.

Laughing softly, she arched upward and tucked his cock between the satiny flesh at her apex. He watched in utter fascination as his length disappeared behind a shield of silky, tight curls.

She landed against him with a tight shudder, her hips quivering, her pussy fluttering like a butterfly's wings.

Behind them, Micah stood, stroking his cock as he watched,

his eyes hooded and intense. For just a moment, Nathan ignored him, wanting this moment when Julie was all his, when her pleasure was his.

He bowed upward, sending himself deeper into her depths. She gasped and reached down to brace herself on his belly. He took her hands, so small in his, and held them as she began to ride him.

Her breasts bobbed above their joined hands. Pale blue veins ran underneath the soft brown skin rendering them delicate looking. He trailed a thumb along the underside of one breast then raised her hand with his so he could brush his knuckles over the nipple. His mouth watered with the need to taste her. It wasn't as if he hadn't had her breasts in his mouth often enough, but he seriously doubted he'd ever grow tired of her taste, of the feel of her on his tongue. Or the way she shivered in delight when his mouth touched her.

She moaned again and arched forward, and it was then Nathan could see that Micah was touching her, his hands running the length of her back, then down again and over her hips.

Knowing his brief moment was over, Nathan scooted toward the edge of the bed so that Micah could step between his legs. As long as he didn't think too long or hard about their relative positions, he could do this. It made him damn uncomfortable, but with Julie clasped around his cock like a warm burst of sunshine, he could easily tune Micah out.

Julie sighed and curled her fingers tighter around her lover's hands, holding on as the second man slipped a finger into her ass, stretching gently as he prepared her for his entry.

Warm oil coated her opening, inside then out again. One

finger, then two. She clamped down on the cock inside her pussy, wringing a soft cry from her love. Then a condom-wrapped dick replaced the fingers at her anus, blunt and pushing inward.

Her body fought the invasion but he persisted, pushing against her natural resistance. She held her breath and pushed back, and with a gentle pop he was in.

Her entire body seized. She crushed the hands she was holding as she bucked, nearly pulling free of both cocks.

Soothing hands gripped her hips, holding her down, petting, stroking. She could almost hear their reassuring whispers floating over her skin.

Two cocks impossibly wedged into her body. So tight she could hardly breathe. It seemed more difficult this way than how they'd taken her before. More intense.

When the man at her ass carefully retreated, she bit her bottom lip, knowing what was coming. His retreat felt so damn good. A lessening of the incredible pressure that bloomed in her lower body.

Then he rippled forward, reopening her ahead of his advance.

She cried out, digging her knees into masculine hips. Again they soothed her, stroking her lightly, stilling their thrusts as they let her get used to their size.

God, it burned. Like fire in her deepest recesses. It was the single most intense sensation she'd ever experienced. If the pressure didn't dissipate soon, she was quite simply going to explode.

She wiggled and squirmed like a trapped fish, wanting them to move, to help her. She needed relief. When they still refused to accommodate her, she reached down and pinched a very firm abdomen.

A chuckle rumbled underneath her fingertips, but he wrapped his big hands around her hips and thrust upward. Finally.

Forgoing their lazy pace, both men surged into her body with strength that took her breath away. She knew they were big. Knew they were muscled. From what she'd been able to feel, they were incredibly built. She'd love to massage both of them. Spend a lazy afternoon seducing them with nothing more than the touch of her hands. And maybe her mouth.

A wicked grin erupted as she remembered running her mouth over Nathan again and again.

Nathan watched her lips turn up in a smile worthy of a siren. She was so incredibly expressive and passionate. The woman burned with it.

Knowing what she wanted and determined not to torment her or himself any longer, he gave himself over to the mindless ecstasy whipping like a hurricane through his belly.

"Oh," she gasped.

Micah pressed his lips to the curve of her neck, his hands sliding up her sides and to the underswells of her breasts. He kneaded and cupped the soft mounds, pushing them outward. Nathan rested his own hands on the tops of her thighs, enjoying the smoothness of her skin as she rode him, as Micah rode her.

The sight of the three of them was erotic as hell. Now he understood some of what drove Micah. Not all certainly, because Micah was as deceptive as they came. Behind that lazy-ass smile and charming exterior lay some fucked-up demons, of that Nathan was sure.

But he left it all behind when he loved on a woman. Nathan had to give him that.

Like rain lashing in the midst of a storm, the current arcing through his body grew stronger. Fire built and rose in his cock, pushing upward until his body screamed for mercy.

Her pussy clenched, spasmed danced around his dick. His fingers curled into her hips, and with a hoarse cry, he let it all go.

As long as he lived, he'd never forget the sight of her on top of him, head thrown back, the red sash a vibrant splash across her eyes. Her mouth open in a soundless scream of pleasure. Beautiful. So beautiful and fucking perfect.

Micah strained against her, pushing her down onto Nathan. He caught her and supported her, stroking her like a colt in need of gentling as Micah lowered his head to rest on her shoulder.

The three were exhausted. When Micah finally pulled away, Julie sank down like a deflated balloon into Nathan's waiting arms. His cock still pulsed and twitched inside her, and for the moment he was content to remain connected to her in the most intimate way possible.

He tentatively touched her hair as she lay on his chest, her soft breaths blowing over his skin. How he wanted to remove that hated blindfold and look into her eyes. After tonight, he wouldn't do this again. And if he had his way, he wasn't going to be replaced with some other guy who didn't give a shit one way or another.

Chapter 19

Nathan hurriedly pulled his clothes on, and with one last look at Julie, he left the room behind Micah. The halls were mostly quiet, only the faint sounds coming from the common room filtered down the passageway to where they stood.

"I need to talk to you," Nathan said in a low voice.

"Come downstairs. We can go into Damon's office and have a drink. He won't care."

Nathan followed him down and through the living room where many people mingled over drinks and appetizers. He didn't see them, though. His thoughts were consumed with Julie and what he needed to tell Micah.

"You seem more bothered tonight," Micah said after he closed the door to the office behind them.

Nathan dragged a hand over his scalp and cupped the back of his head with his palm. "I can't do this again, man."

"Okay," Micah said calmly.

He opened and closed several cabinet doors before finally dragging out a bottle.

"Damon's shit is all too refined," Micah said in disgust. "The man doesn't believe in having a fridge full of beer on hand."

Nathan gave a half laugh and waited as Micah poured them both drinks. Glancing around at the rich furnishings, he felt vaguely uncomfortable, like an interloper.

Micah handed him a glass. "Have a seat."

Nathan sank into one of the leather seats and had to suppress a sigh of appreciation. He was boneless after the last few hours with Julie. All he really wanted to do was go hunt her down and lay down with her for the next forty-eight hours or so. Sex was entirely optional. He wanted to sleep with her curled in his arms, her sweet body pressed to him in all the right places.

"Now what's bothering you?" Micah asked curiously.

Nathan grimaced and set his drink down on his knee, his hand curled cautiously around it to keep from spilling it on his pants.

"I'm going to come clean with Julie."

Micah arched a brow. "Uh-oh."

Nathan shook his head. "I should have been up-front with her from the beginning. This was a stupid idea and it can only come back to bite me on the ass."

"So if she wants another threesome, you're out?"

"Yeah. I'm not coming here again, and I'm hoping to hell she won't either. I don't like the idea of her being passed around like some piece of meat no one gives a fuck about. She's better than that."

Micah blew out his breath. "Okay, you know I don't agree with your assessment that her being here equates to her being treated like some whore or that the men here wouldn't treat her well. I respect your feelings on the subject, but I don't agree with them. That said, this is your gig, man. I'm only along for the ride. At your request, I might add."

"Yeah, I know. Look, this isn't about me being pissed at you or even Damon. It just doesn't feel right. I care about Julie, and it occurred to me that being here fucking her while she's blindfolded isn't the best way to start a relationship."

Micah snickered. "Bet your mama never accused you of being very bright."

Nathan flipped him the bird. Then he grew more serious. "I fucked up, Micah. This was a stupid idea, one I didn't think through. If I have my way, Julie and I will be seeing a lot more of each other, which means hanging out with our mutual friends. It's going to be awfully damn awkward once she finds out you and I both fucked her."

Micah looked genuinely confused. "I don't get it."

"You're my friend. If Julie's my girl, getting together will be awkward, given the fact you two have fucked."

"Ah."

Micah gave him one of those looks that suggested Nathan was still green. He hated that damn look. He continued to study Nathan for another long moment and then looked away and sighed.

"Look man, what I'm about to tell you goes no further than us. Normally I'd cut my lips off before I'd say anything about either of these women, particularly if there was any chance it would get back to them and embarrass them."

Nathan crooked an eyebrow. Leave it to Micah to get all brooding and mysterious.

"Okay, you've got my attention. Spill."

"I've slept with Faith."

Nathan's jaw dropped. "Faith? Our Faith? Little sister Faith Malone?"

Micah snorted. "If all you see is baby sister when you look at Faith, you need your equipment examined. The girl is Hot with a capital H."

Nathan stared incredulously at him. "You're serious, aren't you? When the hell did you sleep with her? Does Gray know?"

"Considering he was there, yeah."

Nathan blinked owlishly. Ooo-kay. "You mean you and him . . . ?"

Micah nodded. "Yeah, a threesome. Right before Gray was shot and Faith was kidnapped."

"Wow, I'd have never guessed."

"Exactly."

"What are you getting at here?" Nathan asked.

"I've also seen Serena naked," he continued.

"That doesn't really surprise me. About Damon, I mean. He seems to have pretty relaxed standards about that sort of thing," Nathan said dryly.

Micah lifted one eyebrow and stared back at Nathan. "I think you'd be surprised. Damon doesn't share what is his. He's pretty damn primitive when it comes to Serena. It's a long story, but I saw her naked. Touched her even, but it wasn't sexual. I never had sex with her. I was there for a get-together, and he and Serena had a slight misunderstanding. She tried to embarrass him in front of his guests. He punished her for it."

"Whoa, he hurt her?" Nathan asked aghast.

Micah scowled. "Do you think I'd have any part in hurting a woman? Ever? That's not what their relationship is about. I don't expect you to understand it. That's not what I'm getting at anyway."

"What are you getting at then?"

"The point is, I see both women all the time. There isn't any awkwardness because none of us has any reason to be embarrassed or ashamed. Julie is a cool customer. I don't think much would make her tuck tail and run. She might twist your balls up for fucking her on the sly, but if you and her keep seeing one another, you aren't going to have to worry about me and her acting like fourth graders around each other."

"You know how to get to the heart of the matter, don't you," Nathan murmured.

"I understand your reluctance to keep doing it this way," Micah said as he stared down into his drink. "If she was my woman, I wouldn't be hip on her fucking another guy, unless it was at my instigation."

Nathan cocked his head then shook it. "I guess it's just not the turn-on for me that it is for you. It's hot in a porn kind of way but it makes me all itchy and knots me up inside to see another man's hands on her body. I've done it her way. I've given her the fantasy she wanted. But now it's time to do things my way for a while."

Micah chuckled. "Let me know how that works for you. Julie doesn't seem like the type of woman you can easily bring to heel."

Nathan gave him a disgusted look. "I don't want to bring her to heel. I just want to be the only guy in her bed."

"Fair enough. Takes balls to own up to what you've done and be honest. Most guys would keep their mouth shut and hope she never found out."

"I may wish I'd done just that if she tries to remove my balls with a rusty spoon."

"She's one hot woman, Tucker. You're a lucky son of a bitch if you rope her."

Nathan grinned. "Don't I know it. Don't I know it. And hey, Micah. This is awkward as hell for me, but I wanted to say thanks." He almost groaned as the words came out of his mouth. What kind of moron did it make him to be thanking his buddy for fucking his woman? But better it was Micah than some other jerk who had no regard for Julie's pleasure and well-being.

A flirty grin curved Micah's mouth upward and a gleam entered his eye. "Not a problem at all. Remind your girl when the time comes that you've got her hog-tied and under your palm that she owes me one."

"Oh? What does she owe you?"

"Nothing yet. But she will," he added with unrestrained glee. "She definitely will."

Julie stepped into the hallway and paused at the top of the stairs. She should go. Exhaustion whispered in her ear and made her muscles sag like overcooked pasta. But the murmur of voices from the opposing end of the hallway drew her.

She'd never actually been by the common room when it was in use. Damon had given her a tour of the facilities when no one had been around. But he'd told her about it, and her curiosity had been firmly piqued.

Straightening her T-shirt and smoothing her hands down her jeans, she walked quietly down the corridor, blinking as the lighting got stronger.

When she stepped into the doorway, she scanned the room,

disappointed that, for the most part, everyone seemed to be standing around. There was one couple stuck in a far corner going at it like rabbits, but that seemed to be it. So much for public debauchery.

Then her gaze lighted on a woman in the middle of the room, a woman that every eye was upon. She was completely nude, her long black hair sliding down her back like a veil of silk. Her hands were bound together at the wrists above her head and then tied to a heavy wooden beam that formed an upside down U.

Dear God, it was Serena.

Julie's breath caught in painful anticipation. What the hell was Serena doing here? Well, here and naked. She shouldn't be surprised that Serena was here, given that the place belonged to Damon. But what on earth was going on?

She leaned against the doorframe, hiding most of her body in the hallway. She gripped the frame with her hand and peered around it to see what was happening to Serena.

When she saw Damon approach Serena, her lips pursed and she frowned. He had a . . . he had a whip in his hand. Good God, was he going to beat her in front of everyone? What the hell could she possibly have done to deserve this kind of treatment?

She knew that Serena and Damon had a very . . . nontraditional relationship. Nontraditional being a code word for Serena being completely and utterly submissive. The slave to Damon's master.

Julie shuddered at the idea, the implication of what that meant. Complete subjugation to a man. Sometimes she wondered if Serena had rocks in her head. Or if she was just completely and utterly blinded by love. What else could explain why such an intelligent, beautiful woman who could have any man with the snap of her fingers would remain in a relationship where the balance of power was severely tilted in Damon's favor?

Silence fell over the room, and Julie found herself holding her breath as Damon trailed the tip of the crop through Serena's hair. He pushed it over until it hung over her shoulder, baring her slim back for all to see.

He moved methodically. No, he definitely wasn't in a hurry. Julie searched Serena's face for any sign of fear, some sign that she didn't want what was about to happen. All she saw was calm acceptance. And love.

Befuddled and still analyzing the softness she saw around Serena's eyes, she jumped and her hand flew to her mouth when Damon raised the crop and struck Serena across the shoulder.

The sound resonated across the room, shattering the stillness.

Anger rose, sharp and furious, heating her veins. How dare he do this to her? Serena trusted him. She'd given him *everything*. And this was how he repaid her?

She shoved away from the doorframe, prepared to march across the room and put an end to this. She'd be damned if she stood by and watched her friend be abused this way. Her heart positively ached for Serena.

Before she could do just that, a hand closed around her wrist. She jerked around to see Cole standing there, silent and watching her.

"Watch," he instructed.

She tried to yank her hand away but he held fast.

"You don't understand," Julie hissed. "He's hurting her!"

"Is he? I think it's you who doesn't understand, Julie." He turned her toward Damon and Serena again just in time for her to see Damon bring the crop down across Serena's flesh again. "Watch," he said again.

"Damn you," she whispered furiously.

Unable to look away, she watched helplessly as marks crisscrossed Serena's back, each one placed strategically, with exacting measure.

How could he do such a thing with such love in his eyes? His motions looked almost gentle, which was absurd given the fact that he was beating her for all to see.

Her gaze found Serena's face, soft and illuminated with . . . pleasure? Julie blinked in surprise, sure she wasn't seeing correctly. But yes. Serena's head was thrown back, eyes closed, lips parted as the blows rained down over her back.

She looked, in a word, beautiful. It was a fact not missed by the rest of the room. As Julie looked around, really looked, the mixture of awe and arousal was stunning to see. Women looked upon Serena with envy while men stared with lust glittering in their eyes.

And still Damon continued until the only sound was the rhythmic slap of crop against skin. Even from across the room, Julie could see the welts against the white of Serena's flesh. They glowed like Serena glowed.

Julie's forehead wrinkled as her confusion grew.

"She's beautiful, isn't she?" Cole said huskily in her ear.

Julie started. She'd forgotten he stood here. Forgotten everything but the sight of Serena stretched beneath Damon's crop. Her mouth went dry. What kind of a friend did it make her to agree that Serena *was* beautiful? Not just beautiful in her normal way because Serena was gorgeous, no doubt. But tonight she shined.

Slowly she turned her face up to Cole. "Why do you find her so beautiful?" It was a question born of genuine curiosity, and Cole seemed to take it as such.

He nodded toward Serena. "See how she trusts him? She's placed herself and her care directly into his hands. She's vulnerable to him and he knows it. Her trust is a powerful thing. More potent than the most powerful aphrodisiac. She knows he'll take care of her."

"Why does he like hurting her?" That more than anything Julie didn't understand. If Damon loved Serena so much, how could he bear to cause her pain?

Cole smiled gently. "If he thought for a moment he was truly hurting her, he'd cut off his arm before allowing it to happen. He loves her, Julie. The deep, bone-wrenching kind that a guy only feels once in his life and that's only if he's damn lucky."

"Then why?"

"Look again," he said patiently. "Look at the pleasure in her eyes. Look at the pleasure in his. Your fantasy revolved around two men to see to your every need. Serena's fantasy is this. Just what you see. How is Damon providing for her any different than your men providing for you?"

She did look, and what she saw was painful. Her eyes opened wide, and the veil lifted away. Serena's fantasy was *real*. She and Damon weren't playacting. He loved her, and she loved him. How much more powerful, how much more sexy did it make the scene playing out before her?

For the first time she understood Serena's struggle, her fear that her love for Damon was rooted in make-believe. But for anyone watching the reverence in Damon's actions, there was no mistaking the reality of his feelings for Serena.

Julie's own romp between the sheets seemed such a farce now. Nothing like this beautiful display of love and devotion. Julie was hiding behind her blindfold just as surely as Serena was standing in the sun, letting the world see who it was she belonged to.

The power of her revelation weakened her. *Hiding.* For a woman who prided herself on taking the world by the nuts, this was hard to swallow. *Coward.* She winced at the word.

"I can't do this again," she said in a low voice.

Cole cocked his head to the side, his blue eyes curious. "Does it upset you so much to see Serena worshipped by the man she loves?"

Julie laughed huskily, ashamed of the tears that swelled in her throat. Worshipped. What an apt word. That's precisely what Damon was doing.

"No, not now that you've explained it. Now that I've seen it and understand. She's very lucky."

The wistfulness in her voice made her cringe, but calling it back would have been impossible when every piece of her yearned to be looked at like Damon looked at Serena.

"What is it you can't do then?"

She met his gaze and wondered if he would ever look at her the way Damon saw Serena. No, he wanted her. Even desired her. But he didn't *see* her. And now it seemed so important that a man look at her with everything in his eyes.

God, she was losing her mind. She didn't want a relationship. She didn't want promises of forever. Words were so damn cheap. But she wanted that look. She would die for that look and never ask for anything else.

"I've been playing games," she said ruefully. "It's what I do best."

Cole moved closer, touching her cheek with gentle fingers.

"There's nothing wrong with games, Julie. Not everything has to be about love and commitment."

She laughed. "Two hours ago that would have been music to my ears. Who knows, maybe when I wake up in the morning and kick my ass around a bit, it'll sound wonderful again. But tonight . . . " She sighed. "Will you do me a favor and let Damon know that I won't be back? I'll call and thank him later. He's truly the best. Serena is one lucky bitch."

Her gaze went back to the center of the room to see Damon's hands gliding over the marks on Serena's skin. His lips followed a similar path. She swallowed against a dry tongue when Damon unfastened his pants and moved behind Serena. God, he was going to make love to her in front of everyone else.

Cole remained silent next to her as they watched. There was no discomfort evident to Serena or Damon. No, they were focused solely on each other. The rest of the world didn't exist for them.

Serena arched against her bonds as Damon grasped her hips and guided his erect cock into her depths. Julie tried to look away. She shouldn't be watching. This was her friend. Their lovemaking should be a private matter. But she couldn't tear herself away from the beauty of the two people allowing their love to shine over the entire room.

A knot formed in her throat. Tears shimmered in her vision. Never had she been so affected by sex. But no, this wasn't just sex. Sex was a paltry word to describe what was before her. Beautiful. Magnificent. Soul stirring. As long as she lived, Julie would never forget this night and what seeing Damon and Serena had done to her on a primitive level. Later she would marvel at how much they had changed her outlook, her own desires and needs.

Damon held Serena, lifting her so that her weight wasn't born by the ropes securing her wrists to the wooden beam. His movements weren't entirely gentle, in fact he made love to her almost brutally, and yet his love for her was so obvious in each touch, the gentle caresses intermixed with the savagery of his thrusts.

The combination aroused Julie. A hot flush pooled in her belly and spread outward until her face flamed. Her nipples thrust outward, beading and straining. Hot, kinky sex was something she'd fantasized about, something she'd gone to great lengths to make happen, and it had been good, but how much better would it be to have a man make love to you with absolute devotion, to know he loved you more than life itself?

She shook her head mutely as if by doing so she could deny that she wanted—no, *needed*—such a thing from a man.

Damon lowered his head to press a kiss to the middle of her back. Such a simple gesture and yet Julie felt that kiss to her soul. Never again would she poke fun at Serena for her relationship choices. How could she, when Serena held in her hand something that Julie could never hope to find? Who was better off? Julie who flitted from stranger to stranger to avoid messy emotional entanglements or Serena who was loved and cherished to her very core?

He continued to thrust against Serena's hips, their bodies shaking with the force of his entry. And then he pulled away, his cock bobbing as it came free. He closed his hand around the base and jerked up and down, aiming at Serena's skin.

Julie watched in absorbed fascination as jets of Damon's semen erupted, splashing onto Serena's back, vivid against the rosy blush of the welts.

"He's marking her," Julie whispered in surprised realization.

Dear God, how primitive. How abso-freaking-lutely *hot*. What the hell was wrong with her that she went positively liquid inside at the idea of being marked by a man?

"Yes, he is," Cole said quietly. "He's showing the world that she's his, that she belongs to him. The marks from the crop are his. Her body is his. He comes on her to honor her. What might seem insulting to others, demeaning even, is hardly that to Damon."

Cole was right. Under any other circumstances, her feminine sensibilities would be screaming in outrage. Damon's public marking would be seen by many to be degrading, like Serena was some nameless, faceless object of his lust.

But all Julie could think was how beautiful and poignant the scene before her was. How sexy it was for this man to proclaim publicly that he loved this woman. Damon didn't know it yet, but he'd just gained a staunch ally in Julie. Never again would she question whether he was right for Serena.

"I should go," she said. "I don't want Serena to see me. It might make her uncomfortable. I feel like an intruder here, like I snuck over a no trespassing sign to watch a sunrise on a private beach."

"I know what you mean. The first time I saw Serena was here, Damon asked me to prepare her. Touching her . . ."

"You touched her?" Julie asked sharply.

He raised an eyebrow. "Yes, much like I touched you. Does that bother you?"

She shook her head. "No, it just seems you have the worst job. Look but don't touch, or rather, don't touch too much. Tell me, is that all you do here? Prepare women to be another man's pleasure for the evening?"

Cole looked startled by her question. A rueful awareness settled into his eyes. "This isn't my job. I mean, I don't draw a salary here. I'm not comfortable with that thought. Damon trusts me. I was honored by his request to ready Serena, and then you."

"So you do have your share of women here," she drawled.

Slowly he shook his head. "No, I wouldn't say that either. I'm rather discerning, or so I'd like to think. I see a lot of beautiful women. Beautiful, *willing* women."

"Then what's the problem?" she asked softly. "Why do you have the look of a man who's very much alone?"

His smile looked more like a grimace. "Why do you have the look of a woman who's very much alone after a night with the sexual attentions of two men?"

"Touché. I'll take that as my cue to mind my own business," she said with a grin.

He wrinkled his nose. "I apologize if that's the way you took it. I get rather defensive when I feel I'm cornered."

"Don't we all?" She looked back to where Damon was carefully untying Serena. The rest of the room was slowly going their own way again. "I need to go. Thanks, Cole. For everything. I mean that. Tonight was . . . eye-opening."

He reached down for her hand and squeezed. "You're welcome. It was my pleasure. Are you sure you won't be back? Even to see me?"

She smiled a little sadly. "Last week I would have not only taken you up on that offer, but I would have taken you into one of these rooms and done my best to make you forget every other woman you've ever had or hope to have in the future."

"And why not now?" he asked with a sparkle of amusement.

She glanced back one more time to where Damon and Serena stood. "Because now I want someone to look at me the way he looks at her." She looked back at Cole whose wry look told her he understood exactly what she was saying. "You want me. You find me attractive, but you'll never look at me that way and we both know it."

"Does it make any difference for me to tell you that if I could look at any woman that way, I'd want it to be you?"

She laid her palm against his cheek. "You're very sweet, Cole. And you'll look at her that way. One day."

He caught her hand when she would have pulled it away and kissed her open palm. "It was truly my pleasure to look after you these two nights, Julie. If there is ever anything you want or need, you have only to contact me. I'll see to it you get it."

She rose up on tiptoe and kissed his cheek. "Good night, Cole."

Not looking back, she hurried toward the stairs, feeling his intense gaze the entire way.

Chapter 20

Julie hugged her arms around her middle as she hurried down the stairs. A chill that had nothing to do with the actual temperature had settled into her bones. After leaving the warmth of the common room, every other place just seemed cold. Amazing how love could make you feel the actual rays of sunshine.

She walked down the hallway with the doorway ahead her only objective. She could hear the buzz of conversation, laughter mingling with the clinking of glasses, but she wasn't in the mood to be social. She just wanted to go home.

Ahead a door opened, and she prepared herself to be assaulted by a couple in the throes of passion. Instead she found herself nearly run over by Nathan Tucker and Micah Hudson.

She halted, unsure of who was more surprised, her or them. A guilty look flashed across Nathan's face about the time she caught his scent. Sure she was mistaken, she inhaled sharply. He didn't smell like Nathan normally did, and she was all but an expert on what the man smelled like. No, he didn't smell like Nathan. He smelled like her mystery lover. Her gentle lover. Which would explain the guilt flashing in those green eyes.

And that could only mean that Micah was her more impatient lover.

"You disguised your scent. You actually changed your smell!"

She babbled like a fool, but she honestly couldn't come up with anything else. She was too freaking stunned.

Nathan held out his hands in a placating manner. "Julie, listen to me, please."

His eyes were soft, his mouth turned down in an expression of regret. Micah wore a grimace that plainly said he'd rather be anywhere but here. Well, join the club. That made two of them.

She laughed. Maybe it wasn't the most sensible action, but she was too wrung out to be all cool and collected and in control.

"Well done. I mean, wow. Changing your scent. That took a hell of a lot of forethought. I would have never even considered that. That would explain why you never let me touch you. I guess this is where I say touché and that we're even, right?"

"No, we're not damn well even," Nathan growled. "That's not what this was about. Or at least, it's not now."

She raised an eyebrow. "Come on, Nathan, be straight with me at least. You can't tell me you didn't want a little payback for what I did at my salon."

He huffed, his face reddening with either embarrassment or anger, she wasn't sure which.

"Yeah, I did want payback, but more than that, I didn't want strange men fucking you. Damn it, Julie, what the hell were you thinking? You were just setting yourself up to be hurt or raped or God knows what else."

"So you fucked me to save me from these men?" she drawled out. "Really, how self-sacrificing of you, Nathan." She slid her gaze to Micah who leaned against the wall, hands shoved into his pockets. "What's your excuse, Hudson?"

"Do I need an excuse to fuck a beautiful woman?" he asked lazily.

"No, I guess you don't," she said quietly. "If you two will excuse me, it's been a long day, and I'd really like to get home."

"Julie, don't go," Nathan said as he reached for her hand. "You and I need to talk."

Fatigue dragged at every muscle. This was just the icing on an already draining evening. The only thing she wanted to talk about was how fast she could get home and into bed. Her bed. Alone.

"We could probably say a lot and not get anywhere. Let's just chalk it up to experience and call it good, okay? I always knew sex with you would be nothing short of spectacular and you proved me right. I should be thanking you, right? You and your fuck buddy here," she said with another sideways glance in Micah's direction.

"You're tired and just got dealt a hell of a surprise, baby doll," Micah said quietly. "Don't make it worse by lashing out and saying things you don't mean. Go on home and get some rest. Nathan and our apologies will wait."

Her smile warbled, and she finally gave up on trying to pretend it didn't matter. "You're right. I'm being a hysterical female, and worse, I'm not taking as good as I gave. I had it coming. It was amusing when the shoe was on the other foot, so I need to suck it up and take it like a big girl. I do appreciate you two making it so good for me, though. I'm not lying about that. The sex was incredible."

She walked past, ignoring Nathan's outstretched hand and his growl of protest. She heard Micah tell him to lay off. Willing herself not to react, not to feel, she left The House and got into her little sports car.

The smooth leather cupped her as lovingly as . . . well, as lovingly as Nathan had earlier. She loved her car. She'd worked damn hard for it. The leather was as smooth as a baby's bottom. Like buttah.

The engine roared to life and purred like a contented cat. Ideally she'd be in bed purring like that contented cat after the bone-melting sex she'd had, but there were two problems with that scenario now.

It felt disappointingly hollow after watching Damon and Serena together. Which was pretty stupid, because she might never find the sort of love those two shared, and what was she going to do, spend the rest of her life comparing herself and coming up short?

She shifted and accelerated out of the gate and onto the highway. Feeling a sudden need to feel the wind in her hair, she slowed and hit the button to take the top down.

Briefly closing her eyes as the sweet evening air blew over her face, she shoved her hair back and sped up.

The other problem facing what should have been a sated cuddle against her pillows was the fact that the man she'd spent the better part of the last several months lusting over had managed to knock her completely off guard. She didn't like being at a disadvantage, and when she'd scented Nathan and realized the magnitude of the deception he'd managed to pull off, she had no snappy comebacks, no flirty teasing.

"This isn't like you, Julie," she muttered.

Her words were swallowed by the wind, but she may as well have yelled. The thought resonated over and over, followed her home nipping at her heels like a persistent pup.

She whipped into her parking space at her apartment complex and wearily climbed out of her car.

"Sleep. A few hours sleep and you'll be your old self again."

As she let herself into her apartment, she wondered if lying to herself had become her new mantra.

Chapter 21

A knock at her door wrung her from the deep dredges of a dreamless sleep. When the person showed no signs of going away, Julie grumbled and rolled out of bed. She didn't bother trying to make herself presentable because the way she saw it, whoever had the audacity to show up at such an ungodly hour deserved to see her looking like a hungover hag.

She glanced at the clock on her way out of the bedroom. Oops, maybe ten thirty wasn't exactly an ungodly hour, but still, it was Sunday and Julie's only full day off.

Almost to the door, she had the unsettling thought that it could be Nathan here to take up where they'd left off the night before. She already felt like a train wreck. Facing Nathan right now would be like getting backed over by a Mac truck. Repeatedly.

Remembering Nathan's admonishment about opening the door to just anyone, she cracked it, leaving the chain on, and peered out.

"Julie?"

She quickly closed the door and yanked the chain off then opened the door wide. Serena stood there, her expression troubled.

"Can I come in?"

Julie tilted her head in confusion. "Of course. Come in. Why on earth would you need to ask a question like that?"

She turned and led the way into the living room, Serena's soft steps pattering behind her.

"I was worried you might be angry with me. Or with Damon."

Julie stopped and turned in front of the couch. "Do you want something to eat or drink? I just got up, so I'm not my best right now."

Serena took her hands in hers and urged her to sit down with her on the couch.

"Are you angry with us?"

Julie smiled. "No, hon, I'm not angry with you and Damon. Why would I be?"

"Damon said you found out about Nathan and Micah. Nathan's worried about you. So are Micah and Damon. So am I. Nathan said you looked . . . well, he said you weren't yourself when you left. I knew this was a bad idea, but I went along with it because you seemed to want Nathan so much, and he wanted you."

Serena gave her an unhappy look as she trailed off.

"You have nothing to feel guilty over, Serena. Damon either. He gave me what I wanted. Anonymous sex."

Serena frowned harder. "So what now?"

Julie laughed and scrubbed a hand over her bleary eyes. "That's a good question. Nothing, I guess. I'd already decided before I met up with Nathan and Micah that I wasn't going back for more."

"You sound remarkably calm about all this," Serena said doubtfully.

"Hmm. Well, to be honest, what am I supposed to get pissed about? I was a little embarrassed when I realized the truth, but that pissed me off more than figuring out I'd been had. I gave as good as I got. I have nothing to be embarrassed over."

Serena grinned. "That's the Julie I know and love. Not this kicked-puppy thing you've got going on."

Julie chuckled. "I sulked a little when I got home, but honestly, it's not some great betrayal. I pulled one over on Nathan. He retaliated. He didn't deceive me, because I *asked* Damon for anonymity. In hindsight I'm a little relieved that the two guys weren't complete strangers. And it certainly helped that they were so damn good in the sack."

"So what about poor Nathan? Are you going to give the guy a break? He's making himself crazy over you."

"I haven't decided his fate yet," Julie said thoughtfully. "I don't want to let him off lightly. I may not be pissed, but he went to some serious lengths to pull this over on me."

"I don't like that look," Serena said slowly. "You're usually plotting evil when you get that look."

Julie gave her best innocent smile. "Who, me?"

"Sooo, tell me the answer to the million-dollar question."

Julie arched a brow. "Which one is that?"

"How are Faith's leftovers in bed?"

Julie's mouth dropped open. "You bitch. You had to go there, didn't you?"

Serena snickered, her eyes bubbling with mischief. "You're the one who said you'd never sleep with a friend's leftovers."

"In answer to your question, he was damn good. Not as good as Nathan, but still good. At least Faith has never slept with Nathan!"

"Now that you have a threesome out of your system, how was it? All you thought it would be?"

"Who the hell says it's out of my system?"

Serena snorted. "Knowing you, it's not."

"It was . . . exciting. Decadent. Had that edgy, forbidden feel to it."

"But?"

"No but."

"I could swear I heard a *but* in there."

Julie smiled gently. How could she tell Serena the 'but' was seeing her and Damon? That before she witnessed the absolute beauty of their love she would have said the nights with Nathan and Micah had been the best of her life?

"Maybe I just want more these days than some hot, sweaty sex and mindless bumping and grinding."

Serena looked at her, mouth open. "But that's precisely what you said you wanted. No messy emotion. No expectations."

"I know. Stupid of me, isn't it?"

"It's not stupid, Julie. It just seemed to have come from left field."

"Put it this way. I saw something pretty damn special, and it made me realize what I was missing. Now, I haven't decided if I want it yet. I'm holding out hope that if I give myself enough time to come to my senses that I'll smack myself on the head and stay the course."

"I wish Faith was here. She'd help me pry information out of those clamlike lips of yours."

Julie smiled. "It was sweet of you to come over this morning. I'm sorry I worried you, but you know I'm glad to see you."

"You had Damon worried too. He struggled over the ethics of allowing Nathan to participate in your fantasy. Micah might be his friend, but he's very protective of the women who come to The House."

"Damon is a great guy," Julie said casually. "When are you going to put him out of his misery?"

A peculiar look crossed Serena's face.

"What?" Julie asked, latching on to that look. "What was that look? You aren't taking a page out of Faith's book and dumping the man, are you? Don't make me hurt you."

Serena flopped back on the couch and stared up at the ceiling. "If I tell you this you're going to think I'm the biggest moron on the face of the planet."

"I'm afraid that particular title is mine," Julie said. "So spill."

Serena sighed. "I've been so preoccupied with worrying over whether this whole thing with Damon would last. What if I wouldn't want the type of relationship he wants long term? What if we got to that point and he couldn't accept that I no longer wanted it? What if, what if, what if until I've driven myself crazy with all the what-ifs."

"Recognizing your illness is the first step in your recovery," Julie said sagely.

Serena laughed. "Oh stop, Julie. I'm being serious here."

"Continue on," Julie said with a wave of her hand.

"When he asked me to marry him, all I could think was that

in his position of power, how could he ever know why I accepted? Every time he's asked me, the power is weighted toward him. I don't know but it made me uncomfortable. I want . . . I want our marriage to start out on equal terms even if during the course of it I cede control and power to him."

"You want it to be your choice."

"Exactly! I don't want him to ever look back and doubt that I came to him freely, doubt that I gave myself entirely to him because it was what I wanted. I don't want him to think I was under some spell and would have agreed blindly if he asked me to jump off a bridge."

Julie snickered.

"Oh shut up," Serena grumbled. "I know it sounds ridiculous. Maybe some of what inspired Faith's ninniness rubbed off on me."

"There does seem to be a lot of that going around," Julie said wryly. "I wasn't immune to it, unfortunately."

Serena gave her a quick hug. "Well, we can all be stupid twit females together."

"You'll only be a stupid twit if you keep refusing Damon's proposals."

Serena pulled away and smiled one of her sexy, secretive smiles that probably drove men insane with lust. "Actually, I plan to ask him to marry me. Today. I figure he can't ever think that he coerced me if I do the asking."

"Oooh, sneaky, devious. I love it! I'd pay real money to be a fly on the wall when you ask him."

"Yeah, I'm pretty fond of the idea myself."

"So? What are you doing over here? Get your ass back to your man and propose."

Serena smiled and squeezed Julie's hands again. "Because you're my friend and seeing you was more important this morning. I had to make sure you were okay."

"Well, thanks. I'm fine. Really. Nothing a day of pampering myself won't fix."

"Want to do lunch this week when Faith gets back?"

"The hell with lunch. When she gets back we need to have a girls' night out. Lots to celebrate. Her marriage, your engagement."

"Okay, done. Faith is supposed to roll in Tuesday morning. Or at least that's when Damon's jet is supposed to land. Knowing those two, it's entirely possible they'd miss their own flight."

"Go, go," Julie said, making shooing motions with her hands. "Go propose to that man of yours. I'm so excited I can't stand it. Call me tomorrow and let me know how it went."

Serena smiled so big Julie thought her mouth might crack. Now she knew what pure, unadulterated joy looked like.

"I will. Catch you later."

Serena got up and with a small wave disappeared down the hallway to the front door. Julie watched her go with a peculiar twist in her chest. There went one happy woman.

Chapter 22

Serena smiled at Sam when he opened the back door for her. She leaned up and kissed the startled man on the cheek and all but flew to the front door.

She burst into the living room expecting to find Damon sitting in front of the fire with his book and a glass of wine, but to her disappointment the room was empty. She quickly weighed her options. He could be in his office, but if that was the case she didn't want to interrupt work with what she hoped to be a special moment. Or he could be up in the bedroom, which offered a whole host of possibilities.

She turned eagerly, only to see Sam walk into the living room.

"Miss James, you left the car so quickly I didn't have time to inform you that Mr. Roche is on the terrace. He wished you to join him when you returned."

"Thank you, Sam," she said as she whirled and hurried toward the glass doors.

Her heart was beating like a freight train. She was breathless, scared, but happy. So very happy.

She came to a halt on the stone patio when she saw Damon sitting at the circular glass table several feet away. In her haste, she'd forgotten to shed her shoes, and she kicked them off now, enjoying the warm concrete under her feet.

He was staring into the gardens, a glass of wine held idly in his hand. He looked contented, a man sure of his place in the world. And now, finally, she knew *her* place in the world. His world. It didn't matter where, as long as he was in it.

A ridiculous knot of nervous energy rolled in her stomach, squeezing until her breaths came out in little painful squeaks. Then he looked up and saw her.

She swallowed the huge lump in her throat when she saw his eyes soften with love. He had the most delicious brown eyes and they went positively liquid when he looked at her. She wanted to lock this moment away in time. If only she could stand here watching him look at her that way for the rest of her life, she would be happy.

"Serena mine," he murmured, holding his hand out to her.

She rushed forward, taking his hand and dropping to her knees beside his chair. She rubbed her face over his leg, closing her eyes as his fingers tangled in her hair.

"No, love, you're going to hurt your knees. The stone is too hard and rough for you out here."

She shook her head. Knees? What knees? All she could feel was his love, wrapping securely around her, holding her when she couldn't hold herself.

"Come here," he said quietly, pulling her into his lap.

When she was settled against his chest, he stroked her long hair from her face with gentle fingers.

"What's wrong, Serena?"

She expelled her breath in a quivering rush and smiled. "I love you. Do you know that, Damon? Do you know how much?"

He looked stunned by her announcement. His pupils flared, and his fingers stilled in her hair.

"I know. I hope I know." He pressed his lips to her forehead, and she could feel him trembling against her. "I love you too, Serena mine. So damn much, I ache."

She pulled away and caught his hand, pulling it from her hair to cradle it between her palms. For a moment she studied their entwined hands thinking of all the times she was bound to him, for him, only this time it was her doing the binding. She was in control.

When she looked back up at him, he was studying her with those deep brown eyes. Dropping his hand, she leaned forward, putting her palms against his face.

"Will you marry me, Damon? Will you be my husband and my lover for the rest of our lives?"

His eyes widened. First shock and then joy flooded them, so warm and vibrant that tears clogged her throat, burning and squeezing. If she'd had any reservations, any concerns, they vanished as she saw his relief. Had he been so worried she wouldn't marry him?

"Yes," he said solemnly. "I'll marry you, Serena mine. Anytime, anywhere. I don't care as long as you'll be mine."

She brought her lips to his, kissing him hungrily. Then she wrapped her arms around him and hugged him fiercely, content to just hold on and feel his strength, and his love.

"I don't want to wait," she whispered against his neck.

"Then we won't wait," he said simply.

"I want to be yours."

"You're already mine, Serena. No ceremony or lack thereof will ever change that. You'll always, *always* be mine."

She smiled and squeezed him a little tighter. "We need to call your mom. And mine. She and Dad will want to fuss." She pulled away and sat up to look him in the face. "I don't want a fuss but I don't want to disappoint my mom either. Maybe we could compromise and keep it small, just friends and immediate family."

He cupped her cheek in his palm and smiled lovingly at her. "Do you know how happy you've just made me? Are you sure, Serena? You seemed to have doubts before. I want you to be sure this is what you want. I won't push you for more. You know that."

"I do know. Oh, Damon, I love you so much."

"It figures you would catch me so unprepared," he said ruefully. "The ring I've carried everywhere with me over the last weeks is sitting upstairs in the drawer of my dresser."

"We can get it later. All that matters right now is you and me." She squirmed with excitement on his lap. "I'm getting married. Holy hell, that's scary!"

He administered a light smack to her hip. "Marrying me should not be in the least bit scary. You should be swooning with joy."

She grinned. "Okay, I'll stand up and swoon but if you don't catch me, I'm going to kick your ass."

"I'd rather carry you upstairs, tie you to my bed and make love to you all afternoon long. Then maybe I'll let you up so we can call our families."

"And they say romance is dead," she murmured as she closed her mouth over his.

Somewhere between the melancholy and the ass kicking, Julie's self-disgust overpowered everything else. Which was good, because there was only so much wallowing she could take.

Yeah, Damon and Serena hit her hard, but they were Damon and Serena. Julie was . . . well, she was Julie. Looking at someone else's relationship for the answers was like reading about a romance novel hero and expecting to find a carbon copy in real life.

Smart women didn't do either. And above all, she was a smart woman.

After boiling in a bathtub for the better part of the afternoon, she applied fourteen different types of girly garb, painted her toenails, did all the waxing she could reach and went digging through her freezer for some Blue Bell Homemade Vanilla ice cream.

She needed a plan. She wasn't going to, in the words of Serena, allow the kicked puppy to take over. No, that wasn't her style. What would the real Julie do when confronted with Nathan's one-upsmanship?

She smiled around a spoonful of ice cream. The real Julie wouldn't get mad. She'd get even. And that posed all sorts of delectable possibilities.

Luring him in for another massage would never work. He'd see that one coming a mile away. Besides, she was nothing if not original. No, she wanted something bold. Something he'd never see coming in a million years. Something that gave her the upper hand.

Easier said than accomplished, however.

She sighed a little mournfully as she licked the sweetness from the spoon. The only thing that irked her about the entire experience—now that she knew who her mystery men were—was that she hadn't been able to look at Nathan and Micah, especially Nathan, while they were fucking her mindless.

A woman should never be blindfolded when making love to men who looked that good. That was her own stupidity, but then again, if she hadn't made that stipulation, Nathan wouldn't have seized his opportunity.

But still. She groaned as her body went all fiery again just thinking about Nathan's naked body lying over hers, his hips flexing, muscles bulging while he thrust. Even ice cream wasn't going to help this burn.

Micah was probably nice to look at too in the buff, but with Nathan in the room, she doubted she would have even seen Micah. Which was too bad, really. When a woman stopped noticing a good-looking man, she was either in love or struck blind. She was going with the latter, since lust didn't equal love in her world.

She let the spoon rest on her tongue as she stared dreamily into the distance. Nathan Tucker in her bed. Powerless. Hers to do with whatever the hell she wanted. Nathan Tucker *tied* to her bed. Oh hell yeah. Her girly parts were singing at the idea.

What she could do to a man who could do nothing but lie there and take it. Oh, she'd treat him very, very well. He'd enjoy his captivity before she turned him back into the wild. *Mreow!* Her chill bumps had chill bumps as she imagined all she could get away with if she had him completely at her mercy.

It would be the perfect payback. A man like him would chafe at being subdued by a little ole woman like her. He'd huff and snarl but in the end she'd bring him gently to heel. He'd be purring like a well-trained kitten by the time she finished pleasuring him.

She frowned as she dug back into the ice cream. As fantasies went, this one was stellar. But the execution. Now there was the deal breaker. How the hell was she going to get Nathan Tucker in her bed, naked *and* bound?

She could ask Faith for handcuffs—the good police-issue ones, because she didn't want the kind he could break out of in two seconds flat. Faith was a kinky bitch, and Gray was an ex-cop. They had to have a few lying around, didn't they? It still didn't answer the problem of how to get Nathan into them, however.

Well, just because she didn't have an immediate answer didn't mean she was going to give up. Some things were just too good to let go of. Nathan naked and at her mercy was one of them.

She polished off the rest of her ice cream and sat back with a satisfied yawn. After last night she had that yummy kind of lethargy that spoke of great sex and multiple orgasms. Going back to bed wasn't a bad idea. She had a full day of client appointments to start off her week. She'd worry about how to take down Nathan tomorrow. Today she was going to stare at the back of her eyelids and dream of all she'd do when she did run him to ground.

Chapter 23

"Where the hell is Micah?" Nathan asked.

Pop looked up from the scattered paperwork on Faith's desk while Connor stood to the side staring over Pop's shoulder as they looked for an invoice.

"I forgot this was his time off," Pop muttered.

"You gave him time off when we're short Faith and Gray?" Nathan asked in disbelief.

"Well, it wouldn't be my first choice, but the only time he ever asks for is every year on precisely the same days. He has a standing request in. Never changes them. Never calls in any other time, so I have a hard time telling him no."

Nathan frowned. Come to think of it, Micah did take off every single year on the same days. Even stranger, he disappeared and no one knew where he went or had heard from him until he came back to work.

"Faith and Gray will be home tomorrow," Connor offered. "At least we'll have decent coffee again."

Pop grunted, his lips curled into a surly line. None of them was worth a damn without their supply of coffee. Problem was, no one knew what kind Faith used. It was her highly guarded secret. She used it as a weapon in case they ever got any crazy ideas about firing her. As if.

"So how'd your date with Julie go, anyway?" Connor asked. "Haven't had a chance to ask you since you two went out."

Nathan blinked. They didn't normally talk about their damn personal lives. But he saw the gleam in Connor's eyes and scowled.

"It went fine."

"Yeah? She stick around long enough for you to call it an actual date?"

"You're asking for it, Malone."

"Leave the boy alone," Pop said with a wave of his hand. "We've got enough to do without you two bickering like a bunch of children."

Connor sent him a sideways look and grinned slyly. "I was thinking, if you two aren't going out regularly, I might ask her out. I've only met her a couple of times but she's seriously hot."

Nathan rocketed to his feet. "Over my dead body!"

Pop gave him a disgusted look. "Sit down, son. You're way too damn easy."

Connor chuckled. "Who says I wasn't serious?"

"That girl would eat you alive," Pop said, not looking up from his search. "Look at what she's done to Nathan. You like your conquests to be easy, and I'd say Julie's anything but easy."

Nathan snickered. "You like 'em easy, eh, Connor? There's a word for that, you know."

"Fuck you. I just like girls who don't rank up there with crazy ex-girlfriend status."

"You've had your share of crazy exes," Pop muttered.

"Oh?" Nathan hooted. "Do share, Pop."

"Don't we have work to do?" Connor asked.

Pop grinned and looked over the paper he was holding. "I'll never forget the one girl who waited for him naked in bed. He was coming home on leave, and he'd broken things off with her before he shipped out last. Only problem was, it was my bed she took position in. I liked to have never got her out of there. Connor hid in his bedroom like a damn coward."

Nathan laughed until his sides hurt while Connor glared holes in his dad.

"There was also the one who painted herself in camo colors and decided that was all the clothing she needed."

"Pop, enough already."

Connor sounded a little desperate, which made Nathan all the more determined to hear Pop out.

Ignoring Connor's frantic attempts to hush him, Pop laid the stack of papers to the side and leaned back in his chair, his teeth flashing in a smile.

"The girl had brass, I have to hand it to her. Connor and I were at the local pizza place having dinner—with Connor's new girlfriend, I might add—when Miss Camo-in-All-the-Right-Places waltzes up to Connor and plops herself onto his lap."

"Yeah, and my new girlfriend dumped me over that," Connor grumbled. "I've sworn off psycho women."

"Julie's not psycho," Nathan growled.

Connor grinned. “I never said she was. I want to ask her out, remember?”

“Quit yanking his chain,” Pop said. “Wouldn’t hurt you to ask someone out, though. I’m not getting any younger. I’d like grandchildren before I’m too old to see them.”

“We could always set him up,” Nathan snickered. “I’m sure Micah knows someone.”

“I don’t need your goddamn help finding a woman. The day I do is the day they put my ass in a pine box.”

Nathan held up his hands. “Touchy today.”

“It’s called not getting any,” Pop said with a perfectly straight face.

The laughter Nathan had been trying to hold back poured out. Connor rolled his eyes and sighed in resignation.

“When you two are through dissecting my love life, I’ll be out in the truck waiting. Someone has to do the goddamn work around here.”

Connor stalked off while Nathan was still laughing. Connor could give with the best, but he damn sure couldn’t take it.

Still chuckling, Pop hauled himself up and grabbed his keys. “Well, come on. Let’s go join my grumpy-ass son so we can get this job done. He’s right about one thing. Someone has to work around here since it seems everyone’s taking off at the same time.”

Nathan walked out ahead of Pop and slid into the SUV with Connor. A few minutes later, Pop ambled over to Connor’s side and motioned for him to roll down the window.

“You two go on ahead. I’ll take my truck. I want to check on a system I just got a call about. Owner says the alarm keeps going off.”

"Sure you don't want us to come along and help diagnose the problem?" Connor asked.

Pop grunted. "I may not be the computer guru in the family, but I'm laying odds it's a damn stray cat or a squirrel that's the culprit. If I have any trouble, I'll holler at you boys."

Connor nodded and backed out of the parking lot.

"Want something to eat before we go?" Connor asked.

Nathan shrugged. He wasn't really that hungry, but Connor and food made a date at least every two hours. Nathan was convinced the guy had tapeworms. There was no other explanation for how he never worked out with the other guys, and yet he was lean and muscled despite the fact he ate half an elephant's weight on a daily basis.

They hit the drive-through of their favorite local fast food joint, and Nathan listened while Connor ordered an obscene amount of food. Nathan got a coffee, thinking it couldn't be worse than Connor's earlier attempt. It wasn't much better, but it was liquid caffeine.

"Julie's salon isn't far from here, is it?" Connor asked casually.

"No," Nathan said tightly.

"Shopping center one block over, huh?"

Nathan turned to look at Connor, his eyes narrowed to slits. "Cut the crap, Connor. Unless you're wanting to schedule a hair appointment, why the hell do you care where Julie's salon is?"

"Or a massage," Connor said innocently. "I guess I could always get my ear pierced like you and pussy boy Hudson."

"Pussy boy Hudson would kick your ass and you know it," Nathan said with a grin.

"Nah, he's old and rusty."

Nathan snorted. "And you aren't? You've gotten soft since getting out."

"Julie's different," Connor said, pulling the conversation back to her again. It was starting to annoy the shit out of Nathan.

"What do you mean, different?"

Connor shrugged. "You know what I mean. She's . . . rounder, a little on the plump side. You usually date the tall, lean blonde types."

Nathan stared at him agape. Plump? Was he trying to insinuate that Julie was fat?

Connor glanced over at him and cocked an eyebrow. "Why do you look so appalled, man?"

"What the hell are you trying to say?"

"Just that she's not your usual type. She's got hips, breasts."

"She's fucking perfect," Nathan growled. "Ain't a goddamn thing wrong with her." Hips and breasts. Was Connor sitting there seriously criticizing Julie's attributes? If he wasn't driving, Nathan would kick his ass on the spot.

"I wasn't badmouthing her, dude. Just citing the differences."

"How about you don't even fucking look at her, and you won't have to worry about her differences."

Connor chuckled and held up one hand in surrender.

"Hey, speak of the devil. Isn't that her?"

Nathan blinked at the abrupt change in topic but looked in the direction of Connor's attention. Sure enough, Julie's sporty convertible darted into traffic from the on-ramp and surged ahead three cars.

Her hair blew behind her head, whipping in the wind like strands of silk. She handled the little car like a pro, and she obviously enjoyed the ride. There was a hint of daredevil in her as she weaved back and forth in the busy traffic.

"On second thought, I can see why you're hot for her," Connor murmured as he accelerated to keep up. "Something about a chick in a hot car."

Nathan rolled his eyes. Julie could be driving a grandma car and Nathan would still be hot for her.

Ahead, Julie moved over to the far right lane and put her blinker on to exit. At that precise moment a truck came barreling up the on-ramp and T-boned the small car without ever coming close to yielding.

"Son of a bitch!" Nathan yelled.

Julie's car spun crazily into traffic, and cars scattered across four lanes in an effort to avoid a collision. The asshole driving the truck never even slowed. He careened wildly around several cars, regained control and roared off.

Julie slammed into the far left concrete divider and came to a halt.

In a maneuver eerily reminiscent of Julie's crazy skitter across the freeway, Connor roared over, executing a sharp U-turn and narrowly missing an eighteen-wheeler that had slowed when the accident occurred.

Nathan was out and running as soon as Connor came to a stop. Connor was already on the phone. Nathan's only thought was to get to Julie.

The car was facing the wrong way and the battered passenger side rested against the concrete dividers. Julie's head lolled to the side, blood dripping from a cut above her eye. So much for the goddamn airbags.

He glanced around and then to the steering wheel. It was the only thing she could have hit her head on. Thank God she'd worn her seat belt.

"Julie? Julie, honey, can you hear me?"

A soft moan was her only response.

He touched her shoulder, too afraid to touch her anywhere else. He didn't want to jostle her or have her move her neck unnecessarily. If she hit the steering wheel, she'd have a hell of a case of whiplash and who knows what kind of neck or back injuries.

Her eyes flickered open and she stared fuzzily back at him.

"Nathan?" she whispered.

"Yes, honey, it's me."

Her brow crinkled in confusion and pain. "Am I dead?"

His gut clenched at even hearing such a thing.

"No, you're not dead. I need you to stay with me, though, okay? Can you keep those gorgeous eyes open until the ambulance gets here?"

By now more than one person had stopped. Two cars had parked in the inside lane to keep traffic diverted around Julie's car, a fact he was grateful for. The last thing he wanted was for them to get plowed again, and he wasn't going to leave her nor was he going to move her out of the car.

In the distance, sirens wailed, which meant either the cops or the ambulance was already en route. The sooner they got Julie the hell off the freeway, the better he'd feel.

"Am I going to be all right?" she asked anxiously, her eyes focusing unsteadily on him. "I don't feel so well."

Panic surged through his system. He reached tentatively for her hand, doing a quick look to see if there were any obvious injuries before curling his fingers gently around hers.

"You're going to be fine, honey. I promise."

Please don't let him have just handed her a huge lie.

Connor hurried up to stand next to Nathan. "Don't move her. Wait for the ambulance."

Nathan tempered his irritation. Connor was only doing what was best for Julie. "I know. I'm just trying to keep her calm."

Connor leaned over to stare at the blood seeping down Julie's face. "Julie, sweetheart, do you hurt anywhere else but your head?"

She clutched at Nathan's fingers a little tighter, her pupils dilating a bit in fear. That had to be good, right? He remembered one thing about head injuries. It was good if the pupils were equal and reactive. And she was awake. Not entirely lucid, but she'd just had the shit scared out of her. He could hardly expect her to act normally.

"I don't know. My head hurts." Her brow wrinkled in concentration. "My shoulder, I think." She glanced down and both Connor and Nathan shouted a quick no.

She blinked in confusion.

"Don't move your neck, honey," Nathan said soothingly. "Try and stay as still as possible." He rubbed his thumb across her knuckles and tried to ease the shaking in her hand.

Connor nudged Nathan's arm. "The ambulance just pulled up."

Connor moved out of the way, but Nathan stayed with Julie, holding her hand until the paramedics hurried up and asked him to step aside.

Though he hated to get too far away from her, he was only in the way as they began the process of extricating her from the car.

Two policemen were talking to Connor, and Connor called him over.

"He and I both witnessed it," Connor explained when Nathan walked up.

"Yeah," Nathan said distractedly as he looked back to see the progress they were making with Julie. "I got the plates on the truck that hit her."

"I'd like your statement," one of the police officers said as he stepped away from Connor and the other cop.

"Uh, look, can it wait? I want to go to the hospital with her."

The cop gave him a curious look. "You know her?"

"Yeah, I do."

"Let me have your contact information. If I don't catch you at the hospital, I'll get in touch with you later this afternoon. We'll need what information you can give us so we can prosecute this as a hit and run."

"Damn right," Nathan growled. "The son of a bitch wasn't looking where he was going and then he left without even slowing down. I'd like to ring his damn neck."

One of the paramedics motioned for Nathan. They had Julie on a stretcher and were wheeling her toward the ambulance.

"Go. I'll get with you later."

"Thanks," Nathan said as he sprinted to the back of the ambulance.

After the stretcher was loaded, one of the medics stepped back and motioned Nathan inside. Nathan climbed up and slid along the bench until he was at Julie's head.

The paramedic got in behind him while the other shut the doors and went around to the cab.

"Do me a favor and hop into the jump seat," the paramedic said, motioning to the seat above Julie's stretcher. "I need to examine her on the way in so I can give the hospital a report."

When Nathan repositioned himself, Julie softly called his name.

"Right here, honey," he said, lowering his hand to lightly stroke the side of her head that wasn't injured.

He watched while the paramedic efficiently examined her for other injuries, checked her vitals, assessed her pupils and fitted a loose bandage to her head to stop the bleeding.

He listened with keen interest when the medic called in his report to the emergency room and breathed a sigh of relief when he reported nothing major in his findings.

A few minutes later they came to a halt outside the ambulance entrance to the ER and the doors opened. He and the medic piled out and he waited to the side while they removed Julie's stretcher and wheeled her inside.

No one shooed him from the exam room, so he stood back out of the way while they poked and prodded, hooked her up to monitors and ascertained her level of consciousness. She looked frightened and incredibly vulnerable. Her gaze skated frantically left and right. Was she looking for him? He told her he wouldn't leave her, but how was she to know that now if she couldn't see him?

He stepped forward just enough that he could get into her peripheral vision. When her gaze settled on him, her eyes flooded with relief. She seemed to relax under the straps holding her to the backboard.

One of the nurses turned to him, putting her hand on his arm. "We need to clear her spine before we remove the C-collar and take her off the backboard. We're also going to get a CT of her head. She's doing fine so far. Her vitals are stable. Blood pressure is good. She's reacting to normal stimuli. You can stay with her until we do the X-rays."

"Thanks."

As soon as she moved, Nathan beat a path to Julie's bed. Her gaze moved upward when he stood over her and their eyes locked.

"Thank you," she whispered.

"For what, honey?"

"I don't know where you came from, but I was so scared, and you made me feel safe. That was the single most terrifying moment of my life. I'm so glad you were there."

He lowered his head to brush a kiss over her forehead. "Glad I could help. You scared the life out of me when I saw that truck hit you."

A shudder quivered through her body, and he touched her cheek with his fingers, caressing lightly in an attempt to soothe her.

"You're going to be fine, Julie. Just a knock on the head it looks like, and hey, if a part of your body is going to get abused, it might as well be your hard head."

She grinned and then winced. He frowned when he saw a little tiny cut in the corner of her mouth. Had she bitten it? Before she could close her lips again, he leaned down and gently fused his mouth to the cut.

She went still, her quick intake of breath her only reaction.

"Better?" he murmured as he pulled away.

"Better," she whispered.

His mind was already doing swift calculations. He knew she lived alone and didn't have anyone to look in on her much less take care of her. Taking her home with him was probably out of the question, and she probably wouldn't appreciate his slobby ass bachelor den anyway. He seriously needed to clean it up because he didn't want her to run screaming the first time she came over. And she would be coming over.

But he could definitely go home with her and make sure she took her pain pills, ate right and didn't fall on her face on her way to the bathroom. She could end up lying there all night and nobody would ever know.

His scowl deepened as he imagined her cold, alone and in pain. No, he could stay with her. It was just as well the independent heifer learn to have him around, because he didn't plan to go anywhere, despite her repeated attempts to shake him.

She might be stubborn—beautiful, willful, a handful of luscious woman but stubborn nonetheless—but he hadn't grown up with four women just to turn out to be some namby-pamby pushover. He was skilled at getting what he wanted. Hell, he had to be in a houseful of hormonally deranged females.

Two male techs entered Julie's room.

"Hi, gorgeous. My name is Steven and my partner here is David. We're going to go take some pictures of you."

He glanced up at Nathan. "We won't be long if you'd like to wait in the waiting room. She won't be coming back to this room. This is sort of our triage holding area. We'll be moving her to a different exam room until it's determined if she'll be admitted or not."

"You'll get me when she comes back?" Nathan asked.

"Sure, I'll holler at you myself. What's your name?"

"Nathan Tucker, and thanks."

"No problem, man. We'll take good care of her, I promise."

Nathan leaned down and kissed her forehead again. "I'll see you soon, okay?"

She gave him a half smile. "Okay."

Nathan waited until she'd been wheeled out before he made his way to the waiting room. Connor was standing there, hands shoved into his pockets leaning against one of the windows. He straightened when Nathan came out.

"How's she doing?"

"Good, I think. They've taken her to X-ray to clear her spine, and they want to do a scan of her head to make sure there aren't any bleeds. She was still conscious. Shaky and scared out of her mind, but that's to be expected."

"You staying?" Connor asked.

Nathan nodded. "Yeah."

"Okay, if you want, Pop and I will run your truck over and park it in the garage. I'll find you to give you the keys."

"Thanks. I'd appreciate that. Not sure what's going on here. They won't know if they're keeping her until they get the X-rays back."

"Not a problem. I called Pop and let him know what was going on. You might want to call her friend Serena. No sense worrying Faith if Julie's going to be all right. She and Gray are flying in tomorrow morning. I don't want to ruin their last night in Vegas."

"Yeah, I agree. I'll give Serena a holler when I know more. I don't want to freak her out."

"Okay, see you in a bit."

"Thanks, man."

"You bet," Connor said as he walked toward the exit.

Chapter 24

Julie breathed a sigh of relief when they unfastened her C-collar and carefully pulled it away from her neck.

"There you go, Miss Stanford. Can you move your head a bit?"

Julie stared up at the nurse and moved slowly from side to side.

"Good. Does that hurt? Any tenderness?"

Julie frowned. "Just a little stiff."

"That's to be expected. You're definitely going to feel it tomorrow."

"What about my head?"

"The doctor is just now getting the report. He should be in to talk to you shortly." She frowned when Julie winced. "Are you in pain?"

"Head," Julie muttered. "And my shoulder."

"Ah, yes, you have quite a bruise forming on that shoulder. As soon as the doctor gives me the okay, I'll give you something for the pain. In the meantime, want me to let your young man back in? He's been pacing a hole in our waiting room floor."

Nathan. He was still here. For a moment, anticipation and something that felt strangely like joy surged through her veins like a shot of adrenaline. Where had he come from? She was still confused by the entire episode. Maybe she'd never really remember it all. One minute she'd been driving down the freeway enjoying having the top down, the next she was staring up at Nathan while he held her hand.

When she realized the nurse was staring at her, still waiting on an answer, she carefully nodded. "Yes, send him in, please."

The nurse smiled, patted her on the arm and turned to walk back out. A few minutes later, Nathan hurried in, concern shadowed in his eyes.

He did feel something for her. Something beyond lust and frustration. There was genuine worry for her reflected on his face. It made her feel warm and kind of funny on the inside. No one had ever really fussed over her like he had on the way to the hospital. It was strangely addicting.

"Hey," he said softly when he neared the bed. "I see they got you out of the bondage gear."

She chuckled softly, careful not to shake parts that didn't need shaking. "Yeah, it's a huge relief. That backboard was about to kill me, and having that C-collar on is like having someone's hands wrapped around your throat just waiting to squeeze."

He touched her face, smoothing her hair back behind her ear. "How are you feeling?"

"I've been better," she said ruefully. "I'd say I feel like I've been run over, but I guess I was."

His expression darkened. "Yeah, you were."

"Can you tell me what happened?" she asked. "I don't remember a whole lot. It all happened so fast. I just remember spinning and thinking I was going to die."

"Are you sure you want to go over this now? I don't want to upset you."

"I'm sure. I'm okay, really. Just stiff and sore. Nurse says I'll be worse tomorrow."

"A truck coming up the on-ramp decided that yield meant run over the nearest car, and he rammed you right in the middle on the passenger side. Sent you spinning into traffic where, thank God, you didn't hit any other cars. You came to a stop against the concrete dividers. Your airbag didn't deploy, and you hit your head on the steering wheel."

She tentatively reached to touch her shoulder, wincing at how tender it felt. "That would explain the shoulder too." She glanced back up at him. "You saw all this?"

"Connor and I were behind you when you got hit."

"Oh."

"They say whether they're keeping you yet?"

She shook her head. "I'm waiting on the doc to go over the results of the scan. X-rays were all negative, so that's good."

"Yeah, that's great. You scared me, honey."

She allowed the endearment to roll around, even testing it silently on her tongue. It sounded good coming from him, all soft and lovey sounding almost. Nothing like the affectionate "hon" she used when talking to Faith or Serena. Coming from him, it sounded damn sexy.

"I scared myself." Then reality hit her square in the chest. "My car," she said mournfully.

"What?"

"My car. She's totaled, I bet."

He looked confused by her emphasis on the car, and she couldn't blame him. She was lucky to be alive, but damn, she loved that car.

Tears brimmed in her eyes, which really pissed her off. The last thing she wanted was to turn into a weepy mess in front of Nathan, but her car. That vehicle represented an essential part of her freedom. It was an absolute celebration of herself, warts and all. She'd bought it the day after she'd gained back her weight and grew back her self-esteem.

"Aw honey, don't cry. I'm sure if the car is totaled, the insurance will pay for a new one."

She sniffed indelicately and wondered for the hundredth time why she couldn't cry like Faith. "It won't be the same. That car was special."

It was obvious he hadn't the first clue how to respond to her, but he still hated to see her cry, which was cute. He probably thought she did have a head injury and was even now plotting his immediate escape.

"I understand. I had a car like that. Well, it was a truck actually. A 1968 Ford short bed. Was the ugliest shade of green you'll ever see. I called it the Green Machine. I rebuilt it myself from a rusty old shell I got from a junkyard. Took me a year but I was driving it to school by my senior year. Man, I loved that truck."

"What happened to it?"

His lips twitched and turned down into a frown. "What usually happens to a man's pride and joy. A woman."

She laughed at the look of disgust on his face. "Girlfriend?"

"Sister. She went a round with one of the local bulls, and needless to say she and the truck came out the loser."

"A bull? Are you serious?"

"Yeah, got out of a downed fence. Ambled across the road about the time my sister rounded a corner. She was forever getting the gas and the brake mixed up when she got flustered. She hit the gas and hit the bull like a brick wall. She broke her collarbone and her wrist. Damn lucky she didn't kill herself. My truck was a complete and utter write-off. I had a funeral for it and everything."

She grinned, knowing just how he felt. "Maybe we can give my piece of scrap metal a proper send-off to the junkyard."

"It's a date," he said solemnly.

They were interrupted by the nurse's arrival. She walked to the head of the bed holding a capped syringe. "The good news is the doc gave me the go-ahead on the pain meds, which means you're just fine. He'll be in to make it official, but we had a trauma patient come in a few minutes ago, so he'll be there for a little bit. In the meantime I'll give you this to make you more comfortable."

Julie smiled up at her. "Thanks. I appreciate that."

"Slight burn when the medicine hits your bloodstream. It should go away about the time it hits your shoulder. Then you'll be feeling no pain."

"Sounds good," Julie said faintly as she felt the slight discomfort of the medicine. Then, as the nurse predicted, she traced the sensation to just below her shoulder and a warm hum settled in.

"Nice," she murmured.

The nurse chuckled. "That's what they all say. Get some rest. I'll be back to check on you in a few."

"Nathan?"

"Right here, honey."

"You can go, you know," she said, amused by how her words slurred. "You don't have to stay with me."

She thought he frowned at her but couldn't be sure. The ceiling and his face were doing this interesting sort of swirly thing.

"You're stuck with me, so deal with it."

She laughed. "You're cute when you get all grumpy."

"Is that why you try to drive me insane? Because you think I look cute?"

"I don't think," she said dreamily. "I know. Men shouldn't be that good-looking. Makes 'em too cocky."

"So now you're adding cocky to my lists of attributes."

There was a thread of amusement in his voice. Was he laughing at her?

"You have a nice cock too."

"Thank you . . . I think. Maybe we should talk about something else."

"Did you like having sex with me?"

He took her hand and pressed his other hand gently to her mouth.

"Well?" she asked huffily.

"Yes," he said in a resigned voice. "I enjoyed it very much. Why the hell can't I get you to talk about this stuff when you're sober?"

Was he talking to her or to himself?

"Do you and Micah have sex together often?"

"Julie!" His voice came out in a strangled, hoarse whisper. "No, the hell we don't have sex together. We had sex with *you*. Not with each other. Jesus Christ, woman. You're a danger to society when you're under the influence."

"That's what I meant," she huffed. "Do you two fuck the same chick together very often?"

"Julie, honey, as much as it pains me to say this, we really need to talk about this another time. Preferably when you know what the hell you're saying. Ask me these questions when you're not three sheets to the wind and I'll gladly answer them for you complete with visual aids and an in-depth description."

"Nathan?"

He sighed. "Yes?"

"I'm gonna go to sleep now."

He leaned down and carefully pushed her hair away from her face. "That's a very good idea, honey."

She literally felt her eyeballs roll back into her head as the room went black around her.

Chapter 25

When Julie next opened her eyes she had the sensation of having cotton balls stuffed underneath her lids. They positively scratched across her eyes. Her mouth hadn't been spared the cotton ball treatment either.

"Oh, you're awake."

"Serena?" she croaked, turning her head toward her friend's voice.

"Yes, sweetie, it's me. How are you? Oh my God, you had me so worried."

Serena sat in a chair pulled up next to the bed, her hand curled around Julie's arm. Luminous blue eyes shone with concern, and Serena's forehead was creased with worry.

"I'm okay. Promise. Just a little stiff."

"Is there anything I can get for you, Julie?"

Julie turned to see Damon standing to the side, his eyes also mirroring his concern. It was damn nice to have friends. Good friends. People who dropped things at a moment's notice when one of their friends were in need.

Damn it, she wasn't going to get all weepy again. Must be the freaking medication.

"I'd love some water," she said around her scratchy throat.

Damon pulled one of the paper cups from a canister by the sink and poured it half full with water. He went around to the opposite side of where Serena sat and carefully slid his free hand underneath Julie.

"Let me help you. Don't try to do too much at once," he murmured.

Grateful for his strength, she leaned forward and sipped hungrily at the water. When she was done, he eased her back down.

"Better?"

"A lot. Thank you so much."

He smiled at her. "No problem, Julie. Serena and I came as soon as Nathan called us."

Her forehead crinkled. "Where is Nathan, anyway?"

"Pop and Connor brought his truck, and he went down to grab something to eat with them."

She frowned. "Have I been out that long?"

Serena smiled and squeezed her hand. "Yep, several hours. Doc was by, said you were doing just fine and you could go home when you came around as long as you were feeling up to it. Scans came back okay."

"Oh, that's nice. Bed." She sighed at the thought of curling up with a soft pillow.

"You're coming home with me and Damon," Serena said firmly.

"I am?"

"You are," Damon said with a smile. "Or so Serena assures me. She's informed me you have no choice in the matter, and truly, we have plenty of room. My staff will fuss over you and spoil you endlessly. Think of it as a holiday."

"I hope you weren't trying to talk me out of it with that speech," Julie said with a tired grin. "Sounds far too marvelous to pass up."

The nurse sailed in, a middle aged doctor on her heels. "Oh good, you're awake. Have a nice nap?"

Julie smiled crookedly. "That was some good shit you gave me. I could have slept through a hurricane."

"You ready to get out of here, Miss Stanford?" the doctor asked in a distracted voice as he scribbled on his clipboard.

"Yes, sir."

"Your tests all came back fine. You'll have some swelling and residual stiffness tomorrow. Bruising too, so don't let that alarm you. I've prescribed muscle relaxers and pain relievers. A few hot baths probably wouldn't hurt, and you can ice the shoulder afterward if it bothers you too much. Follow up with your family doctor in a few days, and if you have any nausea, dizziness or sudden pain, come back to the emergency room immediately."

Julie smiled and reached for the scrips. "Thanks, doc. I appreciate it."

He smiled back and patted her arm. "Take care and stay out of traffic awhile, eh?"

"So that's it?" Julie asked when the doctor stepped out. "I can leave now?"

"Yep," the nurse said. "I need to finish writing your discharge papers. If you want to get dressed, I'll be back in just a minute to give you your copies and you can be on your way."

Julie looked down at her hospital gown. "Oh boy," she murmured.

Serena reached down and picked up a duffel bag from the floor. She held it with one finger and grinned at Julie.

Julie's shoulders sagged in relief. "What would I do without you?"

"Die a fiery death, no doubt," Serena murmured.

Julie shook her head at Damon. "She has such an ego."

Damon grinned. "I'm afraid I'm not very good at tamping down that ego of hers. I encourage it way too much."

"Oooh, Serena!" Julie latched on to her friend's hand and tugged it upward into better light. A huge diamond solitaire sparkled on her ring finger. "It's gorgeous!"

Serena beamed almost as bright as the diamond. "I know. Damon has such wonderful taste."

"Of course he does. He chose you," Julie said loyally.

"You'll get no arguments there," Damon said.

"Not that I don't love you, Damon, but if you don't mind, could you step out so I don't flash you when I crawl out of bed to get dressed?"

Damon grinned. "Not that it wouldn't be worth it to stay, but I'll slide on out and leave you girls to it. Are you sure you don't need any help? I don't want you to fall."

"Serena can help me, and if I fall flat on my face, all I ask is that someone cover my bare ass before you call for the orderlies."

Damon chuckled as he walked to the door. "I'll be sure and do that. I'll be back in a bit. I'll get the car pulled around, and I have a few phone calls to make."

"You sure you're up for this?" Serena asked doubtfully.

"You know you could always spend the night in the hospital just in case."

"They just kicked me out, Serena," Julie said with a laugh. "This isn't like a hotel. You don't get to stay unless they tell you to. Besides, hello? Going to your house. That's better than a resort. All that's missing are the really cute cabana boys. Think Damon could hook me up?"

"Damon's done enough hooking up for a while," Serena said dryly.

Julie's smiled faded. "Oh yeah, Nathan's here. I should wait until he gets back. He was so sweet to me after the accident. I don't want to go while he's eating."

"Of course not. Just take your time getting dressed. Here, let me help you."

With Serena's assistance, she struggled out of bed and when her feet hit the floor, she wobbled and weaved like a drunken bobblehead.

"Damn, either I'm still riding the effects of those drugs or my head got hit harder than I thought."

"Just take it slow. Stand here a minute and take some deep breaths. When you feel steadier we'll get your pants and shirt on."

Julie giggled. "Yeah, screw the underwear. Can you imagine? Me on the floor like an octopus falling out of a tree wrapped up in my panties. They'd be talking about me for a week."

Between the two of them, they managed to get Julie's pants and shirt on minus bra as well. Julie looked down and giggled at her breasts straining against the material.

"Let me guess. One of your shirts?"

Serena flushed. "Yeah, well, it was lucky I had a pair of your jeans at the house. I wasn't so lucky with the shirts."

"Should have gotten me one of Damon's, dork."

"I didn't think. Besides, I wish I looked that good in my own shirts."

The door opened as Julie was buttoning the fly on her jeans. Both women turned around to see Nathan standing in the door.

"Ah, gee sorry, ladies. I should have knocked."

Serena smiled. "No problem, she's decent."

Nathan frowned as he took in the fully dressed Julie. "What the hell are you doing out of bed? Why are you dressed? You should be lying down."

Julie grinned. "I'm getting out of here. Doc just discharged me."

Nathan took a step toward her, his mouth pursed as if he was working up the nerve to say something.

"You shouldn't be going home alone. I—"

"Oh, she's not," Serena piped up. "Damon and I are taking her home with us."

Nathan's face fell. "Oh, I mean, well, that's good. You should have people to look after you," he said gruffly.

Julie took a step toward him and grasped his arm for support. Then she leaned up on tiptoe and kissed him on the cheek.

"Thank you, Nathan," she said softly. "For looking out for me. For staying with me when I was scared out of my mind."

His eyes gleamed and his gaze strayed to her lips. She could feel that small cut there tingling, remembering how it felt when he'd pressed his lips to that tiny wound.

"You're welcome. Take care, okay?"

He brushed the hair from her cheek and leaned in like he was going to kiss her. Instead he rocked back on his heels and took a step back.

"Seems like you guys have it handled, so I'll get on out of here." He looked at Julie once more before turning toward the door. "See you," he said softly.

"Yeah, see you," she echoed.

He walked quietly out the door and let it swing shut behind him.

Chapter 26

"When the hell is Faith getting here?" Julie asked grumpily from her sprawled out position on Serena's couch.

Serena rolled her eyes from her position in the armchair catty-corner to the couch. "They're newlyweds plus they're moving into their new house. Which means they take a load, fuck on the living room floor, move another load, fuck on the bedroom floor, move another load, fuck on the kitchen table. Very exhausting thing, moving!"

Julie burst out laughing. "Oh man, we're going to have to carry her ass tonight."

"She'll be a cheap drunk at least."

"My favorite."

"Would you ladies care for another glass of wine?" Sam asked from the living room entrance.

Since Damon had been banned from the night's activities,

he'd taken it upon himself to hang out at The House and make sure things were running smoothly. Sam, on the other hand, had decided that he would at least see the women off. He was still miffed because Serena wouldn't allow him to drive them around.

But hey, girls' night out was sacred, and that meant nothing with a penis was going to be within ten feet.

"I'd love one," Julie called out. "Come on, Serena, we're getting a cab. Drink up!"

Serena smiled when Sam's glower got all the more disapproving. Julie mentally started counting. She got to three before Sam spoke up.

"I do wish you'd let me drive you where you're going tonight, particularly since there is alcohol involved. Does Mr. Roche know about the drinking?"

Serena rolled her eyes. "Julie's going. He knows."

"Hey! What the hell is that supposed to mean? I'm not the only lush in this group."

Serena snickered. "We'll take that wine, Sam. Better bring us the bottle. We're going to need a head start on Faith."

Just then Faith burst into the living room, out of breath, but looking like a million bucks as usual.

"I hate her," Julie drawled, looking at Serena and ignoring Faith.

"So do I."

"What? I'm only five minutes late," Faith said. "And you two started without me. Ungrateful whores."

"Meow. Marriage has made her feisty," Serena said with a raised eyebrow.

Faith plopped down on the couch next to Julie, concern shadowing her eyes. "Are you sure you should be doing this tonight? Are you feeling okay?"

Julie laughed. "I'm fine, Faith. Promise. I've been a lazy ass for four days, my every whim and desire catered to. Well, almost. Damon refused the cabana boys. My head is fine, my shoulder is great, so I'm ready to go cloud the brain with some alcohol. Besides, we have a lot to celebrate!"

Faith smiled and turned to include Serena in the warm gesture. "Yes, we do. Gray and I are married, Serena is getting married and Julie is alive. It's been a good week!"

"I say we get shit-faced for the occasion," Julie said.

"After you, ladies. Sam grudgingly informed me that the cab has been waiting for the last half hour, and he is at our beck and call the entire evening thanks to Damon's cash and Sam's threats not to leave us even for a second."

"You know I love this house," Faith said as she hauled Julie to her feet. "You can just smell the testosterone as soon as you walk in."

"Money and testosterone," Julie corrected. "I'm strongly considering offing Serena and stuffing her into the trunk of the cab. Think Damon would notice if I showed up in his bed with a black wig?"

Faith studied her for a moment. "Hmm, the loss of five inches might tip him off."

"Not to mention the abundance of cleavage," Serena said dryly. "Although he might not complain about that part."

The girls giggled and headed toward the door where Sam stood solemnly, his expression disapproving.

"May I tell Mr. Roche what time you plan to return?"

Julie snickered.

With a perfectly straight face, Serena said, "Well, you could, Sam, but I have no idea when that might be. You may tell Mr. Roche that I'll see him when I see him."

They stumbled out of the house laughing as they headed toward the cab parked inside the circle drive.

"Where're we going anyway?" Faith asked when they piled into the cab.

Julie looked at them sheepishly.

"You seriously aren't taking us to Cattleman's for girls' night out," Serena said.

"I mean, I like Cattleman's," Faith was quick to say, "but this is a special night. We're back together again."

Julie laughed. "Faith, you dork, we were only apart for less than a week."

"So?" she said with a sniff. "I missed you guys."

"The hell you did," Serena snorted. "If I know Gray he had you six ways to Sunday and a few into Monday as well."

Faith blushed but her grin lit up the entire cab.

"Okay, so I know you guys aren't thrilled with Cattleman's, but I arranged our own little private drinking area, complete with . . . drumroll, please . . . our own private bartender. And he's hot, if I do say so myself."

"Oooh, Cattleman's is looking up," Serena said.

Faith wrinkled her nose. "Since I'm newly married and all, aren't I supposed to be struck blind for at least six months? I'm not supposed to notice hot guys, right?"

"Honey, as long as you go home to your even hotter man, a little window-shopping is not verboten," Julie said.

"Hmm, window-shopping. I like that," Faith said.

Half an hour later, they landed at Cattleman's and entered the pub, cutting past several people waiting to be seated to eat. Julie caught Carl's eye and waved. He smiled and motioned her back.

"Come on, girls," Julie said grabbing their hands.

Seconds later, escorted by Carl, they were given a table in a cordoned off section of the bar. The rounded back corner was theirs and a bartender leaned saucily against the wall.

"Ladies," he greeted. "My name is Drew, and I'm yours for the evening."

"Oh, Julie, good call," Serena murmured.

"Somebody remind me I'm married," Faith squeaked.

"Place your orders," Drew said. "I'm ready to pour."

Fours hour later, the crowd had filtered out, the drinks had slowed and Julie, Serena and Faith were on the floor, their heads touching as they stared up at the ceiling.

"Who knew there were stars up here, or that they glowed in the dark," Faith said in a low whisper.

"Pretty," Serena agreed.

Julie was still trying to get her tongue to work. A face appeared above her head, a grinning face.

"Ready to call it a night?" Drew asked.

"Hell no," Julie muttered. Easy enough to find her tongue when it counted. "I want one more. Just slide the straw down here so I don't have to get up."

He chuckled. "Sorry. I'm going to have to cut you off. It's last call."

"Damn."

"Think Carl will mind if we just camp out here tonight?" Serena asked. "I've lost the feeling in my legs."

"I'm not moving," Faith said. "If I do, I'll probably puke."

"So, we stay," Julie said with a nod.

She held up her hand, giggling when it waved precariously. Serena and Faith held theirs up, and it took three attempts, but they finally managed to high-five.

Julie let her hand fall to the floor with a thump. "Damn it's good to hang out with you guys again. We need to make a solemn vow with you two heifers tying the knot that we don't give this up and become boring housewives."

"Bite your tongue," Serena muttered. "Damon may have me manacled, but he doesn't have me on a leash."

"Yet." Faith snickered.

Julie turned to check out the shiny arm cuff on Serena's upper arm. It looked so exotic on her, and she'd wondered more than once what its significance was. She had a matching one above her ankle. It looked so slave-girlish.

"So is that what he gave you in lieu of a collar?" Julie asked seriously.

Serena stilled and touched the outline of the gold. "Yeah," she said quietly. "It's his mark of ownership."

"Damn, that's hot," Faith said wistfully. "Gray's not into the embellishments and trinkets of the so-called lifestyle. I'd wear something like that though. It's incredibly sexy."

"So collar yourself," Julie said. "Surprise him one night and show up naked save for your owner collar or whatever the hell you call it."

"Your snideness is showing again," Serena snickered.

"No," Julie said. "I'm not snide at all. I think what you guys have is cool. It's not for me, but anyone with eyeballs can see how much Gray and Damon love and worship you two. If Faith thinks it's hot, then go for it. Get a leash while you're at it. I can think of all sorts of naughty things you could do with a leash," she added with a grin.

"Uhm, I guess I'm too drunk or I lack imagination, but now I'm dying to hear these deviant ideas you have about leashes."

Julie snorted. "Come on, Faith. You're the resident wild child. If you can't figure that one out, you need to go watch some porn or something."

"I once raided Micah's stash," she admitted. "He has some, er, uhm, interesting stuff."

Both Serena and Julie raised their heads, or at least they tried. Julie's landed back with a thump, and she groaned.

"We're dying of curiosity here, Faith. Spill," Serena said.

"Lots of bondage stuff. Darker than I would have thought. Kinda scary, but it made me shivery at the same time," Faith said.

"Oh? Well, I kinda figured him for the bondage type. He's all brooding, and he seems to like submissive women," Julie said.

"Uh-huh," Serena said.

"There was something in that agreement," Faith needled.

Serena laughed. "I've felt the sting of Micah's lash," she said ruefully.

"Damon allowed this?" Julie asked.

"Oh yes," she sighed. She went silent, and Julie didn't pry for more.

"So what else?" Julie prompted Faith. She was curious as to Micah's proclivities now that she knew he'd fucked her along with Nathan.

"Dark stuff."

"You already said that," Serena said patiently. "What kind of dark stuff."

"Spankings, but not the light, fluffy kind. Pain, the edgy kind that crosses the line of pleasure. Hot wax. And when I say submission, I mean complete and utter submission. It's hard to explain. Had this dungeon feel to it. He seems to like threesomes too, but then I guess we all know that," she added with a laugh.

"What do you suppose his story is?" Julie murmured. "A man like that has all sorts of juicy secrets, I'm willing to bet."

"Dunno," Faith said. "In some ways he's an open book. In others he's so tight-lipped. For instance, he takes off the same time every single year. No one knows where he goes or what he does. He gets moody leading up to it and then he disappears. When he returns he's back to his old self."

"Oh you're right, that does sound juicy," Serena said. "We're women, which means we're nosy. Now I'm dying to know where he goes."

Julie laughed. "Ask him."

"No thanks. Like I said, I've felt the sting of his lash. I don't think I'd ever want to piss him off. I know he's usually so easygoing, but I don't think I'd want to see him truly angry."

"Oooh, the stars are spinning now," Faith said.

Serena snorted. "That's your head, dumbass."

"Preeettty," Faith said with a giggle.

"You lightweight," Julie said in disgust.

"Who's going to volunteer to get up first?" Serena asked.

"Not me," Faith said.

"Or me," Julie added.

"So we just lie here. Works for me," Serena said.

"What on earth are you girls doing on the floor?"

Julie's eye cracked open at the amused husky tone she'd spent the better part of the last three nights fantasizing about.

"Nathan?"

CHAPTER 27

Nathan looked down at the three women sprawled on the floor and tried like hell to suppress his grin.

He squatted down next to Julie. "I'm surprised you recognize me."

"There can't be that many gorgeous bald-headed guys running around Cattleman's, can there?"

He lost the battle with his twitching mouth and chuckled. "Had a little too much to drink?"

"Hi, Nathan," Faith said, holding her fingers up and waggling them.

"Hey, sweetness, is Serena conscious over there?"

Serena let out a sound that he couldn't quite decipher. It didn't exactly sound human.

He turned his attention back to Julie. "So how were you girls planning to get home anyway?"

"Cab."

"Ah. Well, I have a better idea."

He pulled out his cell phone, still chuckling. He got up and moved a few feet away as he punched in Gray's number.

"You're out late," Gray said as he answered the phone.

"So is your wife."

"Yeah, girls' night out. How did you know?"

"Well, I'm staring at her, Julie and Serena lying flat on the floor of Cattleman's," Nathan said with a chuckle.

"What? What the hell?"

"Relax, man, she's fine. They're drunk as skunks and having a good time as far as I can tell. They said they were catching a cab back to Damon's, but I didn't feel comfortable letting them pour themselves into a cab as drunk as they are. Thought you might want to come get Faith."

"Damn right. Thanks, man. Last thing I want is some joker to see three easy marks. What the hell was Damon thinking? I thought he was at least sending his mountain of a driver slash security guard."

"I'll let you call him to collect Serena."

"What about Julie?"

"I'll take care of Julie," Nathan said softly. He'd been waiting for his chance to pin down the little escape artist.

"Do you mind hanging out until I get there?" Gray asked.

"Of course not. I'm not going anywhere. I'll hang out, keep an eye on them until you and Damon show."

"I'll be right over."

Nathan hung up and walked back over to where the girls hadn't moved.

"You ratted us out, didn't you?" Serena said accusingly.

He winced as he squatted back down to their level. "Sorry,

sweetheart, but I did just that. Guy's code and all that. When your girl's in trouble, you expect your buddy to call. Just looking out for three very special women. I don't want y'all climbing into a strange cab or have some stranger take advantage of you."

"Aw, that's sweet," Faith slurred.

"Yeah, kinda hard to be mad when he says shit like that," Julie mumbled.

He tweaked Julie softly on the nose. "You three sure are cute when you throw a drunk. But next time do it at home. If you don't want the guys around, banish them for the evening."

"Yes, big brother," Serena snorted.

"You, I'll let get away with that crack," he said. "*You*, however, better not ever even think of me in that capacity," he said to Julie as he touched her cheek.

She grinned. "I think we've already established that there is nothing fraternal about our relationship."

Nathan hid his triumph. At least they were getting somewhere. She might be drunk, but at least she'd acknowledged something was going on between them.

"So, uhm, who's coming to get us?" Faith piped up.

"That would be me, the husband," Gray said from behind Nathan.

Nathan stood up to see Gray standing with his hands shoved into his pockets, a wide grin across his face.

"You didn't use to be that big, did you?" Faith squeaked as she looked up at her husband.

He squatted down as Nathan had done and smiled at her. "Better?"

Faith scrunched up her nose. "Are you here to take me home?

I can't be the first to go home. Would be embarrassing. Like I'm an old married lady or something."

Gray chuckled. "But you're my old married lady, and I'd like to have my old married lady in bed with me. It's sorta lonely without you."

Nathan watched in amusement as Faith melted into a gooey puddle on the floor.

"Oh, that's nice," Serena sighed.

"Want help up?" Gray asked as he ran a hand over Faith's shoulder.

"I'm worried," she muttered.

"About what, baby?"

"If I become upright, I might puke."

Nathan chuckled and Gray's shoulders shook.

"Tell you what. I'll lift and get you back onto the bar stool." He glanced up at the bartender who waved a large plastic basin from behind the bar. "If you need to puke, there's a nice big puke bowl on the bar."

"Ugh," Faith moaned. "Like I want to puke in front of everyone?"

"Oh shut up, Faith," Julie muttered. "Like you haven't held my hair up enough times."

"Up you go," Gray said as he pulled Faith to a sitting position.

He let her sit there for a moment as he brushed her hair from her face. "Okay so far?"

She nodded and he helped her to her feet. She weaved precariously on her way to the stool, but Gray kept a firm grip on her arm.

She sank onto the stool with a sigh. Then she stared at the bartender. "Hey, I know you. You're Drew." Then she glanced around the empty bar with a bewildered expression on her face. "Where is everyone?"

"Baby, it's three in the morning. They're all home, which is where you should be."

"Three?" Serena squeaked. "Sam is going to kill me."

"Sam and not Damon?" Julie asked.

"Sam is a little protective. He's already mad because I wouldn't let him drive us around."

Ah, so that solved the mystery of why they had taken a cab. Nathan shook his head. What the hell had they been thinking?

"And you should have let him," Nathan said. "Three young women alone, three young *drunk* women alone, is never a good idea."

"I need to go to the bathroom," Julie announced.

"Uh-oh, you need to puke?" Nathan asked in alarm.

"No, pee."

His cheeks warmed but he reached down to help her up all the same. Damn she felt good, all limber and cuddly against him. Like a kitten after a full bowl of milk. Hell, all she had to do was stretch and purr.

She made it one step in the direction of the bathroom and listed heavily to the right.

"Oops!" Then she turned an accusing eye to Drew who was wiping down the counters. "What was in that last drink?"

Drew's mouth twitched. "Straight juice, doll. Orange juice."

Well, at least the bartender had the sense to know they'd had enough. Nathan shot him a look of gratitude before tucking Julie solidly under his arm.

"Come on, honey, I'm taking you to the bathroom."

He walked her to the ladies' room and went inside with her.

Not like they'd have to worry about running into anyone since Carl had closed the bar an hour ago.

He pushed open a stall for her. "Can you make it from here?"

"Uh, yeah."

She wobbled into the stall and shut it behind her. She fumbled with the latch for a few moments, and he stepped back to wait.

There was a long silence and then, "Nathan?"

"Yeah?"

"Turn the faucet on please."

"Huh?"

"Turn the faucet on. I don't want you to hear me pee."

Holding his laughter in, he shook his head and went over to turn the water on. Then, to make her feel better, he hit the button so the blower on the hand dryer came on.

It had just quit when the stall door opened again and she stepped out. He waited while she washed her hands, and then once again he tucked her under his arm and headed back. She seemed to have regained her bearings, but he liked holding her. Any excuse to touch her, he was going to take full advantage of.

When they got back to the others, Damon had arrived and had Serena on a bar stool, stroking her silky black hair. To most men, seeing the utter domestication of a friend might instill panic, or even disgust. For Nathan, watching the two men with their women filled him with an odd longing.

He'd never been opposed to love and commitment; he just hadn't ever found a woman that made him start thinking about it. Now when he looked at the two couples, the way they communicated silently with just a touch or a look, it made him feel almost lonely.

He looked down at Julie, and his grip tightened around her

waist. If he could ever get her to stay still and in one place long enough, he'd show her just what it was he wanted from her.

His brow furrowed just a bit at the last. What did he want from her? From the beginning it hadn't just been about sex, though Lord knows he'd lusted after her to the point of insanity. He was perplexed by his reaction to her. She befuddled him. Kept him solidly off balance.

Was this how other guys felt when they met their woman?

"You have to go first, Serena," Faith said with a wave of her hand.

"Ah yes, so you don't look like an old married lady," Serena said dryly.

"Come on, Serena mine," Damon said with a chuckle. "Sam is beside himself with worry."

She looked at Damon then looked doubtfully at the floor. "Has the floor moved?"

Damon reached for her, pulling her down into his arms. He kissed the top of her head before tucking his arm around her waist. "Come on, love."

"G'night," Serena called with a backward wave of her hand.

Gray turned to Faith. "*Now* can we go?"

Julie frowned. "Would someone call the cab for me?"

Nathan scowled. Did she really think he was going to leave her here alone? "I'm not calling you a damn cab. I'm taking you home."

"Oh."

Content that she didn't offer any argument, he turned her toward the door and waved at Carl with a mouthed "thank you." Carl grinned and offered a two-finger salute as he threw a towel over his shoulder.

Nathan opened the passenger door of his truck and hoisted her Julie into the seat. When she just sat there, he pulled the seat belt and reached over to buckle it for her.

"How do you do that?" she asked in bewildered tone.

"Do what, honey?"

"Pick me up like that. Like I don't weigh any more than a child."

He chuckled. "A little five foot nothing like you? Piece of cake."

She turned and locked gazes with him, her eyes shining a little brighter. "You honestly don't notice those extra pounds I'm carrying, do you? I love that about you."

Nathan was reminded of the conversation he'd had with Connor in the truck before Julie's accident. The idea that she was somehow not perfect baffled him.

He leaned in until their mouths were just an inch apart. "What I notice is that you're an incredibly sexy, mouthwateringly beautiful woman. In a word, you're fucking perfect."

She blinked as he drew away, her lips slightly parted as she stared at him with a dazed expression. "Wow."

He closed the door and walked around to the driver's side. The ride was quiet, and he periodically looked over to make sure she hadn't passed out, but she seemed wide-awake, her gaze focused out the windshield.

A while later, he pulled into her apartment complex. As he went around to get her out, he experienced a wave of déjà vu. Unlike the last time he'd brought her home, this time he wasn't leaving. She'd obviously been left with the idea that he wasn't that interested, and he'd be damned if they went through all that again.

Wanting to impress her again, he swept her into his arms and carried her to the door. She sighed a happy little sound and laid her head on his shoulder.

"Where are your keys, honey?"

"Pocket," she mumbled.

He allowed her to slide down his body until her feet hit the ground and then he reached into her jeans pocket to pull out the keys.

A few minutes later they were inside, keys placed on her kitchen table. Nathan carried her to her bedroom.

The first time he'd brought her home, he'd undressed her as quickly as possible, feeling like a guilty voyeur the entire time. This time he was going to savor every moment.

"Nathan?"

They stood at the foot of her bed, and she looked up at him, her expression so trusting.

"Yes, honey?"

"You're about to see me naked, aren't you."

"Uh-huh."

"Do I get to see you naked?"

He chuckled. "You've already seen me naked, you little tease."

"You look good naked," she said with a sigh.

"So do you," he said huskily.

He reached for her shirt, pulling it over her head. She raised her arms in cooperation. Every part of his body started humming when the pink lacy bra came into view. Her breasts were thrust forward and straining against the cups, the darker peach of the aureoles playing an erotic game of peekaboo.

He was so going to hell for lusting over a drunk woman, but at the moment he couldn't see a downside in that.

When the shirt fell to the floor, he reached for the button of her jeans, loving the feel of her soft belly against his knuckles. He popped the fly and peeled the denim over her hips only to find the thinnest, silkiest pair of underwear that exactly matched the frothy confection that was her bra.

As he worked his hands over her ass to push the pants farther down, he discovered that the panties were a thong.

Ah hell. He closed his eyes and shook his head, sure that instead of hell, he'd be assured sainthood if he survived this without throwing her on the bed and burying himself inside her.

Deciding there was no way he'd be able to make it if she slept naked beside him the entire night, he acted quickly and stripped off his T-shirt. He dropped it over her head and pulled her arms through the holes, satisfied when it fell below her hips. There. Almost completely covered.

He kicked off his shoes and hastily stripped down to his underwear, ignoring the way his damn dick was about to bust a hole in the material.

"Come on, honey, let's get you into bed."

She docilely let him lead her around the side of the bed and urge her onto the mattress. She crawled under the covers and laid her head on the pillow, closing her eyes immediately.

Well hell, he thought ruefully. Passed out already. But when he climbed in beside her, gingerly easing the covers over his body, she turned into him, curling up like a contented kitten seeking warmth.

A massive wave of satisfaction rocked him. This . . . this was nice. Julie in his arms, sweet and warm, her soft breaths easing over his neck.

Careful not to disturb her, he wrapped on arm around her waist, pulling her in closer. He gently maneuvered his other arm underneath her neck so that she was cradled against his shoulder.

"Good night, Julie," he whispered against her ear.

She responded by snuggling a little closer and inserting her leg between his. Content to wrap himself completely around her, he slid his leg over her hip so that there wasn't a part of her not touching him.

He blew one silky strand of hair from his mouth and then kissed the area right above her ear.

Yeah, this was nice.

Chapter 28

Angelina Moyano watched from a distance as Micah stood over the two headstones in the small graveyard. She peeked from behind a large oak tree, her small hands gripping the rough bark. It was always like this. At dawn he'd come to honor their memories. Just as he did every year.

The sun's rays were barely peeking over the horizon, but the Florida humidity was already thick and heavy, each breath a struggle in the cloying heat. She chanced a look over her shoulder, damning her paranoia that she'd been followed, but she couldn't afford to take chances. Seeing nothing, she turned her attention back to Micah.

He knelt at Hannah's grave and carefully laid a single yellow rose, her favorite, just below the marble slab that marked her death. He kissed his thumb and ridge of his forefinger then laid his hand over the flat ground.

Angelina sucked in her breath. It was different this year.

Before he'd always stood there looking so haunted, his eyes filled with grief and regret. This year . . . this year he seemed to be saying good-bye.

Her eyes filled with tears when he turned to David's grave and drew a simple rosary from his pocket. He kissed the beads and then laid them at her brother's headstone.

Sadness knotted her throat. She missed them too. She missed Micah, but he was as lost to her as David and Hannah. Maybe now he was ready. Ready to let go. He had grieved long enough. *She* had grieved long enough.

He rose, shoving his hands into his pockets. For a long moment he simply stood there as the early morning light grew a little brighter.

Warmth flooded the little place where Micah stood, and Angelina took it as a sign that it was time.

"I love you," she whispered, letting the wind carry her words away.

When he finally turned and walked back toward his truck, she waited only long enough so that she wouldn't be seen before she darted back to her car. She would have to hurry if she was going to get to Twilight before he did.

It was where he always went after he paid his homage to his former wife and to David, his best friend. Only Angelina understood the need that drove him. Only she understood his pain, knew his private demons. She would help him because she could do nothing else. She'd loved him far too long. Maybe now he could finally love her in return.

She took the shortest route to the club and whipped into the back parking lot ten minutes later. Though it operated twenty-four hours a day, at this time of the morning it was usually empty, and she knew that was one of the reasons Micah always chose this time to come.

Grabbing her bag, she hurried inside the employee entrance and checked with Rose who manned the front door.

"I'm here, Rose. Just give me a minute to change. If he gets here, put him in room one."

"Hey, baby. I see him walking up now, so scoot on back so he doesn't see you."

"Thanks, Mama Rose." She blew a kiss to the older woman and ran for the dressing room.

She didn't go for garish dress-up. No leather, no high-heeled boots. No, save the mask that protected her identity, she went with black jeans and a long-sleeved black shirt. Her long, dark hair was drawn into a braid and tucked down her shirt. She was as nondescript as they came.

The last item was the leather mask that covered her from the neck up. Only her eyes were visible, and they blended with the dark leather, dark, almost black.

David would have killed her if he were alive. He and Hannah would both be horrified that David's little sister was for all practical purposes a surrogate daughter to a woman who owned one of Miami's most successful bondage clubs.

Micah would look at her with those dark eyes and ask her what the hell a little girl like her was doing in a place like this.

And it was all because of him.

A soft knock at her door had her whirling around as Mama Rose stuck her head in.

"He's ready for you."

Angelina nodded and walked out the door and down the hall to one of the flogging rooms. When she entered, she sucked in her breath so hard her chest hurt.

Her reaction to him never dimmed. The sight of such a powerful, proud man standing in the middle of the room, bared to the waist, his hands high above him, tied to a spreader. He was utterly magnificent.

On another man, his pose might seem submissive. Weak. Only she knew better. Underneath the seemingly calm surface was a man who seethed with emotion. Dark and boiling. And she would call it to the surface.

His head rose when he heard her footsteps. There was a vulnerability to his eyes she hadn't seen in the past. Like the emotion bubbled that much closer to the surface. Before he'd buried it, only releasing it with his pain.

Not everyone would understand his needs. But she did. Oh how she did. She would set him free. She would give him what he needed.

"I need . . . Don't go easy," he said in a low voice.

She nodded her acceptance of his request. She alone understood his need for this kind of pain. They were more alike than he would ever know.

She uncoiled the whip and let the end fall to the floor as she circled behind him. Such beauty. His back was broad, his waist lean and narrow. The muscles coiled and bunched between his shoulder blades as he readied himself for her strike.

How long she had practiced, relentlessly perfecting her method, so she would never disappoint him. He was safe in her hands.

The first lash landed against his skin with a deafening crack.

He jerked but quickly righted himself and went still, waiting the next. She flicked her wrist again, exerting just the right amount of force, and placed an identical stripe across from the first.

She forced herself to relax, to not allow the welling emotion to bubble up. Calmly and methodically she kissed his back with the lash, watching as he jumped and bowed under the whip.

Sweat glistened on his back, dampened his hair until it fell in limp curls past his neck. Still she continued, sensing he needed more. She striped one side then the other, working a path down to his waist.

As she worked her way back up, blood beaded and shone in the low light. Finally. Release. Lightly, like a lover's kiss, she whispered the whip across his shoulders until they were slick with blood.

It was like making a cut in a festering wound. The relief was profound as pressure—and pain—escaped the seething cauldron. His hands clenched in their bonds, his wrists flexing as he raised his head, looking upward as if he was seeking redemption.

With every stroke, she lavished him with her love. It was bizarre to someone who didn't understand. An unacceptable outlet for many. But this was his way. She accepted it as she did him.

A heavy sigh escaped him, the only sound he made the entire time. His shoulders drooped and she knew it was enough. She let the whip fall and walked around to face him.

His eyes were closed, but his cheeks were streaked with tears. Her own eyes clouded with moisture. He'd never cried for them. Not at the funeral. Not at the graves. Not afterward when he'd driven her home. And then he'd simply disappeared, dealing with his grief as he did everything else. Alone.

She ached to hold him, to tell him it was all right, that Hannah and David loved him too. That *she* loved him. That he didn't have to be alone any longer.

Instead she stepped forward and cupped his face lovingly in her hands. She pressed a kiss to his forehead and whispered in a husky voice he'd never recognize, "*Vaya en paz.*"

Go in peace.

He looked up at her as she stepped away with glazed, unfocused eyes. Another tear slipped down his cheek, marking a raw trail on his face.

"Thank you," he said in a husky voice.

She simply nodded, knowing that even if she dared, she wouldn't have been able to speak around the knot in her throat. She kissed the shaft of the whip and laid it carefully at his feet.

She left the room on shaky legs, knowing Mama Rose waited to free Micah and to attend to him in whatever way necessary. She also knew he'd refuse the older woman's attentions and would be gone within minutes.

She shed her mask, for the last time. It was all she could do not to run back down the hall and throw her arms around him, beg him to take her with him. Letting him go instilled her with a fierce ache. Because this time he wouldn't be back. With that realization, she knew that it was now or never for her. She'd given Micah the time he needed to heal. Now it was up to her to go after him. Show him it was okay to love again.

He might not be coming back to Miami, but there was nothing to stop her from going to Houston. She had to go. She couldn't stay here. It wasn't safe, and Micah was all she had to run to.

Chapter 29

Julie awoke to the smell of warm, masculine goodness. She inhaled without opening her eyes, because if it was a dream, she wanted to make it last a little longer.

Spicy. Yum. Just yum.

She finally cracked open one eye and collided with the hard wall of a sculpted chest. She knew that chest.

Shifting just enough that she could crane her neck, she looked up to see the chiseled outline of Nathan's jaw, roughened slightly with an overnight beard. Mmmm, she'd love to run her tongue over it.

His right arm was thrown carelessly over his head while the other was tucked firmly around her, his fingers splayed over her ass. The innate possession in his touch sent a decadent thrill up her spine, rebounding and arcing through her body. Her entire ass tingled, and she shifted restlessly to alleviate the burn.

Inspiration struck her right between the eyes, and she sucked in her breath as she weighed the possibilities. He presented her the perfect opportunity. Just perfect. If she could just get out of bed without waking him, she could retrieve the handcuffs that Faith had given her from her dresser drawer.

Then Nathan would be all hers.

She was tempted to rub over him like a cat, but she could always do that later. After he was at her mercy.

Barely containing her gleeful smile, she began the slow, agonizing task of slipping away. After every movement, no matter how slight, she studied him for any sign that he was waking. He never even stirred.

When finally she slid out of bed, she hurried over to get the handcuffs, fumbling with the clasps in her haste.

On his side of the bed, she studied how best to accomplish her goal. Ideally she'd like both hands cuffed to the iron headboard. One would be easy, and if she could get the right wrist secured without waking him, then she could possibly get the left one done as well.

Bottom lip between her teeth, she stealthily moved in, securing the cuffs to the headboard first and then carefully easing the bracelet around Nathan's wrist. When it went together with a slight snick, she held her breath, waiting for him to awaken.

Mentally doing a fist pump, she hurried around to the other side. Now here she would have to forgo stealth and make a mad grab for his wrist. Again she attached the other set of cuffs to the headboard, her eyes darting back and forth between his hand and the cuffs.

Well hell. No guts, no glory, and no one could ever accuse her of being gutless.

Holding her hand an inch above his wrist, she sucked in her

breath and struck. She grabbed his wrist, hauled it upward and, about the time his eyes fluttered open, she snapped the cuff shut around his wrist.

Victory!

"What the fucking hell?"

He looked blearily at her and then at his wrist and then back at her again. When he tried to move his right arm, the cuffs clinked against the headboard and he yanked his head around in surprise.

"Julie, what the hell are you doing? Have you lost your mind? Let me out."

She slid to her knees on the bed, far enough away that he couldn't pin her with his legs, and smiled at him in satisfaction.

"Oh no, Nathan," she said softly. "I've got you just where I want you."

He lifted one eyebrow. "And what do you intend to do with me?"

He didn't look overly alarmed, just confused and a little annoyed. She didn't think he'd be annoyed for long though.

With a saucy smile, she backed off the bed and stood at the end, her gaze never leaving him. The covers were bunched at his hips, but his dick was straining at his underwear in a very noticeable ridge.

She gripped the hem of the T-shirt and looked down, realizing it wasn't hers. Nathan must have given his to her. Slowly she raised it, pulling it over her head and then tossing it aside.

Nathan's breath sucked inward in an audible whoosh. Clad in only her panties, she sauntered toward the bed, gratified to see that ridge between his legs getting a lot larger.

She hooked her thumbs under the thin straps of her thong

and eased it downward, watching as Nathan's gaze tracked the progress all the way to her ankles. Then he returned to her pussy, his eyes flickering with lust. And need.

She reached for the covers and yanked them away until they gathered at the very end of the bed, nearly falling away from the mattress. She reached and smoothed her hand up his hair-roughened leg. Thick, muscular and so very warm.

She hoisted herself onto the bed, straddling his legs. The muscles jumped and trembled against her thighs, telling her without words just how much he wanted her. It was hard not to get a thrill out of knowing a man like Nathan was out of his skin with desire. For her.

Leaning forward like a wanton on the make, she slid her hands up his lean torso, over the scattering of hair on his belly and higher where the hair grew slightly thicker. She came to a stop when her head was nearly level with his.

"Let me free," he said huskily. "I want to touch you so damn bad I'm about to explode."

She shook her head, smiling. "Oh no, Nathan. This is my show. My turn. You had your fun. Today you're mine. All mine."

"God help me," he groaned. "I may not survive you, woman."

She leaned down to nip at his neck and then she nibbled a path to the shell of his ear. "You may not," she whispered. "But I guarantee it'll be a hell of a way to go."

She laced her fingers behind his neck and worked her way up over the smoothness of his head.

"Have I ever told you how hot you look with that bald head?" she murmured.

"Glad Faith talked me into keeping it, then."

"And your earring." She nipped playfully at it, holding the

ring between her teeth. "Not all guys can wear an earring. It just makes you look like a badass. I love badasses."

"Mmmm. I'm afraid that around you, I'm one big pussycat."

She grinned. "You have the hottest body." She sat up, feeling his rigid erection in the cleft of her ass. It was all she could do not to moan as she remembered how delicious he felt deep inside her ass. "Perfectly muscled. You don't look like a steroid poster child, but it's obvious you take care of yourself."

"You're gonna give me a big head in more than one place," he said with a hint of embarrassment.

"Oh come on, Nathan. You have to be used to women throwing themselves at you. Some of them probably make downright fools of themselves. Sorta like I did," she said ruefully.

"Now wait just a damn minute."

"Shhh," she said, placing a finger over his lips. "You're ruining my revenge."

"Revenge?"

"Well, yeah. I owe you one."

He scowled at her, his eyes glittering with annoyance. "That anonymous threesome was your idea, honey. If I'd had my way, your eyes would have been locked on me the entire time and there would have only been two of us in that damn bed."

Oooh, there was a lot in that statement she wanted to explore, but she'd be breaking her own rule. Damn it. She wanted to hear more of this and, more than that, she wanted to know why he went through with it if he was opposed to pretty much everything on her wish list.

"Later? I want to have this conversation. Much later. Right now I want you to shut up while I fuck you."

"I've always said speech was highly overrated," he murmured.

She leaned down again and kissed his belly, flitting her tongue out to circle the shallow indention of his navel. He quivered in response and flinched. She smiled. Ticklish, was he?

Deciding that his underwear had put up with enough strain, she dipped her hand inside the band and pulled his cock free. Oh man, he was built. Beautiful, and she'd seen enough cocks that it was not a word she assigned freely when it came to that portion of the male anatomy. Some of them were downright ugly.

But Nathan . . . Ah, what a man. His natural skin tone was a light tan, and the hair around his cock was light brown, not too bushy. She hated overly hairy men, but he was just right.

He watched her every movement, his eyes glittering with excitement. In her hand his dick twitched and pulsed with impatience.

Part of her wanted to mount up and sheathe him with no workup or preamble, but the more devious part of her wanted to work him into a frenzy. She wanted him to beg again. She wanted to make him so crazy that by the time she took him, his control would be shattered.

She slid down his legs, her pussy clenching as it brushed over his skin. Unable to resist, she slid her free hand down her belly, between her legs and to the soft folds.

Nathan groaned when she closed her eyes and threw back her head, her fingers gliding over her clit, rolling and circling as pleasure worked through her.

"God, I love to see a woman pleasure herself," he whispered. "There's nothing more beautiful."

Tucking that piece of information away for later, she grinned and leaned up, offering him her fingers. He sucked them into his mouth, licking every inch that had delved into her pussy.

Slowly, she pulled them away and returned her attention to his erection. When she let it go, it leaned heavily toward his belly, stiff, the bulging vein on the underside calling to her tongue.

"You have one beautiful cock," she said as she lowered her mouth to the tip. "I've wanted you since the minute you walked into my salon with Faith. Do you know how many nights I've lain awake fantasizing about taking you every conceivable way there is for a woman to take a man?"

"Christ," he breathed. "If you don't stop, I'm going to go off like a damn fire hose."

"Then I'd have to start all over," she taunted.

"Suck me," he pleaded. "Goddamn it, Julie, stop teasing and put your mouth on me."

Instead she stuck her tongue out and stroked one of his balls, weighing it on her lips, absorbing the puckered texture. Then she lapped at the other, rolling it then sucking it into her mouth. He bowed upward, his buttocks leaving the mattress as he followed her mouth.

Enjoying the quiver of his flesh against her tongue, she blazed a trail up the engorged vein, curling her hand around the base of his shaft when the tip danced out of reach of her tongue.

Deciding to end his agony, she let her lips hover over the crown for one long moment before swallowing him in one quick movement.

He cried out, his body arching and convulsing underneath her. The handcuffs clanked against the iron of her headboard and his head thrashed from side to side, his eyes squeezed shut. She smiled and lowered onto him again, tasting him, sucking and swallowing him as he stabbed deeper.

"God almighty, woman, I'm going to come!"

She pulled away, cupping him with her hand and leisurely rolling him up and down as she stared into his passion-glazed eyes.

"Not yet," she murmured.

"I want to be inside you. Please tell me you have condoms. I didn't bring you home intending to seduce you."

"You didn't?" she asked in mock horror. "I think I'm insulted."

"Difficult wench. You know damn well if I'd come armed with condoms, I would have been labeled an opportunistic pig."

She laughed, still keeping her lazy pace with her hand, enjoying the hardness against her palm, the supple give of the firm flesh.

"Yes, I have condoms. Extra large. Just for you."

"You bought them for me, eh?"

"Or maybe I just like my lovers big," she teased.

He shuddered against her hand, and he closed his eyes as strain marred his forehead. "Damn, but you make me crazy. Slow down, honey. Even your hand has me about to explode."

She smiled, let him go and leaned forward to kiss him. He responded eagerly, drinking of her lips as she gently explored his. "I love your goatee too," she said against his mouth. "So damn sexy. Everything about you is sexy."

He stared up at her for a long moment. "I love that you're so honest and open. You say what pops into your head and don't give a damn. It's incredibly arousing."

"Hold that thought," she said as she swung her leg over him to get up. She strode nude to the dresser, knowing his gaze followed her every movement. She put a little extra wiggle in her ass and threw him a teasing look over her shoulder.

He positively smoldered. His eyes could start a blaze. They already had. Her entire body bloomed with heat.

She picked up a few condoms and walked back to the bed.

"Optimistic, aren't you?"

She looked down at the three packets in her hand. "I like to be prepared."

"I just hope I can get it up for you twice," he said with a grin. "You might kill me the first time."

She straddled him again, dropping the packets to the side. The devil in her was prepared to give him a show he wouldn't forget.

Dipping her finger into her mouth, she sucked and slowly pulled it away, then lowered it to her pussy, sliding it between her folds. Her other hand cupped her breast, plumping it, her fingers going to her nipple as she tweaked and rolled it.

Nathan lay completely still, watching her with avid fascination. He was drawn tight as a rubber band at full stretch, and his breaths came quick and ragged.

She closed her eyes, pushing her finger down and into her entrance, feeling the warm, damp tissues close around the tip.

Never had she been watched by such an attentive male. Her arousal was sharp, quick to rise. Already her orgasm swelled, lurking just beyond the edge, waiting for that push.

"That's it, honey, slow it down for just a minute. Take your time. God, you're so beautiful to watch. Do you have any idea how jealous I am of your fingers right now?"

She stroked over her clit again and rolled her nipple between her fingers, pulling it until it was a taut, stiff peak. Cupping the breast, she leaned down, guiding it to Nathan's hungry mouth.

"Suck it," she said huskily. "I want your mouth on me."

His tongue swept out, licking it. Then he nibbled around the point, his goatee scratching at the hypersensitive nub.

"You're just as much of a tease," she complained.

He chuckled and sucked the nipple between his teeth, laving it with his tongue the entire time.

"Uncuff me."

She shook her head. "Nuh-uh. I like you this way. Under me. You take direction so well."

"I can be a good boy when the motivation is right," he murmured.

She pulled away and her nipple left the suction of his mouth with a light pop.

"Make yourself come for me. I want to watch while you sit astride me and come."

She let out a whispery sigh as she tucked her fingers more firmly around her clit. She pressed with one finger, finding just the right spot, and then she gently rotated, gradually increasing the pressure until she was wound tighter than a spring.

"Oh God," she moaned.

"That's it, honey," he encouraged. "Mmmm, just like that. Damn it, I want to touch you."

She smiled dreamily as she mimicked riding motions, undulating her hips over his waist.

"Beautiful," he murmured.

The wave surged, rolling, then faster. Higher it rose until she was bucking wildly over him, her head throw back in abandon. Her fingers moved faster, and finally, the wave broke, scattering her to the wind.

She tensed, her face creased in near pain as she held still, only her fingers fluttering lightly as she coaxed herself down from the intensity of her release. Then she sagged forward, laying her head on his chest as she sucked in mouthfuls of air.

His heart pounded against her ear, and he was breathing nearly as hard as she was.

"Get the condom on," he said through gritted teeth. "Please, Julie, I'm not going to last whether I'm inside you or out."

She dragged herself upward, her body still sparking from her orgasm. She snagged one of the condoms and ripped it open with trembling fingers. Then she hiked one leg so she could move back.

His cock was full and straining, the head dark as the skin stretched tight. He was ready all right.

Carefully she rolled the condom down his length, avoiding too much pressure. Already a thin trickle of semen had moistened the crown. He was so close to bursting.

"You ready for me to mount up?" she asked softly.

His green eyes flashed dangerously, sending a shiver straight down her spine.

"Take me. Ride me hard, Julie. Don't let up."

She grasped his cock and raised her leg so she could position him appropriately. The blunt head nudged against her swollen pussy, and they both uttered sounds of agony.

Then he slipped inside, filling and stretching her. She paused for a moment with him only halfway inside, relishing the feel of this solid male tucked into her so intimately.

"Finish it," he said in a hiss.

"Beg," she taunted.

"Honey, if I could, I'd be on my knees. Fuck me. Make me yours."

She lowered herself onto him, taking him deep. His possession took them both by surprise. Her instant reaction was to place her hands on his belly to ease some of the pressure. Her gasp of shock mingled with his moan of sheer ecstasy.

"Jesus, you're big," she gritted out.

"Not too big. Not for you, sweetheart. Take me. Show me how well we fit."

"You're going to kill me," she groaned.

"And you said you were going to kill me."

Cautiously, she rose, allowing him to ease out of her a few inches. When she was sure she could take him, she followed back down, taking all of him this time.

"Ah hell, honey, move. Please. Ride me."

Bracing herself on his hard abdomen, she began a sensuous ride that, though designed to make him crazy, already had her climbing toward another orgasm.

"Harder," he urged.

With a cry she let loose and began to buck up and down, the slap of her ass meeting his thighs filling the room, mingling with their sighs and groans.

He pulled futilely against the cuffs, his hands flexing as though he wanted nothing more than to grab her ass and ride her as hard as she rode him.

"Oh God, Nathan, I'm going to come again," she panted.

His smile of satisfaction was brief and then he threw his head back, arching his hips into her thrusts.

"Me too, honey. Me too. Ah shit."

Her movements became frenzied as she rode him hard and fast, grinding her ass against his thighs. She lifted until she was nearly free of him and slammed back down, sending shockwaves over them both.

His agonized groan split the air just as her own world shattered into a million colorful pieces. She slowed when he flinched below her, taking a more tender pace as she milked the last of his release.

As she'd done before, she rested her head on his chest, listening to the frantic pace of his heart.

"That had to be what they had in mind when they thought up the word *earth-shattering*," Nathan said in a husky, passion-laced voice.

"Mmmm."

He chuckled. "So who killed who, wench?"

"Mmmm."

She lay there a few more moments but stirred when she remembered the condom. With a regretful sigh she eased off him then reached to tug the latex free. After making a trip to the trash can, she padded back to the bed ready to curl up on top of him again, but he gave her a pained look.

"Uh, Julie? I need to pee."

She flushed. Of course he did. She'd woken him up and jumped him. He was probably about to pop.

With a frown she studied how he was laid out on the bed. "If I free your left hand, the right is close enough to the side that you could stand up beside the bed. I could get you a pan."

Nathan's mouth dropped open. "Are you serious? Have you lost your mind?"

"I can't let you go!" she protested.

He rattled the cuffs and scowled at her. "Julie, it was a fun game, but for God's sake let's be reasonable. You can't keep me locked up here all day."

"No? I thought it would be kind of fun."

Nathan sighed. "You're serious, aren't you?"

She nodded.

He closed his eyes then reopened them to stare at her. "Tell you what. You let me out so I can go pee, preferably in private, and I promise you I'll come back so you can recuff me."

"And I'm supposed to believe that?" she muttered. "You'd probably just cuff me."

"Not that it isn't a highly tempting idea, but I promise you that I'll come back so you can continue to have your wicked way with me."

She was an idiot to be sucked in by that charming, beguiling, *wheedling* smile, but she would be pissed if he tried to make her pee into some pan by the bed. And he had been nice and understanding the night before when he'd taken her to the bathroom. She sighed. "Okay, but if you break your word I swear I'll knee you in the balls so hard you won't be able to get it up for a week."

He winced. "Damn, woman. You're bloodthirsty."

She retrieved the keys from her dresser and unlocked the cuffs, freeing his hands. He pulled them to his chest and rubbed his wrists.

"Do they hurt?" she asked with a frown. She hadn't considered that it might be painful for him.

"Nah, they're fine."

He moved so fast that one minute she was kneeling on the bed beside him and the next she was in his arms, his body over hers, his lips devouring her mouth.

Oh, but the man could kiss.

"I thought we had a deal," she whispered against his mouth.

"I said nothing about kissing you senseless before I go take a piss," he said before taking her mouth again.

Chapter 30

He was crazy for agreeing to this. What self-respecting man allowed a woman to handcuff him to the bed and keep him there as her boy toy?

He grinned even as he walked back out of the bathroom. When it came to Julie, he had no pride. The woman was just it for him.

The thought came as a surprise to him. It? Like *it*, it? As in forsaking all others and that kind of bullshit?

Whoa. That was some scary shit. But in an equally scary way it made sense. Ever since he'd first laid eyes on Julie, all other women had ceased to exist for him.

He'd been attracted to plenty of women in his life. But never before had he experienced an all-encompassing, total obsession with a woman. It wasn't a comfortable feeling at all. Anyone who said love was all hearts and roses and warm, gushy feelings clearly hadn't fallen for Julie.

Ah shit. He'd gone and said it now. Or thought it. He was in love with her.

"You look like a boy who just lost his best friend," Julie said.

He looked up to see her sitting on the bed, holding the handcuffs. For a moment he considered bargaining with her or just out and out reneging, but there was something soft and warm in her eyes. Trust. And maybe something else as well. He was a guy, and guys weren't that good at figuring out woman stuff, but he had a feeling if he backed out now, she'd never let him within six feet of her again. For whatever reason, she was determined to have him at her every whim and mercy, and personally, he could think of worse ways to spend his day than being loved by a gorgeous woman.

He spread his hands out in supplication. "I'm all yours, honey."

She stood, smiling, her plump derriere shaking with just the amount of jiggle that made his mouth water. Then her eyes widened when she saw his cock already standing at attention. Traitorous little bastard. Or maybe not so little, according to Julie. He wasn't above preening a bit that his woman thought he was stacked. It wasn't like he pulled it out to regularly to compare with guys at the gym. If she thought he was impressive then he'd be happy to impress the hell out of her.

When she motioned to the bed, he obediently took position, even offering his wrists up to her so she could cuff him to the headboard. Talk about a man assisting in his own demise.

"Tell me something, Nathan," she said as she secured the last cuff.

"Anything."

She smiled brilliantly at him, and his gaze wandered down to her full breasts. His mouth watered as he imagined the ripe buds on his tongue. Would he ever get enough of her?

She crawled up over him, arching her back like a sleek cat, her breasts dangling precariously close to his mouth. "What's your fantasy?"

"Hell, I'd say I'm living it. Sans cuffs, of course."

She laughed softly. "How do you want me this time? Do you want my mouth? My pussy? My . . . ass?"

"Yes, yes and yes," he growled.

"Did you like fucking my ass before . . . with Micah?"

"Can we leave him out of this?"

She smiled again. "I think it's best if we do. But you didn't answer my question."

"Hell, yes, I liked fucking your ass. I've got wood the size of a tree trunk just thinking about it."

She glanced down at his cock that was straining upward to brush her belly. "Yeah, I'd say so."

His entire body was on fire remembering how tight her sweet little ass had felt around his dick.

"I want to take you without a condom. Do you have a problem with that?"

His body shuddered underneath hers. "Christ." Did he mind? He was screaming hallelujah, but he also knew this was where he was supposed to exhibit a modicum of common sense. Clearly no decisions should ever be made when a beautiful naked woman was sitting astride you.

"You're safe with me," he gritted out. "Never not used a condom. You?"

He hoped to hell she wouldn't be offended by his asking. Some women got all huffy, as if you questioning their history made them flaming whores or something.

"Nope. Well, once, but I was in a committed relationship." A flash of pain shone briefly in her eyes but was chased away as soon as it arrived. "It was a few years ago. I've been tested since then."

"Birth control?"

She looked puzzled by his question. But then they had been talking about anal sex.

"I ask because I'd give my left nut if you'd let me have that sweet little pussy of yours bareback just once, a few seconds, but given how excited I am at the prospect, I wouldn't want you to do it unless you were protected against pregnancy, if you know what I mean."

She laughed, shaking against his belly. Then she leaned down and kissed him. "If you come, that means I have to start all over again, and it means you have to stay in those cuffs longer."

He grunted. "That's not exactly an incentive not to blow my load as soon as I get inside you."

Grinning, she sat back and reached down with both hands to circle his dick. He shuddered and closed his eyes. When she rose above him, he forced his eyes open again, wanting to see himself disappear into her tight sheath.

The head nudged her entrance and he clenched his fists with the effort it took not to surge upward and bury himself in her satiny warmth.

Instead he let her dictate the pace, and God almighty it cost him. He was going to lose his mind before this was over with.

He watched in fascination as a host of reactions crossed her face. She sank lower, taking more of him, biting her lips with extreme concentration. Was it as mind-bending for her as it was for him?

For a moment he simply marveled in the exotic feel of her swollen tissues clasping tightly around him, sucking him deeper. He'd never look at condoms quite the same way again.

Up and down, slowly and gently, as if she knew just how close he was to erupting. She controlled the pace, never allowing him to go too far over the edge. The woman was a goddess. The women in his past? All girls. This . . . this was a woman who knew how to please a man. And man did she look beautiful doing it.

She closed around him again, taking him as deep as she could and then she rested there, allowing him to remain buried inside her.

"Oh hell," he whispered when he felt her convulse around him, the tiny muscles in her vagina working him like a vise. "I thought that shit was a myth."

She smiled the warm, sultry smile worthy of the goddess label he'd assigned her. Then to his utter dismay, she rose up, releasing him from her depths. He moaned in disappointment when she got off the bed.

"Be right back. Need to get the KY."

"Hurry," he rasped.

"It'll give you time to come down some," she said with a grin as she stroked him once with her hand.

"Not bloody likely," he muttered.

She returned a moment later with a tube of KY and straddled him again just below his balls. He probably looked utterly ridiculous, cuffed to the bed, flat on his back with his dick waving in the wind like a damn flag. But he could get over it because the way she looked at him told him she saw something else entirely. And that gave him hope.

She squeezed a liberal amount of lube onto her fingers and considerately rubbed her hands together to warm it before she rubbed it over his dick.

The slick sensation of her hands gliding so effortlessly over his cock made his eyes roll back into his head. And when she arched up over him again and positioned him at her anus, he had to start imagining ice. Lots and lots of ice. Covered up in ice. Anything to assuage the inferno that swept over him.

Slowly she bore down and the tip of his dick spread her, opening her as gently as a flower. He held his breath and waited with burning impatience as she adjusted to his size.

"Not too fast, honey," he whispered. "Don't hurt yourself."

She smiled and gripped him a little tighter as she opened up more around him. Finally he felt her resistance give way and he slid into her snug warmth. She took him all the way to the balls, and he lost the ability to breathe.

"Are you okay?" he asked anxiously because if she wasn't, he wasn't going to be. Please, please let her be okay because he needed her to move.

"Mmmm."

She uttered that same purr of contentment she had earlier, and he knew it was going to be all right.

He arched his hips, loving the way he went just a little deeper and how she opened more for him. For a long while she remained still, his cock buried so far up her ass that his balls strained against her tush.

"This is the first time I've ever done this in this position," she said ruefully.

"You're doing fantastic," he breathed. "Just move a little. Mmmm, just like that," he said when she eased up just a bit.

"You like my ass?" she asked teasingly.

"I *love* your ass."

She leaned forward until her breasts swayed intoxicatingly over his chest. "What about my breasts?"

"You're teasing a helpless man, honey. I want to touch them so bad. I want to *taste* them. You have the most gorgeous breasts on a woman I've ever seen."

"And my pussy?" she whispered.

Goddamn. He closed his eyes and took several short breaths that reminded him of all those damn Lamaze advertisements.

"I wanna live in your pussy," he gritted out.

She laughed and settled over him again like a hot glove. Then she grew somber, her hot gaze sliding over him like a razor's edge.

"You're so beautiful, Nathan. Do you have any idea how much I loved giving you massages?"

"Then why the hell did you quit?" he burst out.

She gave him a sad smile. "Because you never saw me."

"That's a load of bullshit. How can any living, breathing male not notice you?"

She rose and sank down, leisurely, rippling over his cock, squeezing him for all he was worth.

"We'll talk about this later," he said in a pained voice. "This isn't the time."

"Agreed," she said huskily. "I want you to come inside me. I want to feel you hot and liquid in my ass."

"Jesus. Move, honey, I'm coming. Damn it."

She took mercy on him and began riding his thrusts, her ass bouncing off his thighs with a loud slap. The rise came swift, gathering like lightning. A bolt of white-hot electricity seared up his dick and exploded outward.

She clutched greedily at him, taking everything he gave her. Hell if she didn't demand more, riding him hard and fast. He loved that about her. No wimpy woman was this. She took what she wanted. She was fierce.

When he couldn't take any more stimulation, he pleaded for mercy. She didn't even tease. She sank onto his chest with an exhausted sigh.

He pulled against the cuffs in irritation. He wanted to hold her. He wanted to stroke her back and say absurdly sweet things to her. Well, he couldn't touch her so he'd have to make due with the sweet stuff.

"Julie?"

She stirred against him, lifting her head so that he saw her dark, sleepy eyes.

"I love you."

Her eyes went round with surprise. Her mouth opened then shut again.

Shit. He hoped he hadn't just made a huge mistake.

Chapter 31

Julie's stomach was in knots. Not just one of those nervous little twitches. She felt like she was going to puke. All because the man said he loved her.

She paced anxiously around the bedroom, stopping to listen every once in a while. Nathan was still in the shower, a fact she was grateful for.

What did she say? What did she do?

She wanted a man that looked at her like Damon looked at Serena. She wanted a man who looked at her with that "everything" glint in his eye.

Well, Nathan had looked at *her* that way. Just before he'd said he loved her. And it terrified her.

She was a coward. An absolute screaming ninny for what she was about to do, but she needed to get out. This wasn't something she could just bumble through. This was important. This was it. This was one of those moments that an entire life path formed around, and if she fucked it up, it would affect the rest of her life.

Okay, she could definitely cut some of the melodrama, but it was true. Nathan had looked at her with forever in his eyes, and she'd wanted to give him those words back. Wanted it badly, but she'd caught herself. He deserved more than just an obligatory utterance. She couldn't—wouldn't—say it just because he'd said it to her. No, by God, she'd mean it.

Did she mean it?

She let out a soft moan. She wished she could believe it. Believe *him*. What if he was just caught up in the moment? What if he did what all other men did and got tired of her strong personality and left her for someone more meek and feminine?

Sweat beaded her forehead as her nausea grew. Was she good enough for Nathan?

Oh God, she did *not* just think that. She was not doubting her self-worth because of a man. She raised a trembling hand to her forehead and knew she had to get out of there before Nathan got out of the shower and she made a royal mess of things.

Before she lost her nerve, she hurried to the bathroom door and knocked. Before waiting for an answer, she hollered through the wood.

"I have to, uh, go out, Nathan. I don't know when I'll be back. You can let yourself out. I'll, uh, see you. I'll call you. Yeah, I'll do that."

She heard a harsh expletive and the crash of the medicine cabinet, but she was bolting for the front door like the scared rabbit she was.

When she spied Nathan's keys on the bar, she had to laugh at her stupidity. She didn't have a car. Her rental was still at Serena's. And she was standing here like an idiot.

Making a split-second decision, she grabbed the keys and flew out the door. Seconds later, she threw herself into the driver's seat and jammed the keys into the ignition. She cranked it and fumbled with the gearshift then put it in reverse.

As she backed away, Nathan came running out of her apartment with just a towel around his waist. He looked pissed, even more so when he saw her in his truck.

"Julie, goddamn it!" he yelled.

She punched the accelerator and left the parking lot, her hands shaking. Okay, not smart. Really not smart. She was too humiliated to turn around and go back though. In for a penny, in for a pound.

Instinctively she went in the direction of Serena's house. It was Serena she needed to talk to right now. Serena had had doubts about Damon and their relationship. She would understand Julie's conflict, and maybe between the two of them they could figure out what Julie's problem was.

Faith was different. She'd known Gray was the man for her from the very beginning, and she'd gone after him with single-minded determination.

Just like . . .

Julie groaned and tightened her hands around the steering wheel.

Just like she'd known that Nathan was the one for her. And now that she'd gotten what she wanted, she was doing her best to screw it up. Just like she did all her other relationships.

Stupid.

As she pulled up to Damon's house, tears swam in her eyes, which only served to piss her off more.

Serena was waiting for her at the door when she pulled up and parked in the circle drive. Had Nathan called her?

No words were exchanged when Julie trudged up to the entrance. Serena took one look at her and pulled her into a giant hug.

"Come in. You look terrible."

"I feel terrible," Julie choked out.

"Aw, hon, it can't be that bad."

Serena led her into the living room and coaxed her down onto the couch. Sam, as well as the housekeeper, hovered in the distance, anxious looks on their faces.

"Give us a while and see that we're not disturbed," Serena said softly. "I'll call if we need anything."

When they were alone, Serena took Julie's hands and squeezed. "Okay, tell me what happened and why you're driving Nathan's truck when he's not in it."

Julie took a big gulp of air and spilled the entire story. From the absolutely awesome sex—not leaving any details out—to Nathan's declaration of love and of Julie discovering that she just might love Nathan back. Hell, there was no *maybe*. It positively scared her how strongly she felt for this man.

"What are you afraid of, Julie?" Serena asked, sympathy ringing in her voice.

Julie gave her a watery smile. "I'm not supposed to be afraid of anything, you know? I'm a confident woman. I own my own business. But he . . . he makes me want things I've never wanted. No, scratch that. He makes me *hope* for things I've always wanted."

"So what's the problem?"

"Remember when you struggled so much with your relationship with Damon? Coming to terms with it? You told me you were so afraid of not being what he needed, of disappointing him."

Serena's eyes softened. "Yeah. I'm still afraid. I've just decided not to let my fears ruin the best thing that's ever happened to me."

"I wish I could be like you," Julie said sadly. "Goddamn it, Serena. I'm terrified. *Terrified.*"

"That he'll leave you?" Serena asked gently.

Julie wavered for a moment, her breath coming out all shaky like she was a hair from crying. She hated that. Hated coming off like a weak-kneed, emotional twit.

"I'm afraid . . . I'm afraid he'll wake up one morning and the very things that first attracted him to me will be the very things that turn him away."

"I'm not sure I understand."

"I'm a bitch, Serena."

"No, you're not!"

"I am. I'm blunt, forceful, headstrong and confident. People often say they admire me, or they appreciate people who say it straight, who keep it real. And for a while they do, until all the new and shiny wears off and suddenly they don't like me so much anymore. I become caustic and abrasive. The things they liked about me now turn them away. And men? They're the worst. A strong, confident woman is sexy to them, but then they become intimidated by me and they think I'm wearing the pants in the relationship."

"There is nothing wrong with you," Serena said fiercely. "Other than the fact that you've dated morons. The right man will love you, warts and all. He'll love your independence.

Contrary to popular belief, men really do love women who can think for themselves. They love women who can be an equal in the relationship."

"Very well said, Serena mine," Damon murmured.

Both women looked up to see Damon standing across the living room, his eyes glowing with pride.

"I'm sorry to interrupt," he said in Julie's direction. "But not sorry I overheard." He walked closer and sat down in the armchair next to the couch. "Serena is right, Julie. A woman who needs protecting, the helpless female persona, can be . . . enticing. But beyond that first brush, that first shine of the relationship, it dulls really fast. A needy woman may appeal to the male ego, but a strong, independent woman is a treasure for the long haul."

Julie cocked her head. "But you . . ." She cleared her throat uncomfortably.

"You can say what you like in front of me," he said gently.

"You like submissive women." She cast an apologetic look at Serena because she didn't want her friend to think she thought she was wimpy. "How can you say those things about a strong, independent woman when you crave submission?"

Damon's eyes twinkled. "Serena is a strong, very independent woman in her own right. She *chooses* to submit to me. I have no desire for a doormat. For as long as Serena is mine, I will always take care of her. However, I need to know she can take care of herself."

Julie's eyes watered. "Do you know why I decided not to go back to The House?"

Both Serena and Damon gave her puzzled looks.

"I saw you that night." Again she looked at Serena in apology. "You and Damon in the common room."

Serena's mouth formed an O.

Damon's expression was no less perplexed. "I'm sorry if you were offended, Julie."

"No," she said huskily. "I won't lie. When I first saw what you were doing, I wanted to run over and kick your ass and then put my arms around Serena."

"You're a very loyal friend," Damon said with a smile.

"You changed something in me that night. I decided I wanted a man who looked at me the way you looked at Serena."

"Ah, Julie," Serena murmured as she stroked a hand through Julie's hair.

"Nathan looked at me like that," she choked out. "He said he loved me."

"And you don't believe him?" Damon asked.

"I do," she whispered. "That's what scares me so much. If I thought he didn't really love me I could laugh it off and know that his infatuation would wear off and it wouldn't bother me because I'd know from the beginning that it wasn't real. But I can't stand the thought of him growing to hate me."

A chill overtook her, and she shook uncontrollably. She rubbed her hands up her arms in an attempt to infuse some warmth. She hated the cold that had settled into her bones ever since she'd run from the apartment.

"Julie, I'm going to be honest," Damon said. "I understood Serena's concerns about our relationship. Because she shared them with me."

Julie flushed and closed her eyes. In other words, Serena wasn't the stone-cold coward Julie was.

"I understood them, but I was frustrated all the same, you see, because all I wanted was a chance."

Silence fell as his meaning settled over her.

"All you can do is give him a chance. Just like I asked Serena to give me. If he loves you, if you love him, you owe it to both of you to give him—and yourself—a chance. What do you have to lose?"

"Everything," she whispered.

"But think of what you could gain," Serena said gently. "Think about it, Julie. You were ready to kick my ass. Remember? You kidnapped me and ratted me out to Damon. Don't make me tell you what a dumbass you're being now."

Julie laughed even as a tear trickled down her cheek. "I love you, you know."

"Yeah, I know. I seem to have that irresistible quality that no one can resist."

"Conceited bitch," Julie said without heat.

Damon chuckled. "I'm going to leave you ladies now. I just wanted to make sure you were all right. If you need—"

The front door crashed open causing Julie to jump. They all looked up to see Nathan barrel around the corner, a murderous gleam in his eye.

Sam appeared from nowhere, stepping between Nathan and the other occupants of the room. To Julie's astonishment, Nathan curled his hands around the big man's shirt, snarled and shoved him out of the way. Sam appeared equally astonished and gaped as Nathan passed him on his way to Julie.

Ignoring both Serena and Damon, he bent over, trapping Julie by placing his hands on either side of her hips on the couch.

"I've tried doing this your way," he growled. "I've tried being patient, understanding, *gentle* even. I didn't want to come across as some knuckles-dragging-the-ground Neanderthal because I was afraid you'd run hard in the other direction. Ha! Well, I'm done with that. This time we're doing it my way."

She squeaked in utter shock when he simply hauled her up and tossed her over his shoulder.

"Damon, Serena," he said in a calmer voice. "I appreciate you being here for Julie when she needed you, but from now on, if I can help it, I'll be one she runs to and not *from* when she does her little panic act. Now if you'll excuse us, she and I have a hell of a lot to discuss, and I'd rather not do it in front of an audience."

"You be careful with her," Serena said fiercely as she rose from the couch.

Julie was getting a kink in her neck from peering around Nathan's back, and why the hell wasn't she putting up a fight? She was honest to God too stunned to do more than just lie there like a complacent twit.

"I'm going to do what I should have done a hell of a long time ago," Nathan said evenly. "And that's show Julie that she damn well belongs with me, and that all these silly games are over."

Chapter 32

Julie sat in stunned silence as Nathan drove his truck through the gates of Damon's home.

"How did you get here?" she squeaked out.

"Well, you damn sure didn't make it easy," he grated out.

She sighed and huddled on her seat.

"Damn it, Julie, don't you look like that. I could cheerfully strangle your ass right now, but you can give up that kicked puppy look."

"I'm sorry, Nathan," she said quietly.

Nathan sighed then reached over and took her hand. "What I want is for you to sit quiet and let me get over the urge to strangle you. We're going to go back to your place where we're going to have a sane, reasonable discussion about the direction of our relationship. And make no mistake, Julie. We *are* having a relationship."

"Damon says I should give you a chance."

"No, you should give *us* a chance. And you damn sure shouldn't need someone else to tell you that."

She acknowledged the truth of his words but fell silent for the remainder of the drive. She had to gear up to say just the right thing or face losing the one thing she most wanted.

Several long minutes later, Nathan pulled back into her apartment complex and they both got out and walked to her door. His anger seemed to have faded, and in its place a wary unease shadowed his face.

They walked into the living room, and Julie stood there awkwardly, not knowing what to do or say next. Nathan saved her from making the decision by pulling her over to the couch. He sat down and then tugged her down so that she straddled his lap, facing him.

His hands rested on her hips, possessively. He eyed her intently, letting her know with no words that this time she wasn't escaping.

The chase was over. For her. For him. They'd danced around each other for far too long. Done some silly stuff, made goofy decisions. And she'd tried to sabotage anything good between them before it ever got started because she didn't want it to hurt so damn bad when he left.

She framed his face in her hands. Her fingers trembled against his cheeks, and try as she might, she couldn't prevent the shaking from invading the rest of her body.

"I love you," she choked out.

"Thank God," he murmured, closing his eyes.

He nuzzled into one of her hands, kissing the palm.

"I thought I was going to have to handcuff you to that damn bed until you admitted you felt something for me beyond simple lust."

She nodded, the knot in her throat too large to say anything more.

"Why did you run, honey?" he asked softly. "What scared you so bad?"

"I don't want you to leave me."

A tear slipped down her cheek, and he raised his hand to gently wipe it away with his thumb.

"Why the hell would you think a harebrained thing like that? I've got to catch you before I can even think about leaving you. And honey, leaving you is the furthest thing from my mind. I know we can't predict the future, but right now? You're mine. All of it. I don't have a future without you. You're going to be in if it kills me, and I'm beginning to think it just might!"

"I'm an artist at self-sabotage," she croaked out. "My relationships . . . well, let's just say I don't have the best track record with relationships. At first, it wasn't my fault. I mean, I went into them hoping for the best. The first couple of guys were drawn to my personality. They liked that I was brassy and outgoing and that I was uninhibited in bed. Soon, though, I grated on their nerves and they moved on, deciding that I wasn't what they wanted after all. I intimidated them."

Nathan scowled but let her continue.

"Then there was the guy who thought I could stand to lose a few pounds. Okay, a lot of pounds."

"What the hell? I'll kick his fucking ass. You don't need to lose a damn thing. My God, woman, you're perfect."

He wrapped his arms around her, pulling her into his chest. He ran his hands over her ass, up to her waist and then back down again as if he couldn't get enough of touching her.

"I'm ashamed to say that I took it to heart. I lost thirty pounds but quickly figured out it wasn't me. I didn't like myself and I wasn't happy. Then I got angry because I allowed the moron to dictate my life. In essence, to control my self-esteem. So I gained the weight back, bought a flashy convertible, started wearing sexy clothes again and said fuck you to any guy who didn't like it."

" 'Atta girl," he said approvingly.

"After that I was wary, I guess. I tended to come on too strong just to let the guy know what he was getting up front, and if he was still interested, I kept the relationships short and sweet. I figured if I was the one doing the ending, it wouldn't hurt so much. I'd never know if they lost interest or not because I was calling the shots."

His eyes softened, and he traced the line of her cheekbone with his finger.

"And then you walked into my salon." She sighed and shifted on his lap. "You walked in with Faith, and I don't know. It felt like a ton of bricks was dropped on me."

"Tell me about it," Nathan said. "You rocked my world, woman."

She smiled. "I wanted you, did everything I could think of to get your attention, and you were so oblivious."

He grimaced. "I was anything but. I just had no idea how to act around you. Every time I got close, my tongue knotted up and I felt like some horny teenager again."

"I was so furious with you," she continued. "I finally decided to hell with you. I'd make you notice me come hell or high water, and then I'd turn you loose. I set up my threesome fantasy with Damon, and, well, you know the rest."

"Yeah, I do," he said softly. "I fell in love with a tenacious, bullheaded, tenderhearted dynamo of a woman. I spent months being in such awe over you that I damn near screwed up any chance I had with you."

She swallowed and her shaking grew worse.

"Honey, listen to me. I love every single thing about you. I love your brass and your sass. I love that you don't need me, but you want me. I think the men in your past were brainless pigs, but you know what? I'm glad they were because they saved you for me. And I swear to God, if you ever get any harebrained notion to lose weight again, I'll kick that ass of yours all over Houston. You are . . . delectable. And you're mine. And I love you just the way you are."

"Oh God," she whispered. "You don't play fair, Nathan."

"I sure hope to hell not. Now tell me you love me again. Tell me you're not going to run from me ever again."

"I love you. I won't run anymore."

He cupped her head and pulled her down to meet his kiss. Hot, breathless, with so much love her heart nearly burst.

"What I'm going to do right now is take you into the bedroom, and I'm going to make love to you until you can't see straight. And then? I'm going to love you some more."

"Tell me again," she whispered.

He stroked his hands through her hair and stared at her with such love and warmth in those green eyes. He didn't need to say it. She could see it brimming there. But she wanted to savor those words again. She'd never get tired of hearing them.

"I love you, Julie Stanford."

She settled into his arms with a contented sigh. "And I love you, Nathan Tucker. If you talk sweet enough, I'll let you finally catch me."

Chapter 33

Micah stood in the back of Damon's garden and watched as the newlywed couple laughingly stuffed cake in each other's faces. He never could figure out the appeal himself, but they looked ridiculously happy, so he couldn't begrudge them.

Then he smiled as he remembered Hannah on their wedding day, all sweet and shining with happiness. She'd very carefully put the piece of cake on his tongue then daintily wiped the crumbs away with a napkin. She was exacting like that though.

He shoved his hands into his pockets, content to remain where he was and observe the festivities. Faith and Gray danced off to the side, which was amusing since there wasn't a band, and no music was playing, and, well, Gray was a pretty terrible dancer. Faith didn't seem to mind though. She was wrapped all around him, her sweet smile warming the entire garden.

And then there was Nathan and Julie. He grinned. Nathan . . . the dude was done. Stick a fork in him. He was never out of touching distance of Julie. He had a hand on her shoulder, or her elbow, sometimes resting on the back of her hair, idly stroking downward. At times he pulled her into his side, his arm around her waist, while other times he linked his fingers through hers.

It was pretty damn funny to see the big, bald guy positively brought to his knees by the tiny package that was Julie. All she had to do was smile up at him, and Nathan's entire face lit up with a goofy, shit-eating grin.

A funny sort of wistful note crept through his mind. He missed having a woman look at him like that. He loved women, but only one woman had loved him.

"Hey man, you made it back."

Micah turned to see Connor walk up behind him.

"Hey, yeah, wouldn't miss the big day for Damon and Serena."

"Good vacation?" Connor asked casually.

Micah stilled. "Yeah. Good."

"Missed a lot of excitement."

"Yeah, I heard. I have a feeling Nathan's boring days are over, though."

Connor snickered. "You aren't lying about that. That woman has him tied up in knots."

"She's a great girl," Micah said with a warm smile.

"Yeah," Connor said easily. "She is."

"Pop here?"

Connor shook his head. "Nah. He doesn't really know Damon. I don't either, for that matter. I guess I'm here as a secondary guest."

Just then Nathan looked up and saw Micah. He lifted his head in acknowledgment, and for a moment, Micah wondered if he was going to avoid the first confrontation between the three of them since that last night.

Nathan lowered his head and said something to Julie, who looked his way and waved with a grin. Then she laced her fingers with Nathan's and pulled him toward Micah.

Micah smiled. Leave it to Julie to head off any awkwardness. He knew he wasn't wrong about her.

"Hey, you made it," Julie said as the approached.

Nathan stuck his fist out to Micah and they bumped knuckles.

"Where the hell have you been, man?"

"Vacation," he said shortly.

"Must have been a good one," Julie said.

Startled, he glanced down at her. "Why do you say that?"

She studied him for a moment. "You look different. Good different."

"Thanks. I think."

"It was a compliment," she said with a grin.

Feeling like needling Nathan just a bit, Micah grinned slyly. "So, when do I get to collect on my bet?"

Unflustered, she raised one eyebrow and looked coolly at him. "Hudson, does it look like I've been tamed?"

He threw back his head and laughed. Oh yeah, Nathan was going to have fun with this one. Damn if she didn't have him on this one. Nathan could be with her fifty years and he'd never tame her.

Nathan scowled. "What the hell are you two talking about?"

Julie patted him on the arm. "Your friend here once bet me that I'd be tamed before he ever would. I was merely pointing out that you don't have a prayer of ever accomplishing that feat."

Nathan's lips quirked upward into a grin. "Nope, and furthermore, I'd never want to."

They turned as Damon called for attention, Serena standing at his side, glowing like a beacon in the sun. Micah listened as his friend thanked everyone for coming and then announced that he and Serena were leaving for their honeymoon but that everyone was welcome to remain for as long as they liked.

Good food, good friends. The evening held a lot of promise, but Micah had a sudden urge to go home. Lately a feeling of restlessness had settled over him, a relentless sort of ache he was at a loss to describe. Or analyze.

He moved forward to congratulate Damon and Serena again and to bid them good-bye. Then he quietly made his rounds so that he could ease away from the party.

"I'm heading out," he said when he reached Nathan and Julie, the last of his good-byes. "I'll see you later."

"Yeah, see you at work," Nathan said.

As Micah started to walk away, he saw Nathan frown.

"Hey, wait a minute. What did you bet Julie anyway?"

Micah started laughing even as he kept on walking.

"Something I never had a prayer of collecting," he called over his shoulder.